Dua^{II} Singular$_I$ty

BY LAWRENCE E. MAYNARD

First edition: February 2025

PROLOGUE

Interstellar News Network (INN) Headlines:

-Negotiations between the Castorian Conglomerate and the Solar Corporation-Gemini joint venture continue on the planet Legos. Vice-president Novas of Gemini hopes to resolve the growing social unrest on her planet led by the insurgents of the K'Tar movement, rumored to be backed by the Castorians.

-In a related story, unidentified sources within the Castorian Conglomerate board of directors are questioning the health of their Chairman. Some allude to the fact he has been unseen for many Polluxian cycles. They challenge the legitimacy of the female Castorian Chief Executive sent to negotiate with Solar Corporation on Legos.

-In local planet Gemini news, Code Enforcement Communications Secretary Selot says that Novas Edison clan member Nimon, biodgen Dual to Starn, is a person of interest in the assault on his own Dual. Wanted for questioning, his whereabouts remain unknown. In the absence of legal precedence, the agency was unable to restrict Starn from resuming his duties on the life crystal facility, *Darwin* after his recovery. Plant Manager Morgan Descartes of the Solar vessel *Darwin* could not be reached for comment.

-Life Rightists held a protest outside the Centar

city laboratory of Dr. Nicholas Edison, well-renowned bioduogenetics expert and co-inventor of life crystal bioduotron empowering technology with his wife, Novas. Demonstrators demanded the cessation of organic life consciousness transference into inanimate life crystal constructs. One protestor was heard to say, "If they can do this for sporting events where contestants look like you and me, what's stopping them from moving in next door?"

-On the legal front, the Castorian Conglomerate has filed suit in Legotian Interstellar Court against Solar Corporation over patent rights for life crystal technology. A spokesman for Solar Corp. defended the company's longstanding monopoly on crystal manufacturing and distribution. Saying, "Castor's claims are baseless and frivolous. Known for their space piracy, they are trying to legitimize their thievery in the halls of justice." The Castorian Executive, in her deposition prior to trial, was quoted, "You have only to look at recent archaeological findings by Helicon of Clio. He discovered the truth on the planetoid midway between Castor and Gemini. A crystal shard, now mysteriously missing, was discovered there. It consists of the identical matrix as the Geminian stone upon which all of bioduogenetics is based. We will show indisputably that the planetoid was claimed by the original settlers of Castor on their journey from Gemini. As such, our Conglomerate has equal claim on all past, present, and future profits from the technology!"

-Religion: On the anniversary of Mitron's

ascension, Kronia, Matriarch of the Council of Elders, spoke to an exclusive assemblage of Phoenos adherents. Her message was delivered amidst the growing unrest from the rift between Life Rightists and those that favor the materialistic exploitation of life crystal technology. Despite an appeal by Nimon, a member of her own clan, for a less spiritual approach to bioduogenetics, she implored, "Ze philosophy of Phoenos still is revered as it vas during the time of Mitron. From ze mists of legend, ve know his teachings gave birth to our Geminian culture. Our goal is unwavering. It is zat of Singular Dualiity. Two lives from one mind. Ze cornerstone of Phoenos!"

Interstellar News Network - *For all the news you need, stay at the INN*

CHAPTER 1

Freefall!

Its jolt of terror was both thrilling and petrifying. If only for an instant.

Hal swung his arctic pickaxe more out of panic than skill to extinguish the fear.

The icy ledge, long unused, had yielded under his weight. His axe, now imbedded in a frozen fissure of the escarpment, tethered him to life. Its carbon fiber thong bit into his wrist. Hal fought through the panic - and pain - to consider his options.

Somewhere from his childhood he remembered:

"Freefall's taste is most sour when sipped a second time."

Old Earth Tibetan monk proverb

"Yeah, I get it!" he scolded himself. "Now, think of something useful, instead. If I swing my legs to reach the jagged edge, taunting me from a mere tred's distance away, it might only pull the axe from its hold," he theorized.

"My grappling cable hanging from my belt could prove helpful, if only I were more skilled with it. I could transmit an emergency code to Eric down below," he thought, "but is Death all that bad versus the relentless ridicule he'd deliver?"

Grimacing behind the plexi-shield of his head gear, he tried to focus on his predicament instead of the reprimand his supervisor would issue for being so careless. His body still swayed precariously as the frigid wind whipped across the cliff's face.

"C'mon, Rookie!" he spat, mimicking his boss's derisive tone. "Pull your butt out of trouble and get on with the assignment! You bragged about your Plutonian mountain assault on our lander ride down to Gemini. Let's see what you've got!"

Grunting as he pivoted to free his right arm from between his body and the snow crusted rock face, he unclipped a second pickaxe from his belt. The adrenaline from his self-induced anger flooded his biceps as he swung mightily. Once fully imbedded, he pulled himself up ever so slightly and kicked the crampon of his left boot into the ice. With the stability the three point hold provided, he stretched his right leg halfway to the ledge.

Another kick and that foot was firmly implanted.

Emboldened, he dislodged the first life-preserving axe. A swift stroke and it again was wedged into ice and stone close to the second axe. Freeing his left foot, he brought it close to the right one and buried the toe once more. Two more sequences of snow-crabbing found him crouched on the craggy shelf. Only now, he had a piton and cable in place as a precaution.

Deeply inhaling the thin Geminian atmosphere through his thermal breather, he re-oxygenated his fatigued muscles and reflected on his situation.

"I shouldn't complain," he thought, despite nearly plummeting eight hundred treds to the alpine ski resort below. "Less than a Solar cycle ago, I was a mere log tech on the interplanetary life crystal manufacturing plant, Darwin. Granted, monitoring a biological's vital signs as he transfers his consciousness into a biodrone on a planet's surface has its merits. But look at me now! I'm the one that gets to go planet-side!"

Vessels like the *Darwin* were a select few. Persons on board these time-space folding facilities were just as special. Highly trained technicians, supervisors, and managers guided the spherical ship on wrinkles of space, harvesting cosmic particles to produce life crystals. As incredible as that seemed, it was the process of *using* the miraculous minerals, once created, that mystified many.

Life crystals embedded in android drones enabled those rare biologicals trained in biodiving to project a conscious version of themselves into the construct. During this process, the biologicals, or *logs* as they were irreverently called, lay comatose. It was up to biodrone safety empowerment technicians, or BEST's, like Hal had been, to monitor the logs to ensure health and safety protocols were followed.

Hal continued his reverie. *"Who knew that biodrones could go rogue? Well, I guess some did, but it's a closely guarded secret. Now that I'm part of the Internal Audit Division, I have clearance!"*

He had been unceremoniously pulled from his BEST role by Eric, a gruff supervisor from IAD, when an obscure condition alert came through on two biodrones under his watch. Thankfully, Eric had given him just enough intel and "butt covering" to get them through his first field assignment in one piece.

Hal Xcorp had truly undergone a transformation over the past Solar cycle. From a bearded, unkempt pudgy technician, he had completed the IAD indoctrination training and emerged a new man. Just under two treds in height, he had trimmed down his body mass index to a 20 and his fat content to 12%. His shaggy red hair and bushy beard had been trimmed and shaved to comply more with the unspoken expectations of Internal Audit Division's management. He had even cut back his more sedentary video gaming pursuits in favor of the healthy alternative of holographic taekwondo. It had come in handy on more than one occasion when dealing with biodgens gone bad.

Somberly, he reflected, *"Even though rogue 'biods' are mechanized, they're part organic, too. The well-guarded secret is that the organic parts, and the biologicals empowering them, can bleed through. Once in a blue Jovian moon, they give in to instinctive urges. And like Eric says, 'It's a law of Nature, biods aren't meant to procreate!'"* Patting his holstered sidearm, he continued, *"That's when we flame 'em!"*

Having rested sufficiently, Hal pulled himself to his feet, planting a firm grip on the cable and piton for good measure. The recall of his first assignment provided the impetus to resume his current one. Not just one but two instances of rogue biodrone activity had been detected by the *Darwin*, currently in high orbit around Gemini. Whether it was two distinct entities, or just one on the move, was unknown.

Hal and his supervisor, Eric, had taken a lander to the surface to investigate. Hal, being the rookie, had been directed to ascend the escarpment to the luxury retreat that overlooked the ski resort below. Primarily accessible by air, he needed to complete his more clandestine approach up the precarious path to the compound to follow the order - *Observe - do not engage!*

Cautiously, the IAD specialist reeled out four treds of cabling from his harness spool and crept gingerly up the frozen trail. Anchoring another piton into the cliff, he affixed a cable clip between the tether and spike and moved further along the ledge. After several repetitions, he looked back to review his handiwork.

"Well, at least I'll have a more secure route back down in case I need a hasty retreat. I can slap on a pulley grappler and enjoy a coaster ride for part of the way!" he mused.

The curvature of the rock face had almost obscured the first piton that marked the spot where the shelf had crumbled beneath him. Turning to look ahead, he noted that the curvature continued.

"Hmmm ..." he pondered, *"that almost looks man-made." Cocking his head back, he squinted up to get a better perspective.* "Sure enough. Natural stones interspersed in faux-crete formed a turret base to a terrace above. The way it projects out from the mountain, I'd wager you could settle a lander up there."

Encouraged by this discovery and its indication that he was close to his destination, he returned to the task at hand. A few more piton plantings later, Hal came upon another finding. Seemingly imbedded in the stone was a ring much larger than those he'd left behind. Only this one server a different purpose.

A smile spread across Hal's face beneath his head gear. *"This should prove interesting,"* he speculated. *"Wonder if Eric is having as much luck as I am?"*

Reaching for the ring, he pulled it outward, twisted it sharply, then pushed. The craggy surface separated along almost invisible seams. On groaning hinges, the door swung inward, the dark recesses all but teasing him to enter.

Ignoring his better instincts, he did.

*   *   *

Eric wove his way through the crowd as deftly as possible, ignoring the downhill performance of the biodrone that held their attention. He was more interested in the activity of a different *biod*, one yet to be identified.

His perspective on the organic-life crystal constructs was jaded, to say the least. After twenty solar cycles of tracking and flaming rogue ones, he had little interest in watching them perform in sports.

"You'd think Solar Corporation had better ways to spend their doubloons than sponsoring an interstellar drone skiing competition," he muttered. "I get it that the performance level is more exciting and with a lot less risk to organics. But give me the thrill of a good crash through the netting and a few broken bones any day!"

To the contrary, Solar Corporation, a conglomerate of ten planetary systems which included Earth and Gemini, saw great profit in such sporting events. Highly trained biodivers were sequestered five hundred kilot-eds away in a transmission center. Through uniquely designed telemetry devices, they projected their consciousnesses into the sports drones. The constructs were equipped in this instance with ski prosthetics, jet boosters, and servo-gyroscopes. As an added element to excite the crowd, drones raced in pairs. Although a non-contact sport, fouls were common. For the cost of a few solar seconds added to their time, a well placed nudge could send a competitor flying.

The throng's roar, followed by a collective groan, told Eric that one such event had happened. A Solar biod had deftly brushed past a gate, slipped out of its lane and cut close to the Geminian opponent. The outer ski of the Solar biodrone clipped its adversary, sending the Geminian biodgen spinning out of control. Unable to recover, the hapless construct plowed into a safety barrier bordering the course. As if on cue, a squad of technicians descended upon the inanimate figure and hurriedly deposited it onto a gurney. Securing it in the compartment of a snow tractor, they disappeared down a trail, leaving another crew to repair residual damage to the course.

A half megatred away, the organic on the projection table convulsed violently. A BEST rushed to the bedside controls, working feverishly to stabilize the log. Thankfully to the biodiver, the tech was experienced. After a well-sequenced series of electric pulses, the organic's eyes snapped open.

"Savage Terran *tinman*!" spat the Geminian, quickly recovering. "Their technology is inferior, so they compensate with dishonor!" His savior, with a deep sigh of relief, simply shook her head.

Back at the tournament, as the swarm of onlookers pushed forward to watch the clean up process, Eric took advantage of the situation. Activating a wrist scanner, he swept it back and forth across the spectators while he moved countercurrent to their flow. A faint blip on the device's screen gradually increased in intensity.

Despite Eric being a full two treds and three hands in height, the taller Geminians made it difficult to gauge his destination until he emerged at the back of the pack. Before him stood an inconspicuous utility building, presumably used for ski course maintenance equipment. Its door, slightly ajar, allowed an eery glow to emanate from within.

Clearly, as indicated by the directional finder attuned to the unusual frequency a rogue biodrone emits, Eric had to enter. He unclipped the strap of his flamer holster and thumbed the weapon's safety, but didn't pull it just yet.

"Best not draw too much attention," he thought. *"Most assignments deal with Darwin-issued units working remotely on some gods-forsaken planet. Can't recall the last time I had to worry about an audience."*

Eric's outfit and sidearm had prompted a few curious second glances already. The sleek helmet with plastene visor was not unlike those worn by the ski contestants, so went unnoticed. As did the form-fitting thermal body suit, woven from polymer designed to disperse high impact energy - whether caused by a fall on the slope or blows from an adversary. But the adornments placed strategically on the outfit were a different matter.

The flamer, a multi-purpose weapon with projectiles ranging from stun charges to immolation gel packs, was nestled in its holster and might be mistaken for a standard issue code enforcement sidearm. Not so the wrist scanner-an eye-catching armlet with pop-up screen and colorful pressure control pads. The distinctive belt held a grappling hook and reel dispenser, plus utility compartments for items such as med supplies, flares, a luminary wand, and food rations. But of greater interest to inquisitive bystanders was the foot gear.

Breathable polymeric fibers were interwoven with a metal mesh to provide a boot that was both comfortable and strong. On the outer edge along each sole a spring mount held a tungsten blade. When activated, the blade snapped out and under the boot. Instantly, the wearer was ready to traverse any frozen surface with ease. Affixed to the back of the snowshoe was a palm's width carbidium slat extending vertically from just above the heel's base to mid-calf. Serving secondarily as armor when performing certain martial arts kicks, its primary purpose was quite different. When actuated, it too could pivot underneath the foot gear. A series of nested slats would then extend forward and rearward to create a ski surface. Albeit much shorter than those in use by the biodrone downhillers, these short runners were much preferred over the alternative of tromping through deep snow.

The footwear served a more practical purpose at the moment. Lifting one and pushing slowly forward, Eric toed the door to gently swing it open. Quickly sliding through the gap, he pressed himself flat against the wall adjacent to the door frame. His visor quickly adjusted from the heavy tint to shield against the snow glare to a more transparent setting.

Upon stepping through the door, Eric surveyed the contents of the maintenance building. His first impulse was to mentally chastise himself for overreacting. But upon closer inspection, he saw that the hardware staged around the room served a greater purpose than mere ski resort groundskeeping. As proof, his scanner, previously toggled into silent mode, vibrated its warning more intensely.

Laboratory grade light panels in the ceiling provided an abundance of illumination - typical of a room where intricate procedures were performed. "Hmmpf," muttered Eric, "no hidden enemy could attack in this brilliance."

Along a side wall to the right hung various devices for biodrone repair. On the left, a work table held a disassembled unit used in the downhill event. The appendages were separated from the torso, and the head had been removed. Its lifeless stare looked out from a bench top glass container with numerous electronic cables running to a control board. Directly ahead, a shorter bench separated him from another door, presumably to an adjacent workroom.

A snap, followed by a scraping sound from the chamber beyond startled Eric, causing him once again to drop his hand to his sidearm. The door slowly swung inward.

Eric's grip tightened.

To his surprise, the figure that emerged seemed less of a threat and more like a treat. The pulsing from his wrist scanner beseeched him to the contrary.

The lithe form of the biodgen smoothly slipped past the short table. Her skin tight bodysuit shimmered as it cycled through a spectrum of luminescent colors. Clearly designed to attract an audience, the construct was quite beautiful. Unlike the robotic versions with body plating and utility hardware used by the *Darwin*, this Geminian design was best described as a living doll.

Slender and fit, Eric could easily imagine her skiing skillfully down the course, sliding mercurially past the gates. Her azure face was framed by a sable, sleek coif. High cheek bones and crimson, feline eyes captivated even the strongest of wills.

Eric was no exception.

Drawing closer to him, she stroked the side of his helmet, triggering the visor to disappear within the shell. The other hand deftly came up to his belt clasp. A twist of the wrist and Eric's protection slipped to the floor.

Mesmerized, he stood rigid. Unwilling - no, somehow unable - to resist. It was her gaze. Peering into his soul.

As if disembodied, floating above the scene, he became aware of something more disturbing than his loss of will. Behind the automaton lay a stripped body. Presumably the technician that worked in the repair shed. She had drug it from the other room. Discarded like a plaything, its head had been twisted unnaturally at the neck.

Still paralyzed, he watched as he became the next object of her lustful desires.

CHAPTER 2

Novas emerged from the portal in the tree's massive trunk, as would a forest sprite from a Geminian fairy tale. The transition from the Legotian chamber - from her former present to her now past - was seamless. Unlike the first temporal journey induced by the mercurial pool of the energy being, Chrislar, this *time* it made sense.

She recalled the Legotian's words.

"In Mitron's past - now *your* past - you can, and *will*, bear a daughter. We know her as the Time Child. She has many fates, as do you. The correct one still awaits. Immerse yourself in the chronal pool to discover which outcome will prevail. For the good of the Geminians, the Castorians, yourself, your biodgen offspring … and the Time Child, resume your journey."

Confusion confounded her during the prior events in this era. She believed herself to be under a mind spell. The clarity of her presence this *time* was refreshing - but fleeting. She knew *when* she was, but not *why*. The cryptic words of Chrislar served only as an enticement to start her mission. They failed to provide her the guidance needed along the way.

To get her bearings, she surveyed the area. The terrain at the edge of the grove was familiar. To the left past the swale of marshy grass was the path back to Mitron's palace. Directly ahead amidst the rocky outcropping stood the escarpment through which she appeared during her first visit to Mitron's epoch. Triangulating those two markers with a third, she knew the trail to the right led to Ravar's lab.

The thought of Mitron's comrade - and her lover - sent a pang of guilt down her spine. *Or was it a sympathetic neurological response reminding her she was with child?*

Working closely with Mitron's brilliant friend and counsel to the tribal court, Novas had been smitten. Though muscular and massive, Ravar also had an extraordinary mind. As a learned astrophysicist, he had foretold the arrival of a meteor swarm that would be apocalyptic. In preparation, his followers had constructed six space vessels to escape the planet's impending doom. The impact of a precursor meteorite not only portended the cataclysm, but provided a crystalline fragment that would determine the future of the star system.

Together, in a fit of passion, Novas and Ravar had unlocked the potential power of the mineral matrix. But in so doing, it was cleaved in two. Novas believed it to be not only the cornerstone to the achievement of Phoenos, but to the unification of the tribes of Gemini and Castor, as well. Ultimately, she had succeeded in creating a Singular Dualiity with her Dual via one of the crystal shards. The thought of what the *two united* could achieve was awe inspiring.

Yet, there were choices. It always came down to choices. Whether past, present, or future, how one chose was what mattered most.

"Should I return to the palace to resume my conflict with P'Teel?" Novas asked herself.

Her previous journey into the past had abruptly concluded with a test of both their Fire Powers. The recoil from the clash of their energy bursts had hurled Novas back through the Legotian portal. P'Teel, the manipulative enchantress and star follower, had won. And in so doing, had earned possession of half the crystalline fragment.

"To what end would vanquishing P'Teel lead?" pondered Novas. *"Ultimately, the miraculous mineral had passed down the Mitronian maternal line to me. Through it, I created the Singular Dualiity, T'Poch, my own self-sustaining bioduogenetron. If I take the stone from the timeline, would that miracle never occur?"*

Continuing to explore the branches of the decision tree before her, she considered, *"Perhaps a better choice exists. I know the destiny of the Mitronian crystal. But what of the Ravarian half?"*

Their last liaison had been tumultuous. From passion to discovery - from epiphany to torment. Novas' psychic burst during the peak of ecstasy with Ravar had activated a prototype mechanical hand via the crystal within. But her revelation of this miracle to Ravar was clouded by the urgency of the moment. He was pressed to save his followers by accelerating the launch of his space vessels. She was driven to fulfill her destiny of empowering the first Singular Dualiity.

Urgency and Destiny - Castorian oil and Geminian water - she knew they would not mix.

So, she had spurned him - throwing the pretense of her desire for Mitron in his face. In his mind, Ravar knew she was only playing a part. Acting out a role in a drama only she understood. But emotion often overwhelms the mind.

"I see in your heart that you believe in what you are doing. Against that, I have no quarrel. But hear me, beautiful one. In *time*, we will meet again ... and as a symbol of our eternal, yet broken bond, I take this crystal fragment." And with that, Ravar spun on his heels, storming out of the lab.

Lost in her reflections, but sure in her resolve, Novas now followed the path to the research facility. Rounding a turn past a boulder and pushing through a brushy overhang, she was stunned! She struggled to process the scene before her.

From the building's sterilization entryway emerged Ravar himself! Striding purposefully, he quickly traversed the walkway to a nearby graviton sled. Before she could do more than raise a hearkening hand, he was gone!

Forcing herself through the shock, she stiffly plodded toward the front of the laboratory. Its exterior facade of adobe blocks and oval glass portals belied the sophisticated facility that existed within. Designed to merge biological science with mechanical engineering, future legends would whisper that it was the birthplace of Phoenos. Yet, as Novas observed through one of the windows, it appeared desolate and abandoned.

Except for one lone figure.

The woman was sitting hunched over a lab bench, her head cradled in the crook of her arm, face pressed against the cool, slatium surface. The sable tresses with silver streak cascaded such that her face was not visible. But Novas knew her identity.

"How is this possible?" she entreated, maddeningly. *"There before me, it is I, wracked with with grief over my loss of Ravar, drifting in and out of consciousness."*

Then, revelation struck her.

"Consciousness ... if a mind can empower two lives simultaneously, as Phoenos proclaims, can the same mind exist in the same time, in a parallel existence, yet experiencing two realities? In essence, creating a Duall Singularity? The possibilities ... the potentials ... are infinite!"

Wavering before the window's glass, she peered through it, seeing herself as she was mere hours - or generations - ago. As the

Geminian sun, Pollux, reflected off the pane, her present image appeared. No longer clad in the tribal skins and lacing of a star follower enchantress, Novas' outfit more befitted a star *traveler*.

Rather than the flowing tresses of her counterpart, her hair was cut short with bangs smoothly blending into a bob angling along the jaw line. The argent streak of her temporal "sister" was more diffuse, creating silver highlights, captivating in their fluid layering.

Clothed in a grey tunic above a darker grey pair of trousers, both with utility pockets placed strategically throughout, she was the model of a space faring crew person from a bygone era. Stretching out both arms and running a hand down one sleeve, she found the fabric to be quite soothing.

The silk of the giant Tarantellan spider was renowned for its tensile strength and durability. Originally used over padded undergarments, when woven tightly into a fabric, it could deflect the sharpest of blades. In this case, the material served a different purpose. The suit had interlocking bands at the cuffs of both arms and legs. They enabled the gloves, tucked smartly on display in one of the vest pockets, and boots to be sealed to the material.

The stiff collar, with ornate brushed silver bands, awaited a helmet to be securely attached. On the wide belt ingeniously interlaced between the tunic and pants were matching silver discs, serving various purposes. One on each side re eased a pressurized gas into the suit. Together with cartridges in the helmet, the wearer could withstand the vacuum of space for a limited duration.

Marveling at what she thought to be an anachronistic costume, wonderment dissolved into comprehension.

"Just as the Legotians dressed me in attire best suited for my first visit to this period, they have done so again. My purpose grows clearer. My past self must also perform hers. As she has already done, and will do so again, once I embark upon mine. I sense that much like biodgen empowerment, distance enables the duality of the singular entity intersecting in two time streams to grow stronger. If correct, I suspect my departure will restore the consciousness of my alternate time self.'

Resolutely, Novas strode down the walk Ravar had taken. The empty compartment of a utility sled beckoned to her. The modular vehicle consisted of a two-passenger plastene-enclosed cockpit. Affixed to the rear were two cubicle containers used to transport a variety of cargo. From the way they sat on their retractable crab legs, they appeared full.

"Most likely valuable materials forgotten in the haste to accelerate the launch of the starcraft," surmised Novas. *"This should serve my purpose nicely."*

Settling into the closest seat, she removed the remote control pad from its center holder. Capitalizing on the security clearance previously provided her during her work at the lab, she powered up the vehicle. Graviton discs glowed, struts retracted.

Noiselessly, Novas surged forward. Following Ravar's dust devil rapidly shrinking on the horizon, the essence of a new time stream coalesced.

*   *   *

Dr. Nicholas Edison labored feverishly over the prostrate form of his duotron "son". Nimon lay motionless, immersed in a sterilizing energy field. A mere two hours prior, he had been fully sentient and mobile. Without warning, while conversing with his father and co-creator, he had collapsed.

Weeks had passed since Edison had successfully extricated Nimon from the Geminian Institute of Mecitative Phenomenon. The cascade of unfathomable events at the facility still left him in awe. Nimon had resuscitated his Life Mentor and organic biodgen dual, Starn. Starn had returned to duty on the life crystal plant, *Darwin,* no longer displaying the psychosis that had him believe *he* was the construct in the dualiity. Nimon had reverted to an inanimate state after a brief moment of Dual sentience. Yet, days later, Edison had discovered his duotronic son staggering in the halls, having moments before awoken from a catatonic state. The stasis condition was normal for a construct when no longer empowered by his life-mentor.

Being mobile was not.

Singular Dualiity. Two lives from one mind. Dr. Edison's wife, Novas, had achieved it. To his knowledge, no one else could claim that accomplishment. Until now.

Knowing this, and the scrutiny that would result, Dr. Edison had urged Nimon to go into hiding. Still wanted for questioning by the Geminian authorities over the near sui-homicide of Starn, Nimon had agreed. The family compound at the arctic pole seemed an ideal haven.

Carved into the rock face overlooking a championship ski resort below, its primitive facade belied a higher order facility within. Laboratories designed for bioduotronics were controversial, despite the beneficial - and profitable - outcomes they delivered to the interstellar corporations that relied upon them. As such, Dr. Edison and Novas were wise to locate this one in a designated geo-political neutral zone on the planet. Being accessible only to the most elite that could afford the transportation and necessary visas didn't hurt either.

The multi-level building had elegant living quarters perched on the peak whose top had been sheared away for the structure. In the first basement where the doctor worked, a laboratory equipped with the most modern and proprietary devices were being put to the test.

Edison knew from his wife's experience with her duotronic other that distance was required to sustain mutual independent sentience. Whether it be high orbit or an equivalent number of kilotreds on the planet's surface, once established, the Singular Dualiity had been attained. Yet, Nimon and

Starn had succeeded in achieving that phenomenon *face to face*, albeit only for a brief period.

Nimon had then faltered, re-emerged to sentience, and faltered once more. Through the use of robotically controlled intra-thoracic probes, the bio-geneticist "father" sought to understand why. By exploring the nuances of the energy spectrum emitted from the crystal imbedded within Nimon, the doctor hoped to unlock its secrets.

That hope would be dashed.

The scraping sound of a door long unused raking across the stone floor startled Edison. Looking up into the reflective surface of the field generator, the sight of the lethal weapon leveled at him morphed surprise into terror.

CHAPTER 3

Hal panned the light beam from his gauntlet across the pitch black interior of the chamber. He tensed, prepared for anything. Except what he saw.

Humanoid figures were scattered haphazardly throughout the room. Lifeless eyes reflected an eerie persimmon glint. Arms and legs dangled akimbo. Stringless marionettes pitifully hearkened for some form of sympathetic succor.

Spying a power strip, Hal flicked at the switches to activate the ceiling lumen panels. Rather than burst forth with brilliance, they gradually increased in intensity - theatre lights revealing the audience to the performer on stage. Hal felt less like a star and more like a voyeur peeking into an alternate reality.

Gingerly winding his way through the serpentine aisles that ensured each mannequin garnered sufficient attention, Hal noted a pattern. All were female. Each was a doppelgänger of the other, to some extent. It was as if individually, a particular anatomical area had been the focus. The constructs were primarily synthetic but enhanced with organic components - essentially trial models to demonstrate a specific technical feasibility.

"No wonder the science is so controversial," pondered Hal. *"The Life Rightists would have a field day protesting this chamber of horrors. The Materialists would argue it's all necessary to advance our society. Reading about it is one thing, but seeing it is something else."*

Since his promotion to the IAD specialist position, Hal had taken a keen interest in studying the evolution of the science of bioduogenetics. *Know thy enemy* he recalled from some ancient text that had survived the millennia. He had familiarized himself with the Solar Corporation models developed over the years - mechanized automatons designed for specific field use. This technology, however, was a quantum level of advancement over anything he had researched.

He had heard stories from Eric about encounters with Geminian constructs - bioduotrons, or biodgens, not the pejorative *biod* that IAD used. But Hal had chalked them up as tall tales spun to incite fear in the hearts of new recruits.

"Riiiiight..." Hal had cynically acknowledged to Eric at the end of one such chronicle. "Superhuman strength in a super-erotic body. And if you hadn't closed your eyes until using the reflection off of your armlet to aim your pulse musket, she would have mesmerized you into a hypnotic coma. Sounds like you heard one too many Greek fairy tales as a kid, o'Perseus, you." Eric had simply shaken his head, figuring if the kid didn't want to listen, he could learn the hard way.

Hal was certainly getting a lesson worthy of a future story of his own. Having made his way throughout the collection of curiosities, he turned and surveyed them.

"It's as if an amalgam of the individuals *could be used to design a* whole *far superior than the sum of the parts. And what a beautiful creation it would be,"* mused Hal.

As he completed his tour of the gallery of figurines, he found himself facing a spiral metal-framed staircase connecting the current level with one above. Although no danger had yet been encountered, his sensor wrist band nagged at him to be cautious. Calibrated to sense synthetic life emitting a frequency outside the norm, it wasn't foolproof, but did serve as an alert to be on guard. Heeding the warning, he drew his flamer and light-footedly ascended the stairs, taking care not to send echoing footfalls throughout the chamber.

The puffs of dust that wafted up from his steps vouched for the testimony that the exterior entrance hinges had given - the lower lab had not been used in some time. Given the surreptitious design of the outside door, Hal wondered if he would emerge through a hidden book case or perhaps look through a pair of eyes in a portrait to survey the next room before entering.

"Okay, enough of the mental meanderings - focus *rookie,"* he reprimanded himself, once more channeling his supervisor's oversight, despite Eric's absence. *"Hmmm..."* he pondered, looking down at the electronic keypad that prevented casual passage to whatever lay beyond. *"As if my inanimate friends here are being discouraged from leaving their sanctuary. Nice try, but that's not going to stop me."*

Flipping open a flap on one of several pouches on his tunic, he slipped out his own small, flat electronic pad with a narrow horizontal screen and touch keys. Magnetically affixing it to the front of the door's controls, he pressed one of the buttons and waited. A series of Geminian glyphs began to flicker on the display, almost too fast for recognition. One by one, a sequence of 12 settled into place. A whirring concluded by a sharp click was a welcomed sound.

Quickly, Hal snatched his device, slipped it into its pocket, and heavily leaned into the door. No secret bookcase or gothic oil painting announced his arrival. Yet, the scraping across the floor dashed all hopes of a clandestine entrance. The laboratory awaiting him was quite the contrast to the one he had just traversed. Well-lit with a hint of ozone scrubbed air, soft classical music floated in the background. In response, his grip loosened ever so slightly on his weapon. But the clinical environs failed to deter him completely from leveling it menacingly at the back of the figure standing across the room.

Tensely, Hal watched as Dr. Edison pivoted from the tell-tale reflection in the field generator, facing his would-be assailant. Two wrist flicks of the flamer signaled the doctor to move aside. Hal wanted to see what his target was doing.

Standing between his patient and the newcomer, Edison casually swept his hand across the control board's track-ball. The transparency of the containment field distorted around the prone figure within. His other hand slipped into the pocket of his lab coat to thumb a remote, triggering a wireless signal to the security system of the chalet.

"Well, it's been quite some time since guests have arrived through the service access way, " Edison proffered, hoping his nonchalant demeanor would be contagious. Glancing at the service patch on the interloper's sleeve, he continued. "Particularly those with ill intent. What is it I can do for the Internal Audit Division?"

Disarmed by his tone, non-threatening posture, and the absence of an obvious threat, Hal lowered his sidearm. He was a little taken aback by being recognized. It's not like the IAD were on holo-posters promoting the general public's good will. Peering more intently at the clinician, recognition dawned.

"Many apologies, Dr. Edison. I've read your papers. Our training sometimes overwhelms our better judgement."

"One can't be too cautious. As I am sure you can understand. " Edison replied nodding in the direction over Hal's right shoulder. Stealthily, noiselessly, a small drone hovered, its defense wand extended, stun tip activated.

"I get it. An interesting succession of strike-counterstrikes averted." Hal's left hand, resting lightly on his thigh, rotated to reveal a palm-sized disc capable of generating a drone-neutralizing electromagnetic pulse.

The doctor smiled wryly, saying, "Your discretion is appreciated. I doubt the electronics in this sensitive equipment would have benefited from your response." Edison made a flourish with his hand, theatrically presenting the sizable assemblage of devices. Unseen was the pulsar musket slowly retracting back into its camouflaged niche in the ceiling.

"No ill intentions, to be sure. Anomalous readings suggested danger. Though, you seem to be fine. Any idea what might be annoying my sensors?" Rotating his forearm so the bioduogeneticist could see, Hal was perturbed that the alarm band was no longer pulsing. Fidgeting, he tried to recover some dignity by elaborating.

"The *Darwin* re-entered Gemini's orbit less than a half rotation ago. Immediately our telemetry detected what may have been two incidences of rogue biods - er, biodgens - in very close proximity of each other. One is being investigated by my supervisor at the resort below." Hal paused. He saw the flicker of annoyance at his slip in the use of the pejorative *biod*. He didn't want to compound the insult by accusing this renowned scientist of harboring a fugitive automaton.

But the astute doctor was not to be mollified. "Supervisor, you say? That wouldn't be Eric Magnek would it?" he asked, testily.

"Ummm, yes, that would be him," mumbled Hal. You know him?" he asked, hoping his cheery tone might redirect the conversation.

"We've had the occasion … let's just say our paths, when they cross, are in opposite directions. You say you're pursuing *two* targets, and you believe one to be here?"

"Straight to the point," Hal thought. *"Sign of a scientific mind, or perhaps indication of a sense of urgency to dismiss an unwelcome guest?"*

"Well, we can't be sure. There's no indication at the moment."

"Do you mind if I review the time stamp on your event log?" The scientist inquired, nodding toward Hal's gauntlet. Without pause, Edison activated a display screen that rose from a bench while simultaneously projecting a holographic key pad on the counter's surface.

"Err, that would be classified," the IAD specialist replied, startled by the request.

The doctor smiled wryly as his fingers raced nimbly across the keyboard. "Yes, I know. I created the protocol. The record will reflect you responded appropriately, despite the information being made accessible to one with appropriate clearances."

Somewhat miffed, Hal reflexively crossed his arms, protectively tucking his wrists under his arm pits, as if that would retard Edison's intrusion.

As the log sequence unveiled the events of the specialist and supervisor's most recent activities, Dr. Edison nodded with an understanding far deeper than he was prepared to share with his uninvited visitor.

Prior to the arrival of the *Darwin,* he had been working on delicate repairs to a damaged sports unit that had been delivered to his lab by the Geminian athletic council. Assisted by his biodgen son, Nimon, an unusual interface had been needed in order to safely disengage the organic from the construct. Standard practice during empowering of a biodgen was for the organic to terminate the link prior to incurring physical trauma. Although independent entities - one conscious, one unconscious - occur as a result of a bioduogenetic link, physical damage to one of the pair can often generate a feedback phenomenon that adversely affects the other. This situation, if not addressed properly, can result in psychosis in the organic and an unstable matrix in the duotron. Field medic units aren't equipped to address the problem, so a higher order lab such as the doctor's was needed.

Edison and Nimon had successfully uncoupled the biodgen pair. Surprisingly, the process had left Nimon increasingly weakened to the point he was placed in the stasis field for monitoring. The sports unit had been transported to the field facility at the complex below while Dr. Edison had busied himself by investigating the condition of Nimon. At that point, Hal had appeared.

The time stamps of events told the scientist much of what he needed to know. The *Darwin* had appeared in orbit just as their efforts with the sports biodgen concluded. Knowing the proximity relationship unique to Singular Dualiity, Edison surmised his organic son's presence in orbit had manifested itself as Nimon's need to enter suspension. What the expert in bioduogenetics did not understand is why the anomalous signal had been detected by the IAD instruments.

"Could Nimon, due to his unique status, shared only by Novas and her sentient Dual,

be generating the IAD alert frequency? Or was something else mysteriously at play?" he queried to himself. "My son's presence, and condition, are of no concern to the IAD. Regardless, he is not some rogue construct to be neutralized. As usual, their interference is ill-timed and unwarranted. Yet, perhaps in this instance the IAD may prove to be useful for once."

"Specialist ..."

"Please, call me Hal."

"Very well ... Hal, your log indicates a sports unit that was here for repairs may be the source of the readings, as she was both here and has been returned to the complex below. Her status, along with her organic Dual, was unusual. Why she would trigger the need for your special skills eludes me. If I recall, you are called into service to eradicate biodrones that have experienced interfaces of either levels 1, 2, or 3 - intimacy of drone to drone, drone to organic, or more sophisticated biodgen to biodgen, respectively. I can assure you none of those events transpired in my lab.

But of note is the current status alert for your supervisor. Is there a reason his bio-signs should be suppressed?"

Dr. Edison stepped aside and pointed to the screen - in particular to the heart and respiratory rate tracks for both Hal and his supervisor, Eric. While Hal's was well within the normal range for a human; Eric, at the sports village somewhere below, was disturbingly not.

Hal's concern over his boss' condition far outweighed his annoyance at Dr. Edison's ability to hack into their control gauntlets. Clearly the scientist posed no threat, and might be helpful in this predicament. After several futile attempts to raise Eric on their secure comm link, he implored, "Doctor, you seem to know your way around our technology. I'm thinking you can give my supervisor a jolt that I can't. With your access, I need you to send a feedback pulse to his suit much like a CPR crash cart does to a heart patient. With your training, you can remotely resuscitate him enough to give me time to get to him. That assumes you have a private transport booth I can use waiting out on the terrace."

"Go!" Edison directed, pointing to a door at the end of a corridor on the far wall, as he turned back to his control console. "And Specialist," he barked after him, adopting a more official and somewhat derisive tone, "whatever is happening, tell Magnek for once to refrain from using his flamer!"

CHAPTER 4

Despite Ravar's head start, Novas easily tracked his vehicle's dust trail over the parched terrain. However, even at maximum output, her utility transport was unable to close the distance between them.

"Maybe for the better," she mused. A kernel of a plan to use this to her advantage took root. *"Perhaps it's wise to delay another confrontation with him. I need to better understood the nature of the new timeline unfolding before me. I know events to this point are real. Not a Legotian mind construct, as erroneously believed during my prior time journey. But to what end have I been enlisted for this venture? The answer clearly must reveal itself, given time."*

As her vehicle crested a rise and descended down a gradually sloping serengeti, her thoughts gave way to the marvel before her.

Ahead on the horizon, six space vessels stood, reaching toward the sky. Not identical, but set apart as three sets of pairs. One structure was comprised of a central inverted teardrop with sinewy appendages extending to the conical ion drive at its base. Encircling the drive were concentric rings that rose up from just above the ground to midway along the appendages. A very few understood the nature of the propulsion system. Novas was one. For her, it was a brilliant, albeit dated, technology. The rings served to create an anti-grav pulse field which simply released the vessel from the inherent pull of the planet. Mini-thrusters for steering dotted the cone, still providing the necessary fireworks to thrill onlookers. Once space-borne, the ion drive converted cosmic radiation into a sub-light propulsion source. The teardrop command module housed the necessary support systems - navigation, life support, inertial dampers, defense systems, and the like. What was less than obvious was the answer to the question, "What about the passengers?"

In response, the second craft of the pair revealed its function. More conventional in terms of achieving orbital escape velocity, an elongated torpedo was centered amidst a cluster of booster rockets. Designed to lift an immense amount of weight into space, the vessel could do little else. Left to its own devices, the payload would soon plummet back through the atmosphere in a fiery inferno.

The marvel was the synergy that resulted from combining the two interplanetary mechanisms. Launched into orbit first, the ship with the tentacle-like extensions seemed to transform into a living kraken from the ocean depths. The teardrop and cone at both ends moved toward each other, allowing the sinews to extend outward, blossoming into a serpentine cocoon. The central capsule of the second vessel, having expended and discarded its boosters, used strategically located steering nozzles to deftly insert itself into the welcoming nest. Once tucked inside, the structure elongated, keeping an ever so slight gap between the coils and the capsule surfaces. Much like a motor winding generating a field to spin the rotor shaft, the cylindrical structure containing the payload and living quarters rotated within the energized tendrils. As such, a natural gravitational field could be generated, making long distance space travel more livable.

Novas saw Ravar bank sharply and head for the furthest pair of vessels to the right. Her trained eye revealed that that combination was entering the final stages of preparedness before launch. In contrast, directly ahead between the other two sets of ships there was a beehive of activity. The frenetic pace by the throngs of personnel were intent on getting their vessels to the same status.

"My chances of gaining entry and eventual access to one of the vessels seems more likely if I can leverage the borderline chaos to my advantage," she postulated.

Ever the scientist trained in logic, she opted to test her hypothesis with action. Throttling back on the transport's speed, she navigated it into a queue of several others approaching the security gate protecting the complex. The guard held a touch pad in one hand as he urgently waved the drivers forward with the other.

Pulling up, he barked at her, "It's about time. We thought we were going to have to go back to the lab and recover your cargo ourselves." He thrust the pad forward and, barely looking at her, waited for her to place her hand on it. As she did, he looked to the back of the line as a personnel carrier arrived. "Hey, not here! Passengers and crew go in at the next gate," shouted the irascible sentry.

The border of the pad glowed a bright lime green. Novas glanced down at it, somewhat surprised. *"Of course,"* she thought, *"I was granted clearance in the system while aiding Ravar with his research."* Quickly, though, she pulled her hand off the pad. The verdant glow persisted, while her image faded from view. *"Even with clearance, my security friend might be overly curious if he saw how much my appearance has changed,"* she speculated.

Returning his attention to her, no less irritated, he commanded, "Straight ahead, second left, park under the gantry. They'll tell you how to get processed for boarding."

Following his terse instructions, Novas found herself exiting the vehicle after positioning it under a set of overhead loading clamps. A logistics tech, after seeing her sleeve identifier chevrons pointed her toward a doorway with only a grunt for directions as to where to go.

"Everyone seems to be disgruntled," Novas observed. *"Urgency plus lengthy checklists equals raw nerves."*

The impact of a precursor meteorite presumably in advance of a more deadly swarm had accelerated Ravar's evacuation plans. Hence the urgency. A select cadre of Geminian followers had chosen to believe

Ravar's prognostications of impending planetary doom. Mitron, ever the inspirational leader, had convinced the majority of the Geminian population that their fate was not as dire as his friend predicted. But the meteor strike had unsettled some of the Mitronian followers. Ravar directed his personnel to launch his limited capacity ships earlier than planned before the panic-stricken mobs could ruin chances of survival for all.

Novas obediently entered the doorway, accessed the elevator, and paused, staring at the choices of floors on the panel. Options ranged from Engineering to Biomedics to Control at the uppermost level, among others. *"Might as well start at the top,"* she concluded, boldly. Again she benefited from the palm print that was uniquely hers, as she held it out for the photon scanner to register.

"Level 1, please," she asked politely.

To which the automated voice replied, "Certainly, Stargazer."

Novas' eyes widened as a mischievous smile tugged at the corners of her mouth. *"Always the jester, eh Ravar?"* recalling the descriptor he had used for her upon their first meeting. *"Apparently you had a direct hand in programming my clearance,"* she surmised.

"Now's as good a time as any to make some adjustments."

"Monitor, new facial scan. Update *Stargazer* Novas ID to   *Council level* Novas de Mitron. a.k.a. Advisor Enn," she commanded, hoping the alternative moniker might provide some level of anonymity to the casual enquirer. The same sensor that registered her palm cast a pulsing grid to capture her new 3D image. Simultaneously, it etched *Advisor Enn* on her as yet blank name badge affixed to her chest.

"Recorded and updated. Any further instructions?"

"Quite sufficient."

"Very well. You have arrived at Control."

The omnivator car eased to a stop, its door scissoring open. Tentatively, newly appointed Advisor Enn stepped out into the chamber. Apparently, the vertical tube was less a stationary conduit from the ground to the top of the vessel and more a flexible appendage that accordioned from one point to another along the length of the structure. Upon deeper consideration, it made perfect sense to Novas.

"Before combining with its passenger module in orbit, the shaft would need to move out of the way to make room. What better

design than to use one of the field generating extensions as a temporary omnivator tube prior to launch. Once united, a central shaft within the passenger section extends through the core to connect the engineering section in the lower ion drive to the upper command levels. Ingenious."

A circular deck around the omnivator provided a hub with several catwalks extending outward to various areas of operation. Some were enclosed in plexiglass, presumably for environmental control and privacy. The material was often capable of adopting gradations of opacity via voice command. Others were open to one another to facilitate a bullpen mode of communication between functional groups. Each section had a utility ladder allowing direct access to the level below, which seemed to be the preferred choice by a very fit looking command staff.

Projecting an aura of self-assuredness, Novas/Enn made her way around the catwalk to better survey her surroundings. Noticing a pair of executive-looking gentlemen in one of the partially enclosed areas engaged in what clearly was an un-gentlemanly discussion, curiosity got the better of her. Using work space partitions and cabinets, she surreptitiously traversed the distance from the omnivator hub to a work station outside the office door. A quick glance partially identified the roles of the individuals.

They were dressed not unlike Novas in that they wore grey tunics above a darker grey pair of trousers. The material and associated ornamentation were less utilitarian, though. Dual purpose functionality to temporarily withstand depressurization had been discarded for more officious decorations. Quicksilver chevrons on the cuffs of the person standing behind his work desk most likely indicated a chieftain rank. This was further corroborated by the tribal war club tucked in a loop on his belt. Lastly, the ornamental ear studs of azure stone glinted against the lighter blue hue of skin. The complexion had not seen Polluxian rays on a regular basis - clearly indicative of a leader versus worker class.

In contrast, the person catching the brunt of the chief's harangue stood with a dejected posture. Carrying no ornamental weapon, save defensive arm bracelets, Novas would not be surprised to see him reflexively raise them against the verbal onslaught he was receiving.

"What do you mean *you were unable to plant the devices?*" hissed the superior to his subordinate.

"*All-knowing* Ravar's miscalculations were troublesome, but to his benefit," the underling replied, sarcastically. "He failed to predict the arrival of the meteorite precursor. Its impact set unexpected events into motion. Of course, his ship pair is ready to depart, while the others must accelerate their preparations. The ensuing chaos resulted in tightened security as Mitronian followers began to break rank in an effort to be numbered among the chosen, as are we. Access to his vessels became impossible."

The aide's eyes widened with alarm as his superior's hand reflexively rested on the head of his decorative, yet lethal, war axe. In an attempt at amelioration, he proffered, "We have an alternative. One that should prove equally disruptive to Ravar's vision. A previously inserted operative among his team awaits our instructions. We have only to ..."

Suddenly, the comm disc at the station where Novas sat warbled loudly. Startled, she knew it would draw the attention of the two in the adjacent cubicle. Without thinking, she bolted from her seat, heading for the utility ladder to the floor below. Though swift of movement, the subordinate caught a glimpse of the top of her head with its silver frosted tresses, bobbing slightly above the partition.

"Someone is out there!" he exclaimed to his chieftain.

"Well get them!" barked the superior.

The aide knew he had better succeed with this assignment, for his leader's patience would not withstand another failure.

*   *   *

Eric stood mesmerized, conscious of his plight but helpless to resist. Or was he *unwilling* to resist?

The Geminian biodgen knelt before him, toying with him in the most sensual of ways. Her beauty was only surpassed by her skills. Eric knew this was wrong, on many levels. The most critical being that of a Level 2 violation of a sexual engagement between a biodrone and an organic. His assignments had yet to involve correcting the outcome of anything more severe than a level 1 encounter - biodrone to biodrone. Not that it mattered. Remediation was the same. *Flame the participants*. Any alternative was unacceptable.

He knew the amok syndrome that resulted from a level 1 was frightful to behold. Without fail, the immediate outcome was the female of the pair in a black widow-esque fashion cannibalizing the heart of her biodrone mate. Instances of the female escaping immolation by an IAD team afterward were non-existent. Fatalities inflicted upon teams were, unfortunately, more common. Both facts were for a sobering reason. The savagery of the biodrone experiencing amok syndrome was fierce. Hence, the need to destroy it at all costs.

The death toll did not stop with amok biodrones and the IAD personnel sent to deal with them. For those with high enough clearance, reports could be accessed to reveal the effect of a level 1 event on the organic biodiver, as well. In most cases, the organic perished from the shock of the destruction of the biodrone while still psionically linked. But not all organics were lost. Known to only a handful of people were rare accounts of biodivers terminating their link prior to the destruction of their dual, *yet the biodrones continued to function.* If only for a short time before being destroyed. Those biodivers survived, but were forbidden to ever empower another construct. A hefty retirement package connected to a non-disclosure agreement ensured their story would never be shared.

The reason for utmost secrecy was clear. It was vital to preserve a peaceful accord within the Solar-Gemini joint venture. Those without reverence to Geminian metaphysics dared make the heretical claim - *are not the animated biodrones severed from their biodiver link manifesting the exalted state of Phoenos?* When Solar executives raised the question within the Geminian halls of power, it received a resounding answer.

NO! The Geminian Council of Elders vehemently denounced the mere suggestion of such blasphemy.

Kronia, the Geminian magistrate over the Council, herself had said, "Ze Solarian constructs, *biodrones* as you call zem, function, but zey do not *live,* as do ze Geminian bioduotrons. Zis functioning, even if independent of ze organic for ze briefest of times, is animalistic, savage. Its mind is no more sentient zan is a monkey a human, simply because it shares 97% of your genetic structure! Phoenos is two *lives* from one *mind.* Your amok drone is neither a life nor does it have a mind. Zis subject is closed."

Eric had learned these secrets. They raced through his mind, confounded by his stupor, as he reflected, *"If such great lengths were taken to shroud a level 1 in such mystery, what unimaginable fate awaits me after this?"*

In answer, his body spasmed, violently. The surge of current coursed through his suit, jolting his body, and that of his assailant.

CHAPTER 5

Dr. Edison scrutinized the biometric readouts of his new "patient". The resuscitating charge he remotely sent from Eric Magnek's battery pack through the disks embedded in his suit appeared to be a success. Pulse rate and O2 content had spiked. From near catatonia, it seemed as if Eric were now engaged in the most vigorous of activities.

The surging jolt ripped away the veil of ecstasy as it coursed through the IAD supervisor. The residual shock surprised the biodgen, causing her to relinquish her hold on her prey. Adrenalin driven, Eric grabbed her by the shoulders, twisting and pivoting his assailant to execute a throw. The nimble athlete deftly countered by tucking and rolling into a crouch instead of crashing into the nearby workbench.

Eric knew he was outmatched in both strength and agility. Only a weapon would even the odds. Unfortunately, she had slid his musket and holster out of reach after unclasping his belt. He'd need to improvise.

Leaping toward his opponent in a pirouette maneuver, he swung a wheel kick across her face, putting the carbidium ski slat on the back of his leg to its alternative use. A gash opened across her temple, allowing a cobalt goo to ooze down her cheek. What would normally be incapacitating to an organic served only to trigger a sinister smile from the automaton. She stood from her crouched position and casually stepped toward Eric.

Without hesitation, the martial artist mounted a second assault. Slapping the side of his footgear, the spring actuator flipped the skate blade out and under the sole of the boot. A jump side kick with a follow-up spin crescent kick left two deep slashes in the chest and neck of the duotron. The smile disappeared. The grimace in its place revealed a hint of concern.

Eric had one more ploy at his disposal. As the wounded fury descended upon him, he pulled the retractable baton from its hip pocket. The attached cord was swiftly plugged into the battery port on his chest. The crackle and hum assured him it was activated.

The biodgen was a trained athlete - strong and fast - but not a trained fighter. The more skilled IAD specialist feigned a strike to her head, causing a reflexive hand to snap up in defense. Eric quickly redirected the blow downward rotating his wrist to maximize the leveraged force. The baton tip cracked against the knee joint like a hammer against an anvil. The baton then was re-applied with the same force to its original target, the side of the dual's head.

Stunned, she dropped to her knees and fell forward, catching herself with both hands to form a table top pose. Eric prepared to deliver what he expected to be the final blow. Raising the bladed boot leg straight up against his chest so the foot was by his head, he quickly reversed its trajectory downward to execute a lethal axe kick.

Unsuccessfully.

The duotron snapped her head up while crossing her hands and arms above it in an X block. Catching Eric's boot just above the ankle, she unleashed the force of her downhill skier legs to spring upward, hurling him heel over head. The forced flip had him arcing into the air with an imminent debilitating impact to the floor. Aikido trained, Eric slapped both arms outward, tucking his chin to his chest, absorbing the brunt of the crash across his back, shoulders, and arms. Kicking both legs up and out, he then vaulted himself into a standing position, ready for the next onslaught.

Not one to disappoint, the femme fatale took two powerful strides as if she were launching herself at the start of a slalom run. Quickly pivoting to her side in a slide, one leg tucked beneath her, she extended the other straight forward. The momentum from the maneuver drove her foot squarely into Eric's midsection. Deflated lungs and surprise prevented another protected fall as he slammed backward to the ground. She was quickly atop him, legs straddling him and pinning the arms that he had reflexively wrapped across his stomach.

Despite the open wounds he had inflicted upon her, she was still a beauty to behold. As she clutched his head, turning his face squarely before hers, the IAD specialist once again felt his will slipping away. She bent close to him and whispered the first hypnotic sounds he had heard from her.

"A valiant effort, one that makes you that much more enticing. The one before you was just an appetizer. He succumbed effortlessly, leaving my hunger unsatiated. True, he freed me from my bond with my Dual. But the madness in its stead is overwhelming. Let us see if you are the cure."

Releasing her hold on his head, she brought her hands down swiftly, grasping the closures to his uniform and ripping them apart. The leggings that were already undone from her earlier attention were stripped away. Completely mesmerized, Eric offered no resistance. Rocking back off her knees on to her heels, she loosened her form-fitting tights. A few well placed twists to her top had it open, revealing perfection no man could resist.

It had the necessary effect on her victim.

Chuckling, she taunted him. "My, my. Impressive. A pity we'll only enjoy this once. But the anticipation for the taste of your heart is irresistible. And it is best served at the peak of our pleasure. Alas, once gone, so are you."

Eric floated in and out of a dream state. Not uncommon to nightmares, he tried to speak, but could utter no sound. Tried to move, but lay paralyzed. He could see, but not completely comprehend. The duotron's words were menacing, but their cadence, soothing. He looked into her eyes for comfort. Awaited her touch to bring pleasure. Once she lowered herself onto him, it would come.

Yet it didn't.

Instead of rocking forward to consummate the joining, she slowly rose out of her crouch. Her back arched, but not to deliver ecstasy. Convulsing, she reached behind her with both hands. Painfully, her mocking smile contorted into a grimace. The compelling gaze controlled Eric no longer.

Now fully standing, one foot on each side of his torso, she pivoted her semi-nude body. Centered on each side of her spine just below her shoulder blades were two darts. A green flash surged between them. A smell of ozone and the popping of electricity followed. Twice more it occurred. Finally, the automaton straightened completely and toppled to the floor like a felled tree.

A figure carefully stepped toward the prostrate duotron and into Eric's view. Still recovering from the hypnotic stupor and residual current that passed through his assailant, all he could do is mutter sarcastically, "Great."

"Whoa. What have we got here, boss?" inquired Hal. He knelt down, placing one hand at the base of the biodgen's skull to search for life signs while keeping his musket trained on her with the other. "Figured you'd survive a little current versus the afterglow of a flamer cartridge. And Dr. Edison pretty much ordered me not to toast her."

Eric raised himself up on one elbow to get a better view of the situation and sniped, "Edison? What's he got to do with this?"

As if in response, a voice came over Hal's wrist comm. "Specialist. Readings and visuals from your chest camera show you both to have survived. What of the duotron unit? I recognize her as the one I treated."

Looking at his supervisor with a raised eyebrow and cocked head as if to say "I've got this", he replied, "Per your direction, I didn't immolate her, but she *is* fried. A couple of electromagnetic pulse darts made sure of that. She won't be assaulting any organics ever again." Hal glanced over at the gutted corpse of the technician.

"Excellent. I'll need the bodies of both the organic and the biodgen for analysis as soon as possible. I have a theory."

Looking around at the mayhem, Eric's sarcasm persisted, saying, "Right. No problem."

*   *   *

Novas/Enn clamped arms and thighs on the outside of the ladder and slid instead of climbed down it. At the third level, she tightened her grip to stop her descent and bounded out onto the deck. She hoped her pursuer felt compelled to investigate the upper two floors she passed, giving her extra time to make her escape.

Surveying her surroundings, she felt more at home. Biomedics, after all, was her forte. A solution to her predicament began to coalesce in her mind. Taking advantage of the absence of personnel, she quickly traversed the floor to a set of glass-fronted cabinets. Using her clearance, she opened the locked door and rummaged through its contents.

Happily, she found what she needed and prepared it.

Making her way back to the ladder, stopping momentarily to grab an additional piece of needed equipment, she took up her position and waited. After what seemed an interminable amount of time, she heard boots contact the rungs. Looking up, she saw their approach. As anticipated, they connected to calves, thighs, and finally her target, the aide's hips.

Once at eye level, she raised the pneumatic infuser containing the tranquilizer she had pilfered from the cabinet. Smoothly, but firmly, she applied it. Her subject jerked his leg, causing him to slip down the last three rungs. Always the considerate caretaker for her patients, Enn caught him under his arms. Carefully, she eased him back onto the gurney she had stationed.

Adrenaline fought the sedative as the aide clutched at his attacker. He looked at Enn's name tag and silver highlighted hair and slurred, "You! Outside the chieftain's office I saw you. Whah..." Speech faltered. Eyes fluttered. The drug fully took hold and he collapsed back on the pillow.

Pulling a sheet up to cover the aide's uniform, Enn then donned a nearby lab coat and surgical mask. She swiftly rolled him to the omnivator and keyed the call button. While she waited, she spied his lapel communicator and formulated a supporting plan to her scheme.

Switching from voice to text mode, she tapped out a cryptic message to his superior.

"Identified intruder. In pursuit. On way to passenger module. Launch imminent. Will apprehend. Full report after vessels connect in orbit."

Smiling as another epiphany occurred to her, she added, "Reserve aide to you notified. She will report as your support, post haste. Out."

With impeccable timing, the omnivator car announced its arrival. Enn wheeled the gurney inside and elbowed the pad to send them to the ground. After scanning her face, the coiled mechanism stretched to its full extent and swiftly, but gently, placed them on the surface below. As the door scissored open, the automated voice from the car warned, "Launch imminent. Final boarding. Instructions?"

Enn responded, "Hold. Returning shortly."

She hurriedly pushed the still unconscious aide forward, aiming toward a parked emergency transport across the tarmac. Two medics were just finishing loading another figure into the back. This one had been restrained and continued to thrash fitfully against the straps.

The senior caregiver looked up, seeing Enn approaching, and voiced ruefully, "Another one? Guess space travel isn't as appealing right before the launch as it is during training. Thankfully, Mitron, in his benevolence, foresaw this. We're here to help indoctrinate these poor souls back into our society. You're just in time. We have to clear the area for launch. I see yours is already sedated due to the neurosis. Are you coming to?"

"No. I must return. But note, this one is highly unstable. One moment, he claimed he was aide to the vessel's chieftain. The next, his paranoia had him believing spies were out to harm him. I suggest he remain tranquilized until all vessels have departed. The option to leave being removed will expedite his reintroduction into society here."

"Understood." And with a respectful nod, the medic added, "Safe journey to you."

In the gesture popular to followers of Phoenos, Enn raised her open hand, her fingertips touching her temple and then extended it toward him with palm up and replied, "The mind is the source of life." Spinning on her heels, she then trotted back to the waiting omnivator.

Once again the door scissored closed behind her. Off came the lab coat and mask. Taking a deep breath and tugging her tunic crisply, she whispered to herself, "And now, into the maw." More loudly, she then said, "Monitor, take me to Control."

CHAPTER 6

Vice-Executive Talor sulked as he sat in the command chair of his partially disabled renegade Castorian probe ship, *Spectre*. The humiliation of being pulled along within a towing field behind his Executive's vessel taxed his endurance to its limit. Worse yet, his counterpart vice-executive Ralek aboard the lead craft took every opportunity to "check-in" to ensure the safety of the skeleton crew left aboard. As if Talor were an invalid unable to protect his own people!

"Of course Executive Stol refuses to sully his image by lowering himself to communicate directly with me," groused Talor to himself. *"Have I not suffered enough? I took two pulsar concussions from that accursed Solarian life crystal facility, Darwin. Then I depleted my energy manifold attempting to destroy escape pods. Despite this, didn't I still successfully extract two critical agents from Gemini? Are we not transporting them safely to Castor? So what if it would have taken a season to get*

them to their destination? Towing only saves four decions!"

Talor's selective memory failed to recall the *other* incident where he bombarded his own Executive's vessel, the *Eclipse*, to oblivion. The *Darwin* had confused Talor's sensors into believing the *Eclipse* was the *Darwin*. Talor had taken what he felt was swift action and attacked. Unfortunately for him, it was the *Eclipse*. Thankfully, Stol's crew had successfully abandoned ship, sparing Talor from a sentence of murder. But to compound the problem, they had been saved by Ralek, further elevating Ralek in the eye's of the Executive.

It was true that the agents on board his crippled craft were a valuable prize. A dozen Gemini rotations earlier, Talor himself had piloted the lander to the planet's surface to extricate two vital members of the K'Tar. If not for Talor, they assuredly would have been captured as Geminian Code Enforcement personnel were descending upon their desert camp. Had they been apprehended, the effort of the K'tar to undermine Geminian society would have been crippled, if not stopped altogether.

The K'tar believed Gemini needed a revolution. Followers contended planetary leaders had grown soft. To their disdain, to put it mildly, the Geminian Council had decided rather than align with their ancestral brethren on Castor, formation of a joint venture with the Solar Corporation was preferred. Conflicting visions amongst profit-driven companies, anti-capitalist Life Rightists, and religious zealots were tearing the future of the planet apart. Members of the K'tar believed only through unification with Castor and its imperialist goals would control be achieved. With it, Gemini could assert its rightful position of power in the galaxy.

The mantel of leadership over the K'Tar movement rested upon the shoulders of one individual - T'Poch. Her hatred for Geminian culture was unmatched. For decades, she believed she had been cast out of the Mitronian familial line, the most renowned on Gemini. Of late, her discovery only compounded her loathing for the planetary authority, and the descendants of Mitron. Her infiltration of the family archives had revealed she was the *biodgen* of Novas, direct descendant of Mitron, father of Phoenos. And not just a bioduotron puppet, empowered only when her organic Dual decided. She was an independent entity. Self sufficient. The first *Singular Dualiity*!

This distinction was of *galactic* importance. And what better way to manifest a role of such magnitude than by leading a revolution that would transform the interplanetary conglomerates of Solar, Gemini, and Castor? The bioduotron had most recently advanced their cause tremendously. She actually believed she had fulfilled a legend.

Whispered tales foretold that the leader of a new era would be spawned by the unification of two halves of a crystal. A very special crystal. The original matrix that made the Singular Dualiity a reality.

Within T'Poch resided one half. In her mind, she was chosen by Destiny. So empowered, she had stolen the other half. As the hand of Destiny, she manipulated an unwitting and unwilling bioduotron, Nimon, to become its host. And more.

Via what many would call an unholy bonding, she unified the energy within the two halves. From that act, she bore a seed. But, it came with a price.

Madness.

Struggling across the Geminian desert, she had sought the only salvation she could imagine. Her matron, P'Teel. P'Teel had raised her when her own mother, Novas, could not.

P'Teel had taught her the Fire Arts. P'Teel had elevated her to become the standard bearer of the K'Tar. Surely, P'Teel could heal her from this madness.

Now, within the confines of their nomadic tent on the barren wasteland of the Geminian desert, the essence of a new age would be spawned. T'Poch could not help but gloat as her tormented mind reached out across the expanse of Gemini to the progenitor of her creation.

"Dear Nimon ... you have survived, yet I sense you are strangely different due to your ordeal. What a pity. None have lived after my previous failed attempts. You have. But no matter. You cannot stop me. None can stop me now!"

P'Teel watched over her ward as she lay, tensing, twitching, almost convulsing. While she observed, she busily prepared the ancient potion necessary for the procedure. Quietly, she chanted the mystic lyrics to accompany the sacred rite. Her ethereal movements emanated a calmness that swept over her adopted "daughter". As T'Poch relaxed, P'Teel, mistress of the Fire Arts, enchantress of the Stargazer order, matriarch of the Mitronian clan, extracted the vital essence from her.

Employing part mysticism, part science - driven by her own part madness, part inspiration - P'Teel preserved the seed. Within its nidus, she arranged for the concubus to be nurtured. Soon, it would be delivered to a trusted one. Protected. Developed. Until the proper time. A time that P'Teel and T'Poch would create for her awakening.

But that time was not now.

P'Teel, confident that the proper measures had been taken, secure in the knowledge the trusted one would fulfill her duty, turned her attention from the future to the present.

T'Poch stirred. Eyes fluttering, she looked through the haze of her waning stupor. Rage gave way to reason. Looking at her caregiver, she allowed herself the luxury of a small, but meaningful smile, and whispered, "Your ministrations over me have proved successful. My sanity is restored."

"As it should be. For we have much work to do," replied the matriarch. "While you convalesce, we can strategize how best to advance the K'Tar cause.

Although the change must occur here on Gemini, we should travel to Castor to manifest it," suggested P'Teel to her ward. "Our agents are well positioned within Geminian society, corporate leadership, and even on the Council itself. But, it takes resources. Resources only Castor can provide."

T'Poch nodded solemnly in agreement as her mentor continued. "I reached out to our contact within the local Castorian network. A recent unsuccessful assault by three probe ships on the accursed *Darwin* may have worked to our advantage. Two remain in this system and have been dispatched to provide us transport to Castor. Hopefully they are more skilled at subterfuge than cyber warfare. They must penetrate the planet's sensor net if we are to secure passage."

As P'Teel and T'poch plotted their revolution, unbeknownst to them, the resources of the Geminian Code Enforcement Agency were busy. Their goal, to tighten the noose that could culminate in their capture.

As if on cue, the remote beacons strategically placed around their desert shelter pinged an alert. P'Teel quickly moved toward a crystal globe resting on an ornate pedestal at the tent's center. Passing her hand above the sphere as would a gypsy fortune teller, its core pulsed a spectral display. Entranced, she gazed into it.

Frowning, the diviner announced, "Multiple vessels have been detected. I fear the authorities have discovered us." Peering more intently into the device, she continued, "Yet only one vectors directly toward us, for the moment."

Several kilotreds away, the pilot of the Castorian lander, *Wraith*, smiled and murmured to himself, "Aaah, there you are. Let's see if I can evade detection from the Geminian Code Enforcement gnats buzzing about long enough to rescue you."

Talor enjoyed the opportunity to actually fly instead of simply commanding a much larger space vessel. What better way to experience it than in one of *Spectre*'s landers. The craft epitomized the design that had for so long fueled Terran stories of unidentified flying objects. Its concave disc shape spoke to the flying saucer moniker used by the Earth savages. The rotating ring at the disc's outer edge served to generate lift and momentum, augmenting the anti-grav lifters positioned just inside its perimeter. In the center of the disc, suspended in a magnetic field, was a command sphere. Within it resided the expansive compartment for passengers and freight. The field provided inertial insulation, enabling the ship to change directions abruptly without crushing its cargo or personnel.

Vice Executive Talor now used that capability to its full advantage. *"I can't signal my prospective passengers for fear of alerting the authorities to my position,"* he contemplated. *"The element of surprise when I reach them, I hope, will not be too shocking. But it cannot be avoided. The authorities are too close. I'll need to provide them concealment and a diversion until we can safely escape."*

Darting erratically just above the ground to further evade detection, he then swiftly approached their position. Hovering above the desert marquee, he activated an ionic cloak across the vehicle's surface. Extending the docking struts, he gently lowered the craft immediately above the tent. Simultaneously, a slot opened in the vessel's surface. A disc torpedoed outward, gliding briefly a mere tred above the planet terrain. At a kilotred's distance, it darted upward. Once at detection level, it began emitting a tracking signal to simulate its mothership's profile.

"That should keep the authorities entertained," quipped Talor to himself.

Its decoy deployed, the larger craft eclipsed the desert sun, casting a shadowy pall over the inhabitants within the tarpaulin enclosure. Reacting, the two mistresses of the Fire Arts prepared themselves for combat.

The elder P'Teel drew upon her mystic skills. She assumed a ready stance with feet shoulder width apart, knees slightly bent, and hands at her sides. Gently, she leaned to her left, extending her hands in the same direction, one slightly in front of the other, as if she were pushing against an invisible wall. Slowly she dropped her left hand below her right, cradling an unseen sphere. Shifting her weight back to her right she transferred the intangible orb across her body as if she were setting it adrift. She repeated a mirror image of the movements and moved again to her left. After several sequences of this kata, her hands began to glow. The space between them began to crackle as energy charges arced from one to the other.

T'Poch took a more practical approach. Moving swiftly to a cabinet tucked into a niche of the enclosure, she flung open the doors. A pulse musket, holster, and belt were quickly donned. Reaching deeper into the cabinet, she pulled an energy lance from its bracket on the back wall. Turning toward her mentor, she could not help but marvel.

A fiery ball had formed and hovered between the enchantress' hands.

Outside, the lander's ionized surface and rotating edge ring delivered the intended effect. Sand swirled and accumulated across the vehicle, cascading over it to form an artificial dune. As the turning edge stopped, nozzles from the craft's underside opened. A cryogenic spray jetted out in a circle on the tent's roof. The canvas material instantly froze, forming a rigid, fragile section.

Before the external invader could continue with its plans to open a portal, P'Teel obliged. Thrusting her hands upward, she catapulted the fiery sphere into the frozen ceiling. Thermal shock did the rest. With a snap and pop, the polymer fabric disintegrated into a cloud of mist and embers.

Talor, observing the attack on his vid-monitor, realized his would-be rescuees were unaware of his noble intent. He hoped the intelligence provided him from the K'Tar was accurate. Otherwise the next energy ball from the mistress of the Fire Arts could prove fatal.

Hand trembling, he activated a control jewel on his console. The access-way on the bottom of his command sphere irised open. From the internal speaker he broadcasted the code phrase, "The Dualiity provides unity!"

The phrase meant nothing to him, unless it worked. If he survived, he swore he would learn its significance.

Below, T'Poch twirled the energy staff into an at-ease pose, signaling P'Teel to stand down. The elder sorceress ceased her preparatory movements to form a new fireball.

Observing this, Talor released a nervous breath, and continued, "Authorities are near. We have cover. I have discharged a decoy drone. But we must bide our time. I will lower the gangway while we wait for their passage."

"No need," T'poch wordlessly signaled with a slice of her hand. She, too, had prepared for combat, only less visibly. Internally, as part of her self-induced convalescence, her metabolism had surged with energized hormones. Crystal matrices powered organic tissue. Hybrid sinews morphed into conduits of superhuman potential. They now needed a release.

Striding over to her mentor, they exchanged a nod. T'Poch slid her arm below one of P'Teel's and across her back. Steel-like muscles in her legs flexed and exploded with a burst of power. Both figures shot vertically 5 treds through the portal above, landing lightly on the edge of the opening.

Talor marveled at the physical display. *"What other secrets do these two possess?"* he wondered. Regaining his focus, he closed the iris and activated the floor lighting to guide them to him.

The mistresses of the Fire Arts circled around the guided walkway and arrived at the door to the command room as it scissored open. Talor swiveled in his chair, gesturing to the two new arrivals to have a seat.

"Now we wait," he counseled.

CHAPTER 7

Dr. Edison waited patiently as the freight elevator door opened. Inside, two orderlies wrestled their gurneys into the room. But they were no ordinary medical aides. Away from the prying security sensory net on the planet below, Hal and Eric twisted out of their lab coats and adjusted their IAD issued weaponry and uniforms.

Wisely, they had confiscated and donned their garb in the lab to avoid suspicion. Apparently, two techs wheeling a prostrate biodgen and dead body into a nearby transport booth were not worthy of attention. Had it been two IAD agents and their armament hauling away their perps, the crowd may have reacted differently.

The doctor immediately took the biodgen and wheeled her to a waiting examination tube that had appeared behind a hidden wall panel. Support runners extended from the compartment to cradle the figure and ease her into its confines. A glassine door hissed closed as an aurora of light flickered its diagnostic rays.

Treatment of the biodgen's victim was less clinical, despite the technician being an organic deserving of some modicum of dignity. Dr. Edison noted the effort taken by Eric and Hal to collect and replace the entrails that had been ripped from the biodgen's victim. To do the same with the heart was impossible, as it had been consumed by the duotron during her amok fit of rage.

Leaving the automated analysis to run its course on the duotron, Edison stood next to the deceased technician, somberly shaking his head. Eric and Hal exchanged a glance before Eric grumbled, "This is why those things need to be flamed into char!" He looked at the doctor to see if it evoked a reaction.

True to form, Edison maintained his professionalism, as he busily took tissue samples and placed them into a tray of vials. Wordlessly, he then slid the filled tray into a drawer in the base of the analytical sequencer. Only then did he look up to meet Magnek's glare.

"As I explained to Specialist Xkorp, I have a theory. I can't prove it if the bioductron is reduced to ash."

"Enlighten us, then," spat Magnek.

"Very well. The duotronic skier had been placed under my care after she was field damaged. I recorded her baseline profile. There was no evidence of amok syndrome. I can now rescan her and compare it to her baseline. Any anomalies may point to the cause of her condition."

What Dr. Edison withheld was an additional source of information he felt was vital to his theory - his son, Nimon. Scans of that Dual before and after his encounter with T'Poch had already proven invaluable. Edison hypothesized the key to unlocking amok behavior in bioduotrons was one word - *nanites*.

Nanomachines, or nanites, were electromechanical devices that had sizes measured in millionths of a millitred. In proportion, it takes approximately 75,000 nanotreds to span a human hair. Such structures had been researched in various fields in the hopes that advances would outweigh the risks. With high operating speeds, incredible durability, and low energy consumption, they theoretically had many applications. Physicians hoped they could be used to diagnose and treat diseases at a cellular level. Engineers speculated they could be used to build other machines that would be smaller, faster, and better. Environmentalists dreamed they could be used to detect and neutralize toxins in the ecosystem.

But the dangers were too great.

After the Nano Plague at the turn of the century, the science of nanotechnology had been banned across the ten stellar systems, which included Sol and Pollux.

At least nanotechnology *artificially created by organics* had been banned.

Dr. Nicholas Edison hypothesized that *naturally born nanotechnology* was somehow involved in causing Amok Syndrome in bioduotrons.

These devices were not normal to the technology used in creating bioduotrons. So, if present, they would have to have been introduced illegally, or, *spontaneously generated* by an as yet unknown process.

It was the age-old debate over the legitimacy of spontaneous generation that made Dr. Edison cautious. Originated by his home world philosopher, Aristotle, in ancient Greece, it was disproved a thousand years later by Louis Pasteur. Yet, scientists since had only recently had access to life crystals. Still used in only a select few applications and limited to the Solar-Geminian patent franchises, the science of biodugenetics was in its infancy. Neither Aristotle nor Pasteur could possibly imagine the wonders of this new field - or the hazards.

"Could the next breakthrough be upon us," pondered Dr. Edison to himself. Continuing his explanation to the two IAD agents, he postulated, "Have you never wondered why your organization insists upon burning bioduotrons and the less sophisticated biodrones after they go rogue? Consider what other situations warrant such harsh actions. Sterilization of contaminated clothing, elimination of biological infestation, containment of biohazards, eradication of *plague-ridden organisms*, to name a few."

"We're not paid to question orders," retorted Eric. "Only to follow them."

"Thankfully, I am not bound by those restrictions. Yet, they have interfered with my studies very effectively, until now." A chime from the examination tube signaled that the analysis of the biodgen had been completed. Edison stepped over to the vid terminal and deftly manipulated several control jewels to access the results. His face darkened at the discovery.

Attempting to lighten the mood, Ha quipped, "I'd love to play Terran poker with you, Doc. You don't have the face for it. What have you discovered?"

Hesitantly, reluctant to reveal all he knew, particularly when it concerned his duotronic son, Edison replied, "The unit *has* been contaminated... with a variant of a parasitic nanite. It appears to have entered through her nasal passages, making its way to the hypothalamus in her brain. This explains the voracious sexual behavior."

"Whoa, Doc," interrupted Hal. "I may be the rookie, but even I know that nanites are banned. How'd she get those, and more importantly, are we in any danger?"

"Fortunately, the field generated by your electromagnetic pulse darts was quite thorough. Not only did it debilitate the life crystals within the unit, it neutralized the nanites within her as well. And as for infecting the rest of us, there is the risk that live contact with her, such as the kind she had with the victim..." he hesitated, clearing his throat while glancing over at the ripped uniform of Eric, "and our good supervisor here, may be an issue."

Eric's face fell as he nervously looked down at his crotch and reflexively started scratching.

Edison, in a rare display of emotion, allowed the corners of his mouth to turn up slightly. Keying a few more control jewels, he quickly scanned the readout coming from the analytic sequencer. "Most interesting," he thought, and then said aloud, after a few more moments of discomfort for Eric Magnek, "There is no nano-technology viability detected in the technician's remains. In fact, it appears the nanites were not transmitted to the organic at all. Their preference for life crystal based structures is most intriguing."

Magnek's shoulders relaxed, while he forced himself to stop scratching. Hal stifled a smirk in the interest of occupational self-preservation, and asked, "So what's next? We still don't know how she picked up a banned technology."

Edison's mind raced, formulating a plan, and a response.

"It's best the Geminian authorities remain uninformed regarding this situation. I suggest treating it as you would any other rogue duotronic event. Have the IAD organization compensate the victim's family, as usual, and classify the episode so no prying eyes will see the report."

"What about the bodies?" pressed Eric, now fully recovered from his psychosomatic rash. "Normally we flame them on site. And again, how was the skier unit infected?"

Edison, fully committed to his half-truth and the security of his son, replied, "I have a crematorium unit in the next room. That will handle the disposal effectively, and respectfully. All labs working on duotronic technology are required to have them.

As for the cause of the nanite infection, as said, I have a theory. I believe it to be the work of the terrorist group known as the K'Tar. Their leader, T'Poch, is suspected of trafficking in banned mutagenic technology. It is critical we use all the resources at our disposal to apprehend her. That includes the *Darwin*. Magnek, you must contact your superiors and learn if they know of T'Poch's whereabouts."

Eric, reluctant to take orders from anyone, much less a *biod lover* like Edison, still complied. He sidled over to a corner of the room and activated his comm bracelet.

Outwardly, Dr. Nicholas Edison projected a demeanor of earnest concern. Inwardly, he struggled with turmoil.

"The findings from the analysis of the stricken biodgen were devastating. The unit truly had been infected by nanites. Indirectly, they had come from his wife's Singular Dualiity, T'Poch. Recalling the confession of Nimon regarding his violation at the hands - and other body parts - of T'Poch, Edison knew this was the source of the infection," the doctor theorized to himself.

"The mating of two Geminian biodgens - a level 3 event as classified by the IAD - must be avoided. The most severe of travesties, if occurred, had to be addressed. Only one response was acceptable. Complete annihilation. Immolation in purifying flames.

Yet, both T'Poch and Nimon still lived!

And Nimon had come into contact with the skier unit. Certainly not in any sexual context, but in the most casual of methods. Touch. "

The edict of the IAD to purify by fire any duotrons having had sexual relations now made sense to the doctor. Within the deepest of classified files there must exist evidence to justify the Draconian acts of the IAD. Whether the studies were endorsed by the authorities, or uncovered in the dark recesses of forbidden labs, they had to exist. Their conclusion could be but one finding -

bioduotronic   procreation created nanites! And nanites threatened the existence of organics! As history had proven, regardless of the planet, survival justified the most severe of responses. As such, the potential for spontaneous generation of viable nanotechnology had to be eliminated. Hence, the protocol of the IAD.

Nimon and T'Poch, together, had spawned a nanotechnology virus. In contradiction to the ingrained fears of the authorities, it was harmless to organics - so far. But, virally infectious to bioduogenetrons. Its symptoms - rage, voracious lust, and eventually, overwhelming madness. Yet, how had Nimon avoided its effects? And what of T'Poch?

Magnek returned to disturb Edison's reverie.

"I spoke with the *Darwin*. They've been briefed on our situation. Our intelligence operatives planted within the K'Tar tell us T'Poch is off world. The speculation is that she is en route to Castor. Her intentions are unknown, but highly suspect."

"Then, to further respond to Specialist Xkorp's question as to 'What's next?', the *Darwin* needs to dispatch a recovery lander to pick us up. While we wait, we can fu fill our responsibilities to the biodgen and the technician. After that, we embark on a hot pursuit to capture T'Poch!"

CHAPTER 8

Confidently, Enn emerged from the omnivator. So close to launch, the stations in Control were fully manned. Anticipating the *Vector*'s chieftain would be in need of assistance, she marched into his office.

"Advisor Enn reporting as assigned."

Bent over the vid screen built into his desk, clenched fists straddling it as if he were preparing to launch himself instead of his ship, Chieftain Mace looked up. The string of expletives caught in his throat. Accustomed to verbally abusing his milk-toast assistant, the replacement standing before him made him take pause.

Eyeing her from head to toe, his dark demeanor brightened somewhat. Although dressed in the standard-issue light grey tunic over darker grey trousers provided her by the Legotians, Enn filled it nicely. But it was her eyes that were the most breathtaking. Not just the normal deep red of a Geminian, they seemed to flicker with hints of orange.

"*Were actual flames there?*" queried Chieftain Mace to himself. Realizing he was staring, a quick shake of his head restored his focus to the matters at hand.

"Well, Enn, we've got our hands full. Our sister duos are already in orbit and executing docking procedures with one another. Our proximity to the breached security cordon is proving to be problematic. Despite Mitron's flowery speech to allay the fears of those staying behind, a few poor souls have seen the light. They broke through and were attempting to board us. We could have departed sooner, but their lives would have been in jeopardy. Had it been left to me, they would be piles of ash from our jet wash." With clenched teeth, he continued, derisively, "But our benevolent leader, Ravar, thinks otherwise."

Enn's processor-like mind assessed the situation, weighed options, and formulated a gambit. Proof of the chieftain's prior plotting with his assistant against Ravar was further reinforced by his present tone. She would capitalize on that. Having just been at the ship's base, she knew the area to be clear. Apparently Mace did not.

"Chieftain, I will order the launch. If there are fatalities, I will face Ravar's wrath."

With one statement, she had shown herself to be as inhumane as her superior, displayed her willingness to sacrifice herself for him, and demonstrated she had no fear, only disdain, for Ravar.

Mace smiled wickedly. "So be it..." Pausing to give himself another opportunity for a lascivious glimpse, he added, "... and Advisor Enn, report to my quarters after we've docked with our cargo module for a *debriefing*."

Pivoting on her heels, she hastily left the Chieftain's office for the command center. Stations for primary functions for ship control were staggered in one quadrant around the the omnivator just outside the door. Scanning across the half dozen technicians, she could sense an undercurrent of tension. Drills on simulators were one thing, but none of them had actually been in space. *She had.* That imbued her with a sense of calm that she hoped would be contagious.

"Eyes on me," she commanded firmly, but with a hint of compassion. Heads snapped up from their consoles. "You've all trained for this. You are Gemini's best. Our goal is before us. *Take the the best to the stars.* Each of you knows your role. I am here to ensure you are successful at it. I lead through your actions. I am but the catalyst. You are the vital ingredients. Employ your minds, your training, and your skills and we will not fail. And so, let us embark on a miraculous journey. Commence launch!"

A petite female sitting to the left of where Enn stood immediately responded, "Stabilizer clamps released. Anti-grav pulse fields activated." She then turned her head, somewhat coyly, to the rugged operator on her right and added, "Time to get it up, Barr."

The chief operator blushed, a navy tinge darkening his cobalt features. Nevertheless, he retained his professionalism and responded, "Increasing flux to coils by one quarter. Radion release contained to 100 treds."

Had there been any stragglers outside the vessel within the launch perimeter, they would have died an agonizing death as the fluids in their bodies vaporized. Astutely, Enn knew that not to be the case. Ravar's orbital sensors would confirm zero fatalities, and Chieftain Mace would receive the credit.

Barr continued with his launch narrative, "Planet pull at 75% and decreasing. Raising flux to three quarter strength."

As it should be, the passengers felt nothing, despite the ship having risen 20 times its height toward the upper atmosphere. The anti-grav coils generated a field of relative force within the craft such that no momentum was created. As the attraction between the planet and the vessel was neutralized, the vessel and its contents experienced a relative field countering any force from lift-off.

A third technician further around the control deck stared intently into a visor extended to eye level from her console. It connected to visual scanners fixed on an event on the surface. "Sister payload module engines igniting. Algorithm shows she will be in orbit within 30 chronal units ahead of us as planned."

On board the passenger module, 2,000 hand selected Geminians floated in their individual gel cocoons for the long journey. The capsules served several purposes. The classic booster rocket design exerted tremendous gravitational forces that were dissipated by the suspension gelatin. The fluid also provided nutrients and pharmaceuticals required for the state of suspended animation during the voyage. Finally, the nested vessels, much like the honeycomb of Terran bees, imparted a structural integrity to the ship beyond any other design.

The concept of hibernation during space travel had been a hotly debated one. Theories were abundant and diverse as to whether organics could survive the psychological isolation and physical atrophy that would occur. Finally, a compromise was reached such that passengers would go through a controlled cycle of dormancy. Programs dictated how shifts of disparate crews would be roused for part of the journey, only to then be returned to hibernation. The scientific community had been placated. The reality of space travel would be the ultimate proof.

As the booster nacelles jettisoned from the central tube containing the precious payload, the main engine fired a final burst. This would carry the rocket to the apex of its solo flight.

The technician at the control desk alerted Enn and the others, "Flux at full. Zero gravitational influence by the planet. Boosters firing to uncoil the umbilicals. Rotation being imparted to create artificial gravity to Control. Docking with passenger module in 8 chronal units."

The command teams of the two other vessels, having already completed their joining with their respective passenger modules, took pause to watch the orbital ballet. From their perspective, they saw a massive tube with blunted nose and incendiary tail expending its last bit of fuel. If sound could travel through the vacuum of space, the observers would hear the roar of the flames snap off, leaving an echo of itself to dissipate into the void. With this last gasp, 2,000 souls waited helplessly for the salvation of the command ship.

Then, seemingly without effort, a twisting coil of writhing tentacles, connected by an ovoid capsule at one end and conical engine at the other, rose from below. As if a sea kraken from old were pulling a schooner into its maw, the passenger module was engulfed. Coils straightened, energy fields flared, and the two vessels were united.

Albeit highly trained and unquestionably professional, the command crew could not resist celebrating. Enn smiled and allowed it. After all, this was the first time outside of simulators for this team to demonstrate their prowess. But it was brief. They knew this was just the beginning of a long journey for them.

The current operating personnel comprised one long term shift out of five. They would be active for two consecutive seasons, or twenty decions, and then cycle into dormancy. An equivalent group in number and skill sets would awaken from their gel tubes and take over for the next twenty decions. Accompanying the first operating team emerging from hibernation would be four hundred of the total two thousand passengers.

Those on the first shift of active duty knew theirs would be unique. A vessel designed for four hundred plus sentient beings would be cavernous to the two dozen currently awake. And even that number was set to be reduced.

During launch, redundancy in personnel had been designed into the system. In case of an emergency, it was believed best to have all tribal leadership on call. With the successful liftoffs and docking of all three sets of starcraft, it was time for specific commanders, themselves, to retire to their dormancy tubes.

That included Ravar.

The rotation of command, ironically, had Chieftain Mace substituting for Ravar to lead the space flotilla on the voyage's first leg. Had Mace's sinister plot against Ravar been successful, he would be leading for the entire journey.

Yet, his subordinate had failed in his mission due to the vagaries of chance. Planet-bound Mitronians having second thoughts caused chaos his underling could not control.

Sub-chieftain Cral's only salvation would be if he replaced his one failure with two successes.

First, he must activate the agent aboard Mitron's vessel to achieve what he failed to accomplish - Mitron's demise.

Second, now that the passenger module was safely nested within the command vessel, Mace expected the delivery of the infiltrator that had possibly overheard their plans.

"The bumbling fool had best not fail me again," fumed Mace to himself. *"The assignment was simple. Instruct the agent aboard Mitron's ship to place circuit overloads on the primary and secondary panels to that accursed Ravar's hibernation unit. Well into our exodus, an unfortunate mishap would terminate the pacifist in his sleep. This would clear the way for me to assume authority."*

Despite Ravar's prophecy and technical prowess that led to their salvation, tribal rivalry still ran deep within a few of the saved ones. Mace represented the worst of the clans. His followers, though outwardly compliant, whispered that Ravar had too easily compromised with Mitron. A mere three ships could have readily been a dozen if the full resources of the Geminian tribes been employed. By yielding to Mitron's assertions that Gemini was not on the brink of annihilation, the unified tribes had only contributed a paltry amount to the effort. And Ravar gratefully accepted the crumbs.

"My leadership will be from a position of strength, not compromise," he extolled to himself. *"Once Cral fulfills his tasks, locating the infiltrator and ensuring the devices are installed, my ascendancy will be guaranteed!"*

Enn appeared at the clan leader's door just as he was clenching a raised fist in imagined triumphant fury. Gathering his composure, he quickly lowered his arm, an azure flush of embarrassment coloring his cheeks.

"You required a debriefing, my liege," Enn reminded, exerting all her self-control to stifle a smile and accompanying raised eyebrow.

"Sub-chieftain Cral has not reported his progress. Show me you are his better ... what do you know?"

Enn certainly knew of Cral's status - in a mental ward on Gemini - since she was the cause. As for the infiltrator he sought, Chieftain Mace would not be pleased if he knew she stood before him. It was time for some well designed mis-information.

"My sources on our sister crafts tell me no-one boarded during the limited time Cral or the infiltrator had once they left our vessel. That said, logic would dictate that the problem resolved itself in a most agonizing manner when our craft launched."

Mace's azure flush of embarrassment darkened - this time from rage. "Your sense of certainty is impressive, but misplaced. The problem persists. Cral had an assignment. His failure leaves it incomplete."

"I am here to serve. What is it you require?"

Mace eyed her up and down once again. This time, less from lust and more to assess her capabilities.

"Cral was a fool, but he was family. I grieve his loss." Pausing for theatrical effect, Mace then explained the true reasoning for his rage. "Our clan survives by compartmentalizing information. He and only he knew who was loyal onboard Ravar's ship. From what clan do you hail?"

Enn steeled herself before speaking. It was time for a bold maneuver. The best subterfuge often came as a disguised truth.

"I am Enn de Mitron, perhaps you have heard of our order?" she said, tauntingly.

"What?!" Mace's hand reflexively fell to the war axe at his belt. It did not go unnoticed by

Enn. Before he could splutter any further, Enn continued.

"I alone of our clan broke ranks with our leader. Like Ravar, Mitron relied too heavily on peace and compromise for my taste. I used it to my advantage. Rather than force me to stay on the doomed planet, he relinquished and set me free. So, I have no clan. Only allegiance to my superior, you."

Mace's ego overcame his anger. Walking around his console, he stood toe to toe with his subordinate. And surprisingly, due to Enn's stature, eye to eye.

Your words serve you well, Advisor Enn. Let us see if your *actions* can serve *me*. Ravar is scheduled to submit to two seasons of slumber, leaving me in charge. It is my right to send my second-in-command to assume authority over his starcraft before we engage the ion engines.

That duty now falls to you.

Reconnect the broken chain of loyalty to me. Determine the identity of the operative known only to Cral."

Raising his hand slowly up to the side of Enn's head as if to stroke her hair, he pulled it away before touching her, placing his fingertips on his own temple. Enn did not flinch. He then brought it down, palm up, presumably in the gesture Enn had used when saluting the attendant that took Cral.

Instead, Chieftain Mace then clenched his fist and said, "The mind is the source of *power*. Show me yours by terminating Ravar!"

Enn's eyes narrowed, yet the fire in them could not be contained. She nodded a crisp affirmative. Pivoting briskly on her heels, she marched out of the command center thinking, *"Ravar, my love, this should prove interesting."*

CHAPTER 9

Vice-Executive Talor's humor had improved after his reflections on his heroic efforts to save P'Teel and T'Poch. Once the Code Enforcement Agency squadron had flown over in hot pursuit of the distraction drone, it had been a simple matter of lifting off through the man-made dune to return to his mother ship.

However, the nature of his improved humor was relative. He now sat in the conference area adjacent to the control room. Absent-mindedly, he toyed with the memory doubloon hanging from the chain around his neck. His patience wore thin waiting for the two enchantresses. They had insisted on cleansing themselves of the Geminian sands before formally meeting with him to discuss their mission.

The chime of the personnel lift signaled that Talor's wait was over. The door whisked open and out stepped P'Teel and T'Poch. Despite her untold age, the matriarch carried herself with poise and ease. She had availed herself of the dispensary and selected a subtle, but becoming belted robe. The lightweight fabric flowed as she walked. It's shimmering purple hue with gold piping hinted at royalty from a bygone era.

In contrast, her ward almost stalked behind her, as would a feral beast wary of capture. A form-fitting cream tunic over sheer leggings and knee-high suede boots projected both power and grace. The intense Polluxan sun had darkened her sapphire skin to a royal hue. Garnet eyes flashed a warning, set above aquiline features beneath a wind blown ebony mane, daring any nemesis to approach.

Talor caught his breath. Remembering his own breeding, he rose and made a gallant gesture for them to be seated. Once settled, he activated a delivery tray to appear out of a wall compartment, bearing a decanter of emerald liquid with an assortment of small, crystalline glasses. P'Teel nodded appreciatively as the vice-executive served her.

T'Poch abstained.

Talor took the cue and dispensed with any further pleasantries, saying, "We have much to discuss before we arrive at."

"We do," agreed T'Poch, tersely, as P'Teel sipped her refreshment, casually looking away as if disinterested.

"Then let me begin," proffered Talor. "Not all of Castor is aligned with our cause. The cadre of supporters assisting with your transport are looked upon as rogues and renegades by the Castorian Conglomerate. At least *officially*."

"And what is the *unofficial* position on Castor?" inquired T'Poch.

"As has been the history of our planet … it is, complex. Rumored but never proven is the lineage between Gemini and Castor. Legend tells of brave explorers cast out into space by your planet's messiah, Mitron. Whispers say that mid-voyage, a change in leadership of the spacefarers occurred. So, from the beginning, tribal conflict has created strife among our people."

Talor paused, as he noted P'Teel beginning to fidget in her seat, her disinterest giving way to mounting irritation. Yet, he chose to continue.

"A segment of our people desire to return to the past. The spirit of exploration and discovery was strong amongst our founders. It grows stagnant under our current rule. They wish our planet to flourish independently. They fear any alliance that could constrain us. Fragments of history doubloons - rare, but still, real - reveal that those followers, then and now, pay homage to one known as Ravar. He is believed to have initially led the pilgrims on their space voyage."

P'Teel all but snorted as she abruptly set her glass down with a sharp rap. "I know all too well of Ravar … and Mitron, too. Each were visionaries, but could be stubborn. Mitron, famous for his peaceful ways, required the influence of a firm hand at the helm. Ravar, often the intellectual, would get lost in his experiments. He had no guidance once he left Gemini. Without a cause, he could wander. So, the ideals of neither, on their own, w ll lead us to the destiny we seek. Instead, they must be reshaped - forged - into a stronger bridge to our future!"

She turned her stony visage toward T'Poch, seeking her affirmation. The younger enchantress narrowed her eyes as if to extinguish the flame that threatened to burst forth.

Steepling her fingers, she slowly nodded. Softly, but almost venomously, she said to Talor, "We are intimately knowledgable regarding the lineage of Mitron - its successes, and its *failures. Those* we seek to remedy. Our goal is to craft a new future for Gemini, beyond the pacifist influence of those that came before. We believe Castor can be part of that future. At least the *right* Castor. Of which Castor are *you*?"

This time it was Talor who fidgeted in his chair. Not borne of anger, but from fear.

Stammering, he implored, "Let me clarify. Ravarians   of the past yielded to a more militant faction that lead the settlement of Castor. Our civilization grew, prospered, and even ventured back into space. Yet, we were always in the shadow of the more affluent cartels from not just our own system like Gemini, but others, such as Solar Corporation.

But unrest is mounting. Many believe our Chairman to be dead. Our society flounders. Leadership is fragmented. A growing number suspect the power behind the Chair seeks to unify with Solar and Gemini in the courts of the Legotians. This would leave Castor but a minion - stripped of power - neutered on the interstellar stage!"

T'Poch relaxed slightly, taking a small bit of solace in the passion behind Talor's words. "Gemini, too, has suffered because of the impure alliance with the Terrans of Solar

Corporation. I personally know all too well the vile influence on biodgen technology because of the Earthers."

The turmoil within T'Poch churned from the conflict between her indebtedness to her creators and her disgust over their roles as corporate profiteers.

"The revered ideals of Phoenos are but a means to a profitable end with their accursed biodrone commercialization," she continued. "That will change once the prophecy for a unified Gemini and Castor   is fulfilled. We will purge the weak-minded from our midst. Those supporting an alliance with Solar will yield to our righteous cause!"

Talor, excited by what he heard, sought further affirmation from the force of nature sitting before him. His hand went back to the memory doubloon on the chain around his neck. This time to remove it. He slid a cover of a small compartment in the table's surface and dropped it in.

A foil screen rose from a slot adjacent to the vid coin's cradle. Before the images appeared, Talor offered an introduction.

"Our records of the Ravarian pilgrimage are limited. They begin after the three arks sought refuge upon a planetoid that follows a non-ecliptic orbit through the Polluxan system. This memory doubloon has been handed down through my family archives. It depicts a patriarch of my line chronicling the events of the voyage."

A flicker in the projection was followed by the appearance of a young azure-toned man. Dressed in a light, airy cloth shirt draping to mid-thigh, a decorative embroidered belt held a tri-bladed short sword at his hip.

The image spoke.

"In response to -glitch- Chairman Ravar's request, I Stev, am continuing his chronicles of our journey. He has honored me with the mantle of chieftain, -hiss- as he adopts his new role. For this, I am grateful and humbled.

-glitch- Our efforts with the asteroid swarm were significant. We are thankful for the counsel of Advisor Enn. Her wisdom was invaluable. Our gratitude for her to the house of Mitron will hopefully manifest itself in our actions against the swarm. We anticipate success with diverting the meteor that threatens Gemini, but have no way of knowing for sure. Only the gods can foresee the outcome. -squelch-

An added bonus was the delay caused by altering course to engage the swarm. Because of it, our arks narrowly avoided the full brunt of an ion storm. Our altered path revealed the existence of a planetoid with a non-ecliptic orbit through our system. We have decided to explore it for possible colonization. -hiss-

During the final orbital approach to the planetoid, a residual ion front engulfed our vessels. None were heavily damaged. However, radiation poisoning affected us to a limited degree. We expect no fatalities. -hiss-

Our healers have -static- cautiously optimistic news. They expect that some exposed may be sterile, while some may experience radiation effects on their offspring. As new chieftan, I share their grief -hiss- as I am forced to watch my people suffer.

Yet, it might have been much worse.

-squawk- Our starwatchers tell me that the storm during our arrival is of a cyclical nature. Their best calculations give us four seasons to prepare for the next one. After much deliberation, we have decided that for our people to remain bound to this forsaken world through repeated sieges by the cosmos would be an injustice.

Rather than shield ourselves, or seek protection underground as would vermin, we will -glitch-resume our voyage. The fourth and last drone-probe sent out before entering orbit has been faithful in its transmissions. The most recent data has identified a planet twenty seasons journey from here. We believe this oasis, orbiting our own star, but in a cycle always hidden from our home-world, gives us our best hope for survival. It will be a difficult journey, but our spirit will strengthen us. Our hope is that one day, we may return home to

-hiss- reunite with our brethren, who, gods willing, will benefit from our struggles."

P'Teel sat dumbfounded, slightly shaking her head. She stared at the screen, watching it waver, as if two were trying to occupy the same space. Turning to T'Poch, she wondered if she was experiencing the same disbelief. But how could she? Unlike P'Teel, she had not lived so many seasons, spanning generations, resolutely anchored in her own timeline. And only P'Teel had possession of the knowledge provided her from Nimon's trial. The Clionian historian had given witness using vid doubloons recovered from the very planetoid mentioned moments earlier. Yet, the messages were not the same, despite their coming from the same spokesman.

Determined to understand this paradox, P'Teel elected to be diplomatic rather than forceful, saying, "Vice-executive Talor, the information you have shared is … intriguing… and I am sure the doubloon is a treasured heirloom. It provides rare insight into a most critical time for our people. As such, it requires more study. Yet, I fear our adventure escaping the authorities - of which we are most grateful to you - has fatigued me more than I cared to admit. I find myself in need of rest."

Talor, desiring to further court the good graces of his guests, responded, "But of course. We have several decions before we reach Castor. I apologize for our condition that hinders our speed. Perhaps it can be used to your advantage to allow time for rest and recovery?"

T'Poch looked quizzically at her mentor. Never one to exhibit the least bit of frailty despite her age, she recognized P'Teel's behavior for what it was - a ploy.

As they rose to leave, P'Teel stopped in mid-shuffle and added, "Ah, if I might trouble you for one more favor?"

"Why of course, anything," Talor replied, perhaps too quickly, as he would discover.

"My ward is highly skilled in archival studies. Most recently she performed a comprehensive forensic review of the Mitronian lineage," P'Teel informed, coyly. "Too proud to mention it, or ask, she would be honored if she had the opportunity to more closely study this valuable portion of our shared history."

Talor hesitated, clearly caught off-guard. It was as if he had been requested to part with his hand.

T'Poch, not oblivious to the impact she had made upon him when she entered the room, saw fit to employ her own rarely used feminine wiles. She lifted the doubloon from its cradle and eased next to Talor. Lifting his hand with her own, she gently placed the vid coin in his palm. Lightly drawing her fingers back to the tips of his, she curled them around the precious heirloom. The warmth of her hands around his was comforting, almost intoxicating.

She whispered, "Of course, I understand your hesitancy. I would not let it out of my sight. Once done, I would relish the opportunity to return it to you ... personally."

His mouth slowly opened, as did his hand. As she softy stroked it, deftly removing the coin, she allowed herself a seductive smile.

Then, like ethereal apparitions, the two women slipped from the room.

CHAPTER 10

Mitron stood at the railing of his palatial balcony, watching as the fiery plumage of the last of Ravar's ships disappeared into the heavens. Dressed in full battle raiments, he had just returned from the tribal senate. There, standing before the chieftains of the lesser orders, he had beseeched them once again to listen.

"Fellow leaders, one strike of a meteor does not portend a cataclysmic armageddon for our planet. Though my comrade, Ravar, believes it to be true, we must be steadfast in our decision to remain on our beloved Gemini.

Records show our ancestors to have survived such events in the past. Though our planet bears the scars of prior celestial events, it remains as a thriving haven nurturing the advancement of our society.

To abandon that which has cradled our people for eons is foolhardy to say the least, and reckless when considering the dangers of the alternative - space travel!

I implore you to be unwavering for your people. Do not yield to the naysayers. Instead, assure them that we …Will … BE … STRONGER by uniting against the diversity that lies ahead!"

Now, watching his friend depart on a journey into the unknown, he whispered, "May Fate yield to Mercy's song, brother Ravar, and guide you into a safe and fulfilling future."

A soothing voice responded to his prayer, as priestess P'Teel eased herself to his side, slipping her arm beneath his. The balm she had applied to her skin worked its magic, as a pheromonal rush swept over Mitron.

"You are a faithful friend, my love, even to the very end. I fear the is the last we will see of our highly intelligent, but over-adventurous oaf."

"Dear Stargazer, you of all people should be optimistic for our friend. Are you not the one who says the heavens have much to offer, if only we were wise enough to heed their message?"

"That is true. But just as the distant sea can provide wealth and bounty, I do not advocate sailing into the maw of its storms. To be so arrogant that we, with all our frailties, could vanquish Nature's wrath, only invites doom as the outcome. Such as it is with our friend Ravar, and his odyssey."

"Speaking of friends, what has become of your fellow Fire Sorceress, Novas? I fear my last encounter with her may have caused a misunderstanding. My misplaced affections hopefully caused no lasting damage to your association with her. How was I to control the chaos of passion you stirred within me?"

P'Teel's sinister smile went unnoticed by Del Mitron, as he continued to peer skyward after the now invisible star crafts. *"There is no way for me to explain the phenomenon of Novas's disappearance,"* thought the mystical temptress. *"I fail to fully comprehend it myself. I am confident, though, that she is out of our lives forever. Just as is Ravar. Why not let my chieftain form his own conclusion?"*

"Aah, delusional Del... your ego knows no bounds," she taunted. "In your mind, all women must have you. 'Tis true, you can be irresistible, when you allow your beast to emerge. But in the case of Novas, she will remain elusive. For Ravar expressed his undying love for her, revealing his innermost desires. He begged her to follow him to the stars."

"No need to say more, my temptress," Del interrupted. "As with me, her passion was like lightening, seeking a place to ground itself. Whereas my uncontrollable fire found you, most certainly Novas' released itself upon Ravar. I only hope their union wil be as fulfilling as ours."

Why Del, my chieftain, is that a proposal?"

Without hesitation, Mitron replied. "Yes, it most certainly is!"

"Then, you irresistible beast, I must accept!"

*　　*　　*

Hal Xkorp and his supervisor, Eric Magnek were in the next room, tending to the cremation of the murdered technician and rogue biodgen. They had insisted Dr. Edison not be present. Claims of security clearances and confidentiality agreements were offered as the justification.

"Just as well," muttered Dr. Edison, as he hovered over the form inside the stasis field. "I have my own secrets."

The nanotechnology within Nimon's body appeared dormant at the moment. Scans showed they were stimulated by the energy signature from the life crystal embedded within him. Yet, with his Dual, Starn, in orbit, the Singular Dualiity phenomenon was suppressed. Edison wondered if Starn could even animate Nimon if he wanted. Did Dualiity forever separate them - Starn able never again to project his consciousness into Nimon? In essence, had Nimon reverted to a typical bioduogenetic unit at rest until Starn was sufficiently distant?

"I suspect once the Darwin leaves orbit with Starn aboard, Nimon will reanimate as an independent entity," pondered the scientist. *"Infected as he is with the nanites, I cannot allow that to happen. His safety, alone, is in question, should madness engulf him. Not to mention the risk of infecting other biodgens. My choices are few. I am forced to resort to drastic measures."*

The bioduogeneticist within Dr. Edison emerged, displacing the reluctant father. He wheeled a cart out of a corner and positioned its mechanism over his patient. A glass bell jar was slowly lowered into place, laser targeting probes ensuring the proper location. Dials were adjusted. Keystrokes entered. Finally, the activation button was pressed.

The matter-energy converter hummed, its sonic tone crescendoing as it increased in power. Within the glass vessel, a kaleidoscope of colors swirled - first above the surface of the biodgen, then slowly sinking into the underlying tissue. Adhesion within synthetic cells dissipated. Bonding forces to the Ravarian crystal reversed.

Slowly, the shard rose from the body, suspended within the glass container. Beneath it, syntho-organic structures were restored.

The doctor released a long sigh, allowing the father within a small smile. Digital displays showed all to be normal. Atrophy within the nanocytes was underway. It was as if Nimon had never been impaled by his sinister duotronic aunt. But the violation remained.

It would be Starn's decision from this point forward. Return to his role as Dual mentor? Work with Dr. Edison to determine if Dualiity could be safely restored? And what of the Ravarian crystal?

A sound from the crematorium stirred the doctor from his reverie. Quickly, Edison transferred the shard from the bell jar to a shielded case. Just in time, he darkened the opacity of Nimon's containment field as the two IAD personnel entered from the adjacent room.

"The process is complete," noted Magnek. "Our lander should be arriving shortly."

"Very well," replied Edison. "That gives me just enough time to finish gathering my things, and our search for the K'Tar leader can commence."

Surreptitiously, he placed the case among some other items on a small gurney and wheeled them to the exit.

*   *   *

A season had passed since the departure of Ravar's space-bound caravans. For many on Gemini, life had returned to normal.

Except for two.

Del Mitron and P'Teel had wed!

Select citizens of the capital city, Centar, along with dignitaries from neighboring tribes, had thoroughly enjoyed the ceremony. Many more attended the ancillary festivities surrounding the bonding. And, if a royal wedding weren't enough to lighten the citizens' spirits, there was the added bonus.

Planet-bound Geminians had enjoyed a respite from celestial bombardments!

The media had heralded Mitron as a vizier of great prowess. Not only was he correct with his prognostication of minimal harm from space, his wisdom to marry a high priestess of the Stargazer clan was inspirational.

Long shrouded in a veil of mysticism and secrecy, the sect had been shunned by many due to fear and superstition. Though some tribal leaders had sought the counsel of members of the order, most yielded to the will of the unwashed masses by spurning them.

For those earnest followers of Mitron's leadership, the presence of P'Tee was a welcome innovation. For those less smitten with the decision, but electing to acquiesce, she would be a necessary evil.

"Del, our honeymoon has been glorious! You have lavished me with the trappings of royalty, while your subjects have accepted me as your rightful mate!"

Mitron stroked the silver laced ebony tresses of his new wife as they lounged together before a crackling fire. Matching robes of finely woven Tuzzarian silk trimmed in gold loosely covered their glistening bodies after yet another vigorous session of love-making.

"It has truly been wondrous these past rotations, my love," murmured the chieftain, still immersed in the narcotic influence of the temptress's wiles.

"That is why I am reluctant to end our fabled time with the burden of ominous tidings."

Half-lidded eyes struggled to open, barely able to cast a misty gaze upon the enchantress. "Then do not..." Del replied, lightly chuckling at his meager effort to be witty.

Seeing she had dosed him with just the right amount of elixir to blunt his rage, yet comprehend her words, P'Teel continued. "But I must, dear husband. It is for the good of the people. My advisers tell me the eye of the celestial storm will soon pass. Their calculations portend a coming event that will deliver devastating results. More calamitous than ever before experienced by our world."

Propping himself on one elbow to face her, allowing P'Teel to do the same, clarity began to disperse his mind's fog. "And what makes your experts so sure this time is any different than before?" Del probed.

"The science is complex, but the explanation is quite simple. Picture Gemini circling our sun, Pollux, taking five seasons, or fifty decions, to complete one orbit. It's companion planets circle the star similarly, but at varying distances in the same plane. As such, there is no fear of collision."

Mitron interrupted, his irritation building, displacing his stupor. "I am not a dunce. I understand the basics of astronomy."

"I meant no offense, my lord," P'Teel soothingly replied. "Consider it my suggested speech for you to deliver to the less informed populace."

"Ah, very well … wise counsel as usual," he mumbled, apologetically.

She continued, "Now visualize yet another celestial body, eons older than the planets girding our sun. But it is a rogue, in that it orbits in a different plane, some 45 degrees removed from Gemini's, and at a different velocity. To add further complexity, it is not even a sphere, but a collection of irregularly shaped asteroids, stretching in a cloud through space."

"Most likely a shattered planet, or even an assembly of matter that never successfully coalesced *into* a planet during the formation of our system," Del speculated, more alertly.

"Exactly! Over the millennia, on rare occasions, Gemini's orbit coincided perilously close with fringes of the space bound swarm. Hence, the archival stories of past near cataclysms and scars across the surface of our planet. Unfortunately, the timing for just such another intersection is upon us."

"So Ravar was right after all," Mitron groused. "And I am to look the fool by ignoring his warnings!"

"Not so, my love. Chances for your people's survival planet-side are far greater than those who challenged the savagery of space. Especially if we execute my plan for our salvation!"

Mitron raised a skeptical eyebrow, but wisely chose to cloak his disbelief with a show of support. "You are certainly a woman of many wonders. Tell me more of your strategy to save our people."

"Patience, my liege. Rather than tell you, instead, let me *show* you."

*   *   *

Mitron and P'Teel disembarked from their graviton sled, so adeptly piloted by the enchantress. They stood at the base of a sheer cliff in the mountain chain, Mal Gar. The fractured crust of Gemini rose relentlessly skyward, formed ages ago from heaving planetary magma induced by meteorite strikes. The stony barrier served as the only sentinel separating Geminian civilization from the onslaught of an immense desert. T Bok Vri, the Silent Giant, relentlessly bombarded the rocky surface with sand, hoping at some future time to be victorious with its assault.

Thankfully, the pair saw no need to challenge the wrath of nature and approached a rocky outcropping from the leeward side. Both wore loose-fitted linen robes layered over breathable undergarments to defend against the Polluxan sun. Turbans of like material swathed their heads, with a surplus length available to protect their face, if needed. Genetics served to shield their eyes, as nictitating membranes filtered out the harmful rays.

Mitron, obediently submitting to P'Teel's clandestine behavior during their journey, could no longer contain himself.

"Though my love for you knows no bounds, dear Stargazer, my patience is at its limit. What has compelled you to abduct me only to deliver my to this gods forsaken spot?"

P'Teel could not help but giggle at her mate's theatrics. Matching his melodrama with her own, she retorted, "Kneel before me, my captive, for I finally have you in my clutches. Behold, as I command the very child of Gemini's core to open it's maw. It's purpose, to devour you if you do not heed my command!"

In a sweeping gesture, she pivoted, one arm flourishing toward the craggy surface, her other slipping discreetly within the folds of her robe. A small transmitter noiselessly emitted an encoded signal.

Mitron dropped to his knees, half from an improvisational flourish, and half from a reflexive act of astonishment.

True to her proclamation, a massive stone swung effortlessly inward, leaving a gaping opening. The mighty chieftain shuddered as he imagined being consumed by the stalactite teeth revealed within.

P'Teel ushered her reluctant companion into the gloomy chamber. Once inside, motion detectors powered energy to strategically placed crystals. The illumination added warmth as well to dispel the chill of the dank and dreary confines.

Another touch to the controller within the Stargazer's robe prompted the entrance doorway to close, while a smaller one on the back wall opened. Urging Mitron forward, they both stepped on to a pneumatic lift.

As it began too slowly rise, P'Teel explained.

"It would take days to show you the entire complex hidden within these peaks. However, from the control center, I can explain many of the marvels of the facility."

"How long has this existed, and how did I not know of this place?" pressed Mitron, unwilling to wait until the elevator stopped.

"For generations, dearest Del. And none of the tribes but for my own clan are privy to the secrets that lie within. Oh, there have been a few who have stumbled onto our location. Ravar being one. If not for the introduction of a precisely designed potion into his system, I am confident our secrecy would have crumbled beneath the weight of the oath's loyalty to you."

"The story of the day you two met ... I recall. Supposedly he became lost within the myriad tunnels somewhere within this mountain range. You claim you rescued him. He was unable, though, to clearly recollect the details of the event."

"Rescue him, I did. For if the potion had not had the intended effect, death would have been the only alternative."

A chill trickled down Mitron's spine at her cold, ruthless tone. He had not glimpsed this side of P'Teel's personality before. Discreetly, he placed his hand on the hilt of the short sword resting in its scabbard beneath his robe.

"And what is to become of me, Enchantress? Am I to taste the sweet nectar of your elixir - or perhaps something far worse?"

"Calm yourself, Warrior Del. No need for fear - or for the weapon you now clutch. Behold."

The lift halted its climb. As its door slid open, P'Teel took the lead into the waiting control center. Immediately, the collection of personnel at various stations halted their work, turning to stand at attention and face their mistress.

"Please continue," she directed, allowing them to return to their duties.

Del Mitron, awestruck, took in the scene. He had never before seen such a collection of stunning women. Of course, all paled when compared to the beauty of his wife, but not by much.

He discerned some of the tell tale attributes of neighboring tribes. Some with deep indigo skin. Others with gold inlaid tattoos on their arms. Even a few exhibited albinism - their white hair and just a shade of aqua tone to their complexion.

To his dismay, being what he thought to be a world traveler, there were a few he did *not* recognize. One seemed to have a texture to her skin. Almost as if covered by translucent scales, suggesting the watery habitat of the distant Geminian sea. Yet another was adorned with vestigial feathers tracing an outline along her shoulders and arms.

One trait, though, was shared by them all. An undeniable loyalty to their leader, Ɔ'Teel.

Stepping closer to her he whispered, "I am stunned, dear wife. I feel as if I am under a spell. What I see defies belief."

"Ah, my husband, prepare yourself. For until now, you have seen nothing."

CHAPTER 11

A silvery glow fluoresced at the bottom of the door to the utility room on board the *Destiny*. Within, the essence of the Castorian Executive coalesced, her energy particles transforming back into her physical self. The experience was unnerving. Just moments ago, she had been in what she could only describe as a thought counsel with the Legotian, Chrislar, and the Solar Corporation delegate, Novas of Gemini. They both had learned that the Legotians were far more than interstellar negotiators. Having revealed themselves to be non-corporeal beings, they had also demonstrated other capabilities. For one, the ability to transform others from matter to energy to facilitate communication virtually at light speed.

Thankfully, the process was reversible. She preferred her solid form. As her internally generated radiance dissipated, she sensed she was no longer in the Legotian chamber with the mercurial pool. She groped the walls of the small enclosure until she found a switch to activate the lumen panel overhead.

"Somewhat of an unceremonious return to the real world," she thought. *"From a forum negotiating a venture between the Castorian Conglomerate and the Solar Corporation ... to this,"* she mused. Looking around the oversized closet, she saw shelves of cleaning solution, various brushes, and the ever-present mop. *"Well, there must be a method to the madness of the Legotians. Best that I explore where I am."*

She triggered the switch causing the door to whisk open. Stepping into the hallway, a tingling chill bloomed at the base of her neck. An eery sense of familiarity engulfed her. Pausing to get her bearings, she murmured, "Where in the stars am I?" Tiptoeing down the main hallway, she noted its curvature. Dotted along the walls sporadically were small communication panels with archaic glass screens and control buttons. Taking in the dated style of the devices, she pondered, *"More importantly... when am I?"*

Continuing to follow the arc of the hallway, she came upon a series of large glass windows. Peering into the room beyond, she saw the sign, "Hydroponics." Stretching the extent of an auditorium-sized room were tables filled with suspended trays of various plants. Flexible tubing with colored liquids draped from boxes overhead supplied vital nutrients to the vegetation.

The Executive gasped. "I know this place … all to well. But how can it be? I visited this facility as a child, purloining fruit delicacies to the chagrin of … *my father*?! But that would mean, I'm on board the *Destiny*!"

More mature legs carried her further down the corridor than the much shorter ones did so many seasons ago. She stopped at a heavily covered oval panel on the wall that she knew would be the outer hull of the vessel. Opening a plastic covered security box, she turned the handle within. The metal screen slid noiselessly to the side to reveal a breath-taking view.

The planet Gemini!

But not the sight she would see in her era. The surface was lush and green over much of it. Expansive seas formed blue blotches around the sphere where arid deserts should be. As far as she could see, not another hint of technology could be found orbiting the planet.

She had seen artist renderings of the planet as it was thought to look before a near cataclysmic strike of a meteor during the time of Mitron. As best as she could recall, they got it right. Historical accounts varied - often morphed by myth and legend - as to the number and sizes of the strikes. The one consistent version had that moment in Gemini's past as the catalyst that led to the exodus rumored to be the birth of Castorian culture.

"Could it be the Legotians have sent me to that most critical moment in the past of both Gemini and Castor for a reason? Theorists speculate that time travel is feasible. Yet we know of no beings able to achieve it. Until now! But how would my presence here connect to any success with the negotiations between our planets?"

As the Executive mulled over the possibilities, skepticism began to emerge. It *could* be a ruse. But it felt so real. Further inquiry was definitely needed. Her childhood memories floated to the forefront of her mind. *"It all seems smaller and more compact than I remember. Further around this curve and into one of the branch halls should be the stellar cartography lab. I recall learning to read the stars before I could read our language,"* she reflected. *"From there I can authenticate both the vessel as being real and where in time and space I am."*

Arriving at the laboratory's entrance she all but barged in through the frosted plexi-steel door. Most of the technicians were hunched over their control boards. A few supervisory personnel stood with their backs to her. They watched on a large wall screen with intense interest as a sister ship to the *Destiny* choreographed the union between its two modules.

The Executive moved from console to console, her authoritative bearing born from years of practice. Occasionally, an operator would glance up, snap to a seated attention, and give her a sharp nod with their head, as if in salute. After several instances of this, she became emboldened and approached one of the supervisors as an experiment to elicit a reaction.

Smoothly taking a position next to a fit looking male with gold piping on his grey tunic, she waited quietly to be acknowledged. As the *Vector* completed its docking sequence, a murmur of appreciation spread across the room. The section chief noticeably relaxed, turned his head casually toward her to share the moment, and immediately tensed once more.

Nodding his head briskly, as did the others previously, he spoke. "Priestess. My apologies. I did not see you. I was focused on Chieftain Mace's successful arrival to orbit. That makes three, as you know."

"*Priestess?*" thought the Castorian Executive. "*What is he talking about?*" For the first time since her exit from the closet, she had need for a mirror. Glancing down past the chief as if to convey a sense of indifference, she eyed herself in the reflection of one of the inactive video monitors.

Her trim figure was wrapped in a chamois bodice partially covered by a linen stole with elaborate stitching adorning its edges. A matching linen skirt draped to the floor. A leather border protected the hem and rose up the front of the split skirt, revealing the smooth-muscled legs of the wearer. A silver pendant on a gold chain nestled delicately against her ample bosom.

The flicker of shock across her face was quickly suppressed. The section chief mistook it for displeasure. Attempting to recover, he added, "But of course you know. Our fledgling knowledge of space pales compared to the eons of study by your sisterhood. Your insights surpass science, extending into the realm of mysticism few can hope to understand."

The Executive barely heard him. Vague memories swirled in her mind. As a child aboard the *Destiny*, she had encountered an acolyte of the Stargazer sect. Members had counseled the tribal leaders of Gemini, as well as Castor, for generations. With skills residing on a spectrum that ranged from black magic to astrophysics, their prowess had become legendary.

Her garb clearly placed her as a member of the Stargazers. Hence the deference and access to the control center. Leveraging this advantage, she pointed to the console on which her hazy image resided.

"I wish to see our projected course … sub-chieftain …?"

"*Thresh*, my lady."

"Very good. You may address me as Tempora."

"I am honored." Sub-Chieftain Thresh tugged at his tunic and nervously brushed an imaginary piece of lint from his sleeve. He stood there, relishing the opportunity to garner the attention of a Stargazer. Tempora stifled a smile at his servitude. She folded her arms and cast a raised eyebrow toward the monitor, tapping her sandaled foot.

"Oh! Of course … let me." Thresh bent over the worktable, hurriedly tapping jeweled buttons and positioning the microphone for voice recognition. He then commanded, "Display course projection, Ravarian Ark Flotilla."

Instantly, a graphic display appeared. Gemini's orbit around the star Pol ux was represented. Neighboring stars were in their generally relative positions. However, Tempora knew that *precise reckonings* of the astral bodies ' locations would translate to a specific point in time.

"Monitor, *Destiny* location, right ascension and declination, Mitronian epoch time stamp. Overlay known astral bodies, meteor class zeta size and larger," the Executive, now priestess, commanded. A few pulses passed before the display refreshed. "Overlay optical view. Magnify this quadrant," she added, touching a specific spot on the screen. The monitor obeyed.

Tempora remained stoic. Thresh couldn't help but gasp. Internally, she felt the same, though, for a different reason.

The chart revealed the information Tempora sought. She was no longer in her present. Instead, she was somehow in the past

- 12 Geminian cycles into the Mitronian epoch, within 1 cycle of the great cataclysm.

The meteor impact with the planet was imminent.

As for Thresh, the reality of his planet's demise was shocking. "We were so pre-occupied with reaching orbit, no-one thought to investigate the meteor's path from our vantage point in space. Without atmospheric interference, we can clearly *see* what, up until now, was only hypothesized. We now have solid proof supporting your sisterhood's predictions. Predictions only Ravar had the courage to defend and act upon." He half-bowed, almost reverently, in deference to her skills.

Tempora gave him a short nod to acknowledge the praise. But her attention was still focused on the screen. "Monitor, spectroscopic analysis of meteor swarm. Proportional categorization of known and unknown minerals."

The Monitor responded, "Estimated time for task completion, 0.10 rotation."

Tempora responded, "Understood. Results: security protocol *-Eyes Only-* Ravar, mine..." and pausing, she glanced at the section head, "... and Chief Thresh."

The sub-chieftain beamed, puffing out his chest noticeably with pride. "That should allow sufficient time for my staff to take a much needed nutritional respite. Before they are dismissed, might I ask the hypothesis you wish to investigate, Priestess?"

Coyly, Tempora replied, "Why, if I revealed *all* my secrets, where would be the mystery? Instead, I will continue my rounds and you wi l learn upon my return."

With a hint of a smile, she turned smoothly and exited the center.

*   *   *

Tark, third-in-command to the *Destiny*, stalked the corridor, seething. He understood the rules of ascension, as well as the need to rotate leadership through their dormancy cycle, but it did not mean he had to like it.

Through duplicitous means, Tark had discovered a vital piece of intelligence. His immediate superior, and Chieftain Mace's second-in-command, Cral, had bungled his assignment to terminate Ravar. Adding cowardice to incompetence, Cral had then escaped punishment by disappearing.

This left a communication void with Chieftain Mace as to what to do next. As protocol demanded, orders for such a sensitive matter prohibited all but a face-to-face exchange.

So much the better for Tark. He would take matters into his own hands. *He* would decide to implement the contingency plan to eliminate Ravar. The outcome would be more than he could hope for.

Knowing that Mace was sending his *new* second to command the *Destiny* during Ravar's sleep, Tark's opportunity to advance in rank was doubtful. His link to Chieftain Mace was severed with the disappearance of Cral. *"Who knows where the new second's loyalties lie? For all I know, I could suffer from the fallout of Cral's ineptitude, unless I take action!"* Tark schemed.

Always innovative, some said *devious*, Tark would transform this detriment into his benefit.

He knew Ravar would insist on greeting his new sub-chieftain in person. Always the arrogant one, he often dismissed his security detail. Tark would capitalize upon this. Both he and his second would be in the cargo hangar together.

"Similar to the plan to use the excuse of new technology glitches to cause a dormancy tube failure, why not a hangar deck?" postulated Tark to himself, sinisterly. *"It's just a matter of timing. Once he enters, all that is needed is to simply lock the portal and slowly decompress the room. They'll collapse, suffocated, to be found later. Mace will be forced to elevate me to command the Destiny while he leads the flotilla onboard the Vector. At the appropriate time, I will inform him that it was me, not Chance, that was Ravar's undoing."*

*   *   *

Tempora wandered the corridors of the *Destiny,* passing the time until the meteor swarm analysis was complete. Still wading through mists of memories from her childhood, she all but chuckled at how mischievous she had been as a little girl. Despite repeated warnings from her father, she had explored areas where a casual mistake could have meant certain death. She approached one such location - the hangar deck.

It was the largest room on the ship, so ideal for games of all sorts. Although a mere twenty-six seasons old by the time their journey had ended, she had grown up quickly. Her play had prompted her to experiment with many of the ship's systems. One particular favorite was the panel that controlled gravity and pressurization in the cargo hangar itself. Several times she had returned to her quarters nursing a bruised tail bone or strained shoulder. Eventually, she had mastered partial gravity gymnastics, unbeknownst to her father.

As she rounded the side corridor leading to that part of the ship, she gasped. Further down the hallway, a statuesque figure, his back to her, approached the door to the cargo bay. Just as suddenly, he disappeared within. But she was not mistaken. It was him.

Ravar.

Her emotional impulse clashed with her rational thought. She had known him throughout her childhood, and even as an adult.

After all, he was her *father*.

Yet, he had forever carried with him a deep sorrow. One that he never shared. One that had made him distant.

Now, he was so close. *"Would knowing him at this point in his life help me understand?"* she questioned, inwardly. *"Possibly. But it could also interfere with my purpose for being here. My instincts tell me to be wary."*

Edging forward, still debating her next actions, another figure appeared. Tempora's internal alarm became even more heightened. His posture bespoke of evil intent. She pressed herself up against the curve of the wall to avoid notice. He nervously twitched his head to and fro, as would a raptor on a branch, searching for its prey. Content that he was not being watched, he turned toward the control panel adjacent to the door.

CHAPTER 12

Enn lifted herself from the gel cocoon that had been her transport between space arks. Little more than a missile to contain at most three prone bodies, it still served its purpose. Albeit not without making a mess. Similar to the dormancy tubes for the ark's passengers, the living payload was immersed in a viscous substance. This served to dampen the inertia from the transport process. But it did not provide life support. Hence the need for the uniform that the Legotian had so conveniently provided at the start of her adventure.

The capsule had been accurately fired from the *Vector* to match speed with Chieftain Ravar's vessel, *Destiny*. A utility umbilical had then plucked it from space and deposited it in a cargo hold at the base of the teardrop shaped command module.

Once secured, Enn emerged from the pod and made her way over to a personnel shower. She slipped behind the shoulder-height translucent privacy screen and uncoupled the helmet from her compression suit. She then peeled off her gelatin-soaked garments. Activating the shower, Enn used her hands to sluice off the slick substance. Catching her reflection in a metal panel on the wall, she allowed herself a brief moment of vanity.

Although pregnant with Ravar's child from their liaison during her first time trip, she was not showing. One hand slid across her flat abdomen while the other lightly felt the ridge running from the base of her neck down between her shoulder blades. True to Geminian female physiology, a warm wave of arousal spread outward across her bare back. Thoughts of seeing Ravar again melted her inhibitions. Her fingertips wandered playfully to her breasts. Lost in her fantasy, she did not hear the door to the cargo bay whisk open.

The tall, well-honed muscular figure entered, accustomed to appearing unannounced. His garb conveyed an air of unbridled privilege, as well. In contrast to the near monotone grey tunic over trousers worn by his staff, his chieftain battle dress bespoke of one who treasured independence and proudly displayed it.

A leather vest studded with black lactonite crystals overlapped a brief loin cloth of the same design. Thick leggings laced with mercurial bands were tucked into calf-high boots. A side-arm tri-blade dagger hung at his side. Its crystal encrusted hilt was suspended by a multi-colored belt embroidered with flame-eagle down and sand-serpent skins.

Ravar scanned the bay, his gaze settling on the female figure behind the translucent screen. Moving closer, he was mesmerized by her silver-tinged black tresses swaying fluidly as her head moved rhythmically from side to side. Strangely familiar, he could not help but stare. As her body writhed beneath her touch, Ravar could not contain himself. He audibly gasped at the sensual display.

Looking more intently, he questioned his own sanity. "Could it be?"

Enn, hearing the sound, caught herself just short of ecstasy. She glimpsed at the figure over the shoulder of her reflection. Reflexively, she snatched her helmet and whipped it over the screen at the voyeur's head.

Side-stepping the projectile, Ravar's massive hand snapped upward, plucking it from mid-air. Shaking his head and chuckling at the memory of his first encounter with this star vixen, he thought, *"Though impossible, it could be no other. As she did with her foot upon our first meeting, she seems intent upon damaging my skull!"*

Moving around the screen, Ravar held out the helmet to her, as his eyes drank in the luscious beauty of her naked form. "Did you drop this, Stargazer?"

Still feeling the effects of her self-induced raptures, Enn wordlessly took the headgear and lowered it to the floor. From her kneeling position, she looked up at the warrior standing before her. Sliding her hands slowly upward along his leggings, loosening them as she went, she amorously replied, "Why yes, sire. Just as I plan to drop these, as well."

*   *   *

Outside the hangar, less affectionate, although just as impassioned, acts of physical contact were underway.

Tempora knew of no good reason for anyone to be at the panel while others were inside. So, she assumed the worst. And acted.

Although in full gravity, she still remembered her gymnastics. Executing a running cartwheel into a full flip, she landed with one leg extended, bringing her heel down in an axe kick to the right shoulder of her target.

Tark dropped to one knee in anguish, reflexively grabbing his cracked collar bone with the opposite hand. Tempora deftly reached forward, smoothly slipping her opponents "ceremonial" short sword from its scabbard. She used the point pressed into the side of Tark's neck to pivot him around, a single purplish bead of blood emerging to convince him that she was serious.

He looked up at her. Seeing her garb, he all but whimpered, "Priestess, why do you assault me?"

Tempora, not to be dissuaded, laid the edge of the sword on his undamaged shoulder. Peering at the gold rosette pinned there, she said, accusingly, "I see you are no technician, *sub-chieftain*." With a flick of the wrist, the blade sliced off the emblem of position, ricocheting it off the adjacent wall. "So, you have no reason to be at this panel. Why cause harm to his Excellency?"

Her use of the tribal honorific was more than a formality. An unprovoked assault of *any kind* on a chieftain, royal born, was punishable by death. Although a coward, Tark *was* intelligent. Full disclosure might provide information to occupy her sufficiently enough not to kill him.

"I act only on orders, Revered One," he pandered. "Who am I to question the motives among chieftains?" Without saying it directly, he had revealed his actions were guided by one of two people, Chieftain Mace of the *Vector* or Chieftain Jasen of the *Argo*.

"I have neither the time *nor ear* for your subtleties. Perhaps you would like to join me?" Tempora raised the weapon such that its razor edge etched a violet line where his lobe connected to his jaw.

Tark winced, but continued to stroke her ego. "Your swordsmanship is as sharp as your wit, enchantress. But no need for that. Sire Mace has the most interest in ascending the rungs of power." Tark paused, studying her expression. Any sign of relaxing would mean she believed him. Tension would convey the contrary. But he saw neither. "Indifference, Stargazer? Perhaps your curiosity is born of the god, Opportunity, rather than his cousin, Loyalty?"

The question gave Tempora pause to reflect. Tark saw his opening. Still in anguish from his damaged shoulder and without a sword to counter hers, thoughts of combat seemed foolish. He seriously doubted he could overwhelm one of her clan even if the roles were reversed. But his legs were fully functional. From his kneeling position facing her, his left hand nursing his right collarbone, her blade hovering by his left cheek, he had but one recourse.

Run!

He backhanded the blade out and away from her and sprang forward. His left shoulder caught her in the ribcage, sending her spinning backward. His momentum carried him forward, his legs keeping up just enough to propel him further down the corridor. He chortled with glee at his success.

Prematurely.

Tempora lithely recovered her balance by tucking her leg as she pirouetted down on one knee. The short sword still in hand, she flipped it into a flat spin with a quarter twist. Her thumb and index finger plucked it from the air along its two cool sides. Coiling her arm, she paused momentarily, deciding how many revolutions to impart on the weapon as she hurled it.

End over end it sailed. One half rotation … one more full rotation … and lastly, another half rotation.

With a resonating clunk, the handle of the sword struck Tark at the base of his skull. As is often with a knockout punch, a moment passes before the body realizes what just occurred. Another step followed. Then both legs stiffened, nerves no longer receiving impulses from a conscious brain.

Tark pitched forward, falling like a petrified Castorian cactus. Tempora rose and casually strode down the hallway. Picking up the blade and tucking it into her belt, she murmured, "Hmmpf. I need more practice. Was trying for only one *half* rotation. Oh well…"

Unceremoniously, she bent down and clutched the back of the collar of the prostrate sub-chieftain. Despite his dead weight, she hoisted his head and shoulders slightly off the ground, dragging him along. She debated on hauling him all the way to the stellar cartography lab. Spying a familiar door, she formulated an alternate plan. A few more labored treds brought her before the same storage closet from which she had emerged earlier.

"I'll leave this space flotsam locked in here until I can alert Thresh in the lab," she considered. *"He can notify Security and they can deal with him. And just to be sure he doesn't go anywhere…"* She looked down at

her linen stole and the leather laces interspersed through eyelets along its decorative stitched border. Removing two portions of it, she quickly wound one around Tark's hands and another around his ankles. As he stirred, she pulled him to his feet. Standing him up before the now open door, she used the blade she'd grown quite fond of to slice a strip of sleeve from his tunic. Lashing it around his head as a gag, she stepped back to admire her handiwork.

Tark's lolling head and teetering stance were apparently a ploy. He had gained just enough consciousness to attempt one more escape. As he lunged forward to use his head as a ram against Tempora's chin, she reacted. Side-stepping to her left, she brought a knee up into the assailant's solar plexus. With him partially bent over, she cupped her hand behind his head and bounced it off the hall's opposite wall. Not yet satisfied, the trained martial artist brought her other hand up under her opponent's chin and thrust him back in the direction he came. The unconscious dolt tumbled feet over head into the closet.

Tempora briskly brushed her hands together, as if to cleanse them of imaginary debris and signal a job well done. Toggling the control gem, she actuated the storage room door to close without another thought of its contents. As she started off in the direction of the lab to see what the meteor analysis would reveal, she heard giggling. Unable to resist, she turned and crept back down the corridor toward the cargo hangar.

The curvature of the walls provided some degree of concealment. Sliding a ong the inner one, she peered around its horizon. As she approached the nexus of the hangar entrance and the opposing passage that branched into several routes, the laughter she heard waned. That served only to heighten her curiosity.

Picking up her pace, she decided on the course that would take her back to the omnivator. Her choice was rewarded. Throwing caution to the stellar wind, she briskly speed-walked the last section of the hallway. Once more, her timing served only to frustrate her.

Entering the omnivator, she saw the same rear profile of her father. Only this time, he was carrying something.

A woman!

Cradled in his arms, hers draped around his neck, one hand toying with his long hair, was Novas of Gemini!

*　　*　　*

In his bedchamber, Ravar collapsed next to *his* Stargazer after their third round of lovemaking. Her foreplay in the hangar had unleashed a passion even he was unaware he possessed. From the hangar, he had swept her up into his arms and carried her into his private omnivator pod. As the transport rose, so did he. Her cries of ecstasy only encouraged Ravar to continue once they reached the privacy of his suite. He had given strict orders not to be disturbed.

"Though clearly pleased to see you, over and over..." Ravar quipped, "...I am at a loss to understand how this dream is a reality."

"I was wrong to think our *time* was at an end," Enn huskily replied, enigmatically. "I came to my senses and realized there is still much for us to do."

"It appears much has already been done - a new look and a new name? Had I not recognized the sounds of your passion, I might have believed you to be a goodwill offering from Chieftain Mace."

"Aah, so you are aware of his duplicitous nature. Yet ready to avail yourself so easily of his pandering?"

Grinning lustfully, Ravar buried his face in her neck and retorted, "How could I resist, if he is able to enlist someone as enchanting as you? And I sense there is more than just a name and hair change afoot. What other mysteries have you to reveal?"

"I must rethink my opinion of you, my chieftain. Here I thought you no more than an amorous oaf, good for only pleasuring me. And yet, you have a sensitivity rare to most males. Impressive," she playfully jousted.

Ravar lifted his face and replaced it with his hand, gently stroking the nape of her neck. The technique elicited the desired reaction, as Enn shivered while releasing a small gasp. He pulled back a little further, and intently peered into her eyes.

"The male within me is gratified by your reaction. The scientist in me knows physiology sufficiently to recognize your response, and wonder 'How?' But the lover within is joyous, and asks 'Can it be true?'"

Reaching up to lay her hand on the side of his face, Enn whispered, "Yes, my warrior. You have conquered me. I am with child."

Ravar beamed, saying, "Ah, yes. There still is so *much more* for us to do!"

CHAPTER 13

Edison fidgeted nervously as he sat in his quarters onboard the *Darwin*. He didn't know why he was uneasy. The lander transport from Gemini to the life crystal plant in orbit went smoothly - except for the tense silence among him and the two IAD agents, Supervisor Eric Magnek and his subordinate, Specialist Hal Xkorp. He surmised that despite their experience with terminating rogue biodgens, it never got easier. Reflection and time were the best medicine for remorse.

Dr. Edison mused, "*Hmm, reflection. Physician, heal thyself.*" He wondered if the upcoming opportunity to see his son, Starn, was the source of his anxiety. He felt a pang of guilt for not being there for him when he emerged from his coma, thanks to Starn's Dual, Nimon.

Nimon had successfully revived his Life-Mentor, Starn, at the Institute of Meditative Phenomenon. No small feat, and highly significant to the philosophy of Phoenos. The two had demonstrated, if only briefly, independent consciousnesses - *and in close proximity!* Even Novas and T'poch, despite being the first Singular Dualiity, had not demonstrated that capability.

But Nimon had quickly faltered, while Starn thrived. Starn had returned to limited duty on the *Darwin's* staff. Once the life crystal plant entered a time fold away from Gemini, Nimon, in a weakened and disoriented state, once again awoke. Truly demonstrating a state of Singular Dualiity, it was eerily reminiscent of the phenomenon between Novas and T'Poch. After they were sufficiently distant from one another, each was free to live independent - and distinctly different - lives. One entity good - the other, maniacally driven. *"Was it Nature or Nurture..."* Edison asked himself, *"...that caused T'Poch's megalomania? Is it an inherent syndrome of Dualiity, or is it the outgrowth of T'Poch having been left in the care of the matriarch of Novas' family, P'Teel?"*

Regardless of the cause, Novas had had no choice. If her Dual were to have *any* life, it would have to be separate from Novas in order to survive. Edison had recognized the trauma the decision caused Novas, and had further devoted himself to his wife and her care.

In the case of Nimon and Starn, Edison had felt compelled to support the biodgen, leaving Starn to rely on his *Darwin* colleagues. Perhaps it was the scientist in him that influenced his decision. Dualiity within close proximity was a momentous breakthrough! Not just from a technical perspective, but a philosophical one, as well. Edison knew the followers of Phoenos on Gemini would quickly swoop in exert control. He had seen how unwavering fanaticism had impactec T'Poch's development. He was determined not to allow a similar outcome for Nimon at the hands of the Geminian Elders.

Normally known to adopt an advisory role, Dr. Edison in this instance took action. He had secreted his "son" away from the Council-controlled Institute of Meditative Phenomena to the polar facility of Novas' clan. Intent on discovering the secret to Dualiity, he found himself at odds with his original motives. He glanced at the case on the credenza. Within it lay the Ravarian crystal shard he had extracted from his biodgen son. It dawned on him why he was anxious. *"How can I tell Starn that his life goal of achieving Phoenos must be abandoned?"* he pondered.

A chime stirred him from his revery. "Enter, please," he prompted.

The door scissored open. Starn stepped hesitantly into the room. His father immediately rose, approaching him with open arms. His anxiety melting away, he embraced his son in a firm hug. Then, stepping back and clasping his shoulders between outstretched hands, he looked up at the much taller Starn.

Starn stood awkwardly, receiving the embrace with hands hanging at his sides. The normally powder blue complexion of the hybrid Terran-Geminian flushed a mauve hue, triggered by embarrassment mixed with a hint of irritation.

Dr. Edison spoke first. "Your recovery serves you well, my son! You look healthy and strong. I trust your colleagues have accepted you with eagerness?"

Suppressing the urge to snap a retort like *"Better than my own family!"*, Starn simply shrugged and replied, "As well as could be expected."

Unsaid was the realization by both that Starn had a significant adjustment to overcome. He for his entire tenure on the *Darwin* staff had believed himself to be the biodgen half of the Dual pair with Nimon. This psychosis artfully manifested itself to the point that the two were a highly functioning team.

Despite his family, Edison and Novas, and a select few on the Geminian Counsel having knowledge of his condition, his colleagues were completely unaware.

Starn's revival by Nimon had changed that. Though limited to Plant Manager Descartes and Personnel Manager Jefferson Brown, the understanding that *Starn was the organic* had prompted a decided shift in the plant's organizational dynamics. Nimon had served as the very visible and highly utilized plant Technical Superintendent. Starn had been relegated to serving on various task teams and special projects, but had been given no managerial responsibilities. Even after his return, he had been classified as being on "reserve status" as the plant's senior management decided how best to employ him.

Nevertheless, Starn had put his free time to beneficial use. He recalled his meeting with Kronia, Geminian Council of Elders Chairperson shortly after his recovery.

"Starn. Thee has returned to us. A rare few knew of your plight. Even fewer know of your return. Those who do are both pleased and concerned as to its meaning. I sense thee are troubled as well."

169

Starn was more than troubled. He was enraged! During the brief moment he and Nimon consciously coexisted, Nimon had shared his memories with Starn. He learned T'Poch had committed the basest of evils when she defiled Nimon. Implanting the Ravarian crystal shard within him while consummating her sinister lust had spawned an unknown danger.

A biodgenic life essence!

Ultimately, the threat from that concubus must be addressed. However, Starn was more immediately concerned with T'Poch herself. Through her, the K'Tar movement could lead to interplanetary revolt and chaos. As a child of two worlds, both of which would suffer, he felt duty-bound to disrupt her plans.

The wizened matriarch mistook his concern as being one more metaphysical in nature.

Kronia had implored, "Can the sensitive life force between you and Nimon exist for others? Can we fulfill the dream of Phoenos without plunging our culture into the fiery ways of the K'Tar?" The slight upturned twitch of her mouth, belying her deception, escaped Starn's notice.

"Thy task is clear. It must be determined if thee and Nimon can be sustained. If thee are successful, thy name will take its place in humble reverence with that of Mitron!"

The mists of memory from that meeting dissipated as Starn thought, *My task is clear, but it is not as Kronia hopes. Her flowery words that I am to `give life to the future as the new father of Phoenos' ring hollow. Prophesies have a way of being misinterpreted. Those surrounding Phoenos I sense are still in flux.*

Of greater import is the responsibility that befalls me because of the actions of my mother and father. If Phoenos is the justification they used to spawn a creature such as T'Poch, then how noble a philosophy could it actually be?"

He stared intently into the eyes of his father. It was time to reveal just how he *had* been utilizing his time.

"We could exchange pleasantries, Father, but time is rarely on our side. Pressing matters always seem to arise. There are things you should know, now that I am free of the self-inflicted burden of my psychosis."

Dr Edison all but flinched at the verbal slap from his son. He responded only with a pained expression.

"My manic preoccupation with the search for Phoenos and the empowerment of my biodgen is at an end. If a Singular Dualiity such as T'Poch is the outcome of the efforts of you and Mother, what abysmal fate awaits me with my efforts for Nimon's independence?"

Before Dr. Edison could respond, Starn held up his hand to silence him.

"Let me finish. I am redirecting my energies. My expertise in the arena of bioduogenetics is rare, but clearly not *singular,*" he continued, letting slip a delirious giggle at his own pun. "Rather than seek the unattainable - a *viable, positive contribution to humanity* - through Phoenos, I have other plans. I seek to *correct* the travesties that are caused by bioduogenetics, not create more of them.

With that in mind, I have contacted the head of the Internal Audit Division within the Solar Corporation. She was ecstatic to hear from me. We are refining the details of how best to apply my unique skills."

As Dr. Edison struggled to digest *all* he had just heard, he elected to address the most positive revelation. In that way, perhaps some slight favor could be garnered from his son.

"It seems you have chosen a fateful path, Starn. One that your god, Destiny, seems to favor."

This time it was Starn's turn to respond wordlessly, as his hairless, deeply furrowed brow smoothed, his brilliant orange eyes widened in surprise.

Dr. Edison continued. "Dualiity, whether it be your Mother's, or yours, has not yet been perfectly achieved. Though T'Poch lives independently, her weakness is proximity to Novas. Brought close to her Life Mentor, the Dual T'Poch would falter. As for your achievement, for a brief moment, you and Nimon were simultaneously conscious, while together. Yet, it was unsustainable. Only after you departed Gemini was Nimon able to exist independently. So, you have demonstrated a higher level of achievement in the search for Phoenos, but not the defining goal.

And that achievement has come with a devastating price."

Edison paused. Not for dramatic effect. Rather, to collect his thoughts. Starn, recognizing the torment in his father's face, patiently waited.

"Your Dual is self-sustaining only because of banned technology," Dr. Edison blurted. "The interaction of the Ravarian crystal matrix with the duotronic cellular bonding between you and T'Poch has triggered spontaneous

173

generation of nanites! I had to take immediate action…"

Starn could no longer contain himself. "Stop. Slow down. You're not making sense. For one, spontaneous generation of life is a millennia-old scientific myth. Secondly, T'Poch has the same crystal matrix imbedded within her. Why is her existence not a source of banned nanotechnology?"

"My son, like all bioduogenetic constructs, the organic cells are replicated via meiosis in the presence of the life crystals. No union from male and female organic cells occurs. The genetic design is closely controlled *artificially*. *Such was the case for T'Poch's creation.* In that way, the variation and impurities caused by *natural* cellular unification and subsequent duplication are avoided. That is the primary reason the joining of biodgens with others is restricted. The *uncontrolled variation* that can result is incomprehensible!"

Starn's pinched expression relaxed slightly. His childhood training by the foremost bioduogeneticist was not completely lost on him.

"So, the assault upon my Dual, though bestial, was more natural than anything allowed by your science! And from it, a plague is spawned. How ironic. The synthetic life that fuels our interplanetary development can also trigger its demise." Pausing, Starn's expression of understanding contorted into one of fear. "You spoke of `immediate action'... what did you *do* to Nimon!!"

Starn's posture became combative. His upper body tensed as he took a half step toward his father, leaning slightly forward. Reflexively, the doctor raised both hands, palms outward.

"Calm yourself!" he barked, reigning in his son. "Despite your resentment toward me, I am still your father. I have simply provided treatment for Nimon such that he is as he was before T'Poch's assault ... I hope. In his inanimate state, it is impossible to say with certainty."

Starn's shoulders relaxed. His expression, though, remained hard. "Inanimate, you say? I am far removed from him. Why is he not conscious?"

"As I said, I have restored him to his state before the attack. The crystal shard has been removed. The nanites eradicated. Only by your will can he be re-animated."

"Then the level of your success will remain a mystery. I repeat, my empowering of my

Dual is at an end. My focus is retribution against the one who left me comatose, assaulted my biodgen, nearly released an interstellar pandemic, and leads a rebellious group that could take our star system to the brink of war!"

Dr. Edison took in a sharp breath, then released it. "To your point earlier, my son, time is rarely on our side. Your motives to confront T'Poch not withstanding, there is the greater danger. She, *too,* is infected! We must employ all the resources the *Darwin* can bring to bear on capturing and quarantining her."

Starn's flaming orange eyes narrowed. His mouth formed a thin, grim line. To himself he whispered, "Capture, quarantine... and *dispose* of her, if I have a say in it!"

CHAPTER 14

Tempora was rigid with fury! She stood in disbelief looking at the closed omnivator doors. *"What in the flames of Pollux is she doing at this point in time!?"* she raged to herself. *"Clearly the Legotians are behind this. But what can they hope to achieve?"*

She sorely needed counsel. *"If only Threads were here,"* she reminisced. *"Hmmm, funny that his name would rise from the depths of my random recollections."* Often as a child flitting from one area of the ship to another, she would find herself in the lab to which she was heading a moment ago. The science section head would take time out of his busy schedule to ask about her activities. He would show her the projects underway and sincerely engage her as to her opinion about them.

She smiled at her thoughts' faded image of him. He had a shock of ebony hair growing from a bare, azure scalp. Like his beard, it had white streaks reflecting his age - almost like threads - woven chaotically throughout. Hence her pet name for him, *Threads*. As her rage dissipated, replaced by the memory of better times, an epiphany dawned.

"Threads ... Thresh ... the sub-chieftain from earlier is the same as the section chief then, or should I say in the future from now!" She pressed the backs of her fists into her closed eyes, suppressing a blossoming headache. *"Time travel paradoxes - quickest way to a migraine,"* she groused. *"He does not know me now, but I know him. I can trust him. Not only to deal with my prisoner, but perhaps to shine some light on the mystery that is Novas of Gemini."*

More determined than before, she hastened back to the stellar cartography lab. Once more pushing through the frosted, plexi-steel door, she found Thresh at a terminal, peering intently at the screen. He instantly looked up, his eyes wide with excitement.

"Priestess, your timing is impeccable! The analysis has been completed. I'll not bias your interpretation of the results. Please see for yourself and tell me *your* thoughts."

Tempora smiled at her mentor, amused at his boyish excitement and warmed from the reunion with an old friend. Nodding an acknowledgement, she glided to the work station and pivoted the viewer for better access.

Spectrographic results were presented in both tabular and graphical formats. Each object hurtling toward Gemini was depicted three dimensionally with a rainbow of colors, a different one associated with each chemical component. The tables explained relative content of each mineral, labeled with its chemical formula.

Tempora's eyes widened to match Thresh's.

"Over half of their content is labeled with a question mark! This unknown substance is in striations throughout each meteoroid. The normal stone, iron, and nickel often found in formations like these are at a minimum. Crystalline patterning is remarkable!" she exclaimed.

"Look at the energy profile!" Thresh interjected, unable to contain himself. "More specifically, see how it mutates when exposed to varying wavelengths."

Tempora observed the area of the report Thresh highlighted. "Chief Thresh, I admit, although part of the Stargazer clan, I favor some areas of expertise over others."

Thresh noticeably ducked his head, as if bowing for forgiveness. Tempora had just exposed a vulnerability, essentially saying '*I don't understand*'.

"Of course, Priestess. I had the advantage of running diagnostic subroutines. They point to the ability for portions of the meteoroids to be explosive in nature, if excited by the appropriate energy signatures."

Although stretched to her technical limits, Tempora's logical processes worked at light speed.

"Gemini is doomed, unless action is taken," she whispered. *"But how is this possible?"* she wondered. *"In my time, Gemini is a thriving society on the interstellar corporate stage. The projections from these figures indicate the planet will be reduced to space rubble. Is my presence here the pivotal event to change this timeline ... or is it the role of the Solar Executive? The answer is obvious. It seems it is up to me. Here I stand while she frolics in the arms of Ravar!"*

With steely determination, she decided. Turning to Thresh, she postulated, "Chief, I suspect no-one understood the magnitude of this calamity. Certainly my sisterhood could not predict the outcome based on elements of an unknown origin within the meteoroid field. However, as their representative, I give counsel that something must be done. Escaping the cataclysm is not enough. Despite their differing beliefs, the Mitronians we leave behind must be given a chance. They are the flock. We are the shepherds. We must protect them from the predator!" Tempora pointed at the multi-colored objects on the screen.

"But of course, Stargazer. Yet, what can we do? Time is limited. Do you have a plan?"

Tempora looked more closely at the swarm's configuration and distance from Gemini. She often had to formulate alternative policies for her Castorian subjects. Hidden behind the veil of leadership required due to the passing of the Chairman of the Castorian Conglomerate, she was the true source of vision for her people's future. *It seemed that responsibility extends to the Geminians, as well,*" she acceded to herself.

An idea emerged. Wordlessly, she picked up a stylus and began to draw on the screen. With her opposite hand, she tapped the gem controls on the keyboard. First she drew an arc from their current position toward the collection of space debris. As the subroutine she had entered generated results, the speed of the virtual object she drew was calculated.

Still some distance from the target, she used the stylus to accelerate two more points from the original arc. Tracing their path into the lead meteoroid, she then toggled some keys to extrapolate the results.

The outcome was less than she hoped, but intrigued Thresh. "You like to bowl, hmm? But with two balls instead of one. And your pins explode instead of fall. An interesting game," he quipped.

"But unsuccessful. The result only reduces the field by 40%. The primary body is fragmented, but fails to disperse sufficiently. You can see from the projections a number of the deadly objects still reach Gemini."

"I am curious. What did you plan on using as the two missiles?" the section chief asked. "Our defensive armament consists of only pulse fields and space mines to deter *hypothetical* pursuers - given we know of no other space faring life forms."

Tempora, drawing upon her childhood memories, replied, "Do we not have two passenger modules for the occasional transport between arks? My thinking is to pack them with the mines and just enough nuclear ion fuel to create an explosive torpedo. To detain the full flotilla for this fool's mission is unacceptable. Hence, one ark and two projectiles."

Thresh reset the computer model, with one slight change. He added a third explosive device. "Actually, we have *three* modules. We were alerted that *Vector*'s second-in-command has come aboard. That still leaves Mace with one in time of dire need." He then flicked the appropriate jewel to start the display.

This time, the third explosion was slightly delayed after the first two. The primary body fragment was struck once more. It's energy profile spiked exponentially. A series of subsequent explosions cascaded back through the swarm. A fine powdery mist resulted, dispersing through the cosmos.

Excited, Tempora exclaimed, "It could actually work! We need to inform Ravar!"

"Aah, if only we could. The analysis sent to him prompted his security to alert us he was not to be disturbed - for *any* reason. Though mostly an amicable fellow, his temper is well known. No-one is willing to test it."

The executive-turned-priestess seethed. Neither persona liked to be told "No." Especially if it was as a result of the Geminian meddler from the future playing seductress to her *father!* Yet, she understood Chief Thresh's awkward position. And she did not want to unduly pressure her past and future mentor.

"Let me suggest this, sub-chieftain," Tempora whispered, her tone a mixture of firmness and charm. "On my authority, let us prepare the missiles. As shown in the calculations, we have only a narrow window of opportunity. I am sure his excellence will grace us with his presence by the time they are ready. Certainly he will want to be at the helm when his flotilla leaves orbit. By then, we will have presented him with the plan. Our sister ships will head out as scheduled, while we take a detour to save our doomed comrades. And you, my friend, will receive the full credit. After all, clearly you are the better bowler." She smiled, watching his model replay itself on the screen.

All but hypnotized by her, he nodded his agreement.

*   *   *

Tempora stood in the hangar overseeing the preparations for the three exploding modules. As the seal was established on the last one's compartment, she stepped over to the holographic communication globe.

Indifferently, she updated the ship's navigator in the control center as to their status. Thresh had insisted since Ravar was indisposed, protocol dictated that at a minimum, Stev be apprised of their actions. As his image faded, Tempora absently looked beyond the comm globe. On the wall, she spied the warning sign that would alert occupants to a depressurizing event.

"Death's clutches!" she cursed to herself. *"I completely forgot about my captured assassin. Surely he's conscious by now - not that he can go anywhere bound like a Terran fly in a web."* Once more she passed her hand across the communication sphere, activating it. *"I'll inform Thresh about him along with an update on our progress here."*

As the image of the section chief wavered into view, she began, "Thresh, we are ready. Is Ravar accessible yet? Along with presenting our plan, he needs to be aware of another little inconvenience." She relayed the events of her foiling the killer's scheme and where he was being held.

"You *are* the resourceful one, eh Priestess? I am certain a security breach such as this one will gain us access to the High Chieftain. Give me a moment to explain it to his guard. Then someone, I am sure, will meet you at the utility closet."

*   *   *

Ravar admired the rear view of Enn as she stood in front of the mirror, bending over to straighten the crease in her uniform's trousers. He, too, had donned a more conservative attire than his tribal outfit. Instead of the sleeved tunic worn by the command staff, he wore a tight fitting vest of the same color and material. His bare arms, rippling with toned muscles, were adorned with a leather, decorative band around his biceps and long, dark metal bracelets around his forearms. Keeping with his tribal roots, outside the standard trousers he had strapped an ornamental scabbard and highly functional short sword.

Enn straightened, pivoted, and noticed his lecherous gaze. "Settle down, my liege. We have the orbital departure ceremony to attend."

"Aah, the rigors of command. If only I could return to my   scientific pursuits, and the occasional mock combat exercises with my comrade, Mitron." His face adopted a theatrical pout, but Enn knew he truly missed simpler times … and his friend.

"Fate seems to have other plans, o' burly one," she quipped, attempting to lighten his mood.

And it did. A chime shook him from his reverie. With three quick strides, he traversed the chamber and opened the door. Before him at attention stood his security head.

"At rest, Mach. What is it?"

"Apologies, High Chieftain. Despite your orders against being disturbed, there are two subjects requiring your attention...' Seeing movement in the mirror over Ravar's shoulder, Mach added, "...and your second-in-command is also indisposed."

Ravar looked closely at his security head to see if he detected even the slightest of smiles. Always the professional, Mach resisted. "Then out with it. What is so urgent?"

In command mode, Mach succinctly relayed the situations with both the meteoroid threat *and* the personal threat. In typical fashion for a true leader, Ravar placed the concern for his people above any for himself. Although the Mitronians had opted to disregard his warning, they were *still* his people.

"Mach, come with me to the stellar cartography lab. I need to learn more." Turning his head so Enn would be sure to hear, he added, "My second will attend to the security threat."

This time the corner of Mach's mouth twitched, expressing his self-satisfaction at knowing his chieftain had sufficiently welcomed his new second aboard.

*   *   *

Tempora crouched slightly in front of the utility closet, readying herself before she opened the door, just in case. *"This one is cagey, I must admit,"* she mentally coached herself. *"One cannot be too cautious."*

Keying the lock mechanism, she tensed. Although unnecessarily. Within the storage room were only the items she noticed when she first arrived. Except for the fact it looked as if a Clionian had organized it by thrashing his tail haphazardly. She edged forward, pausing at the threshold.

Further down the hall, Enn rounded the curve and abruptly halted. On her way to investigate the imprisoned assassin, she was stunned to see the Castorian Executive entering her destination. Despite seeing her very *self* at the beginning of this temporal episode, she was still unsettled at the concept of chronal displacement. And now, tc discover a *second* time traveler! Especially since it was the Castorian masquerading as a sister of the Stargazer clan.

Before Enn could call out to halt, Tempora stepped into the utility room.

The would-be priestess scrutinized the interior, searching for any signs that might explain what had happened to Tark. The door latch was undamaged. There were no remnants of failed leather bindings. Even the gag cut from his sleeve was nowhere to be found. *"The disruption of the contents must have been from my initial tossing of his body,"* she hypothesized. *"Yet, something else is amiss…"*

Running her hand across the edge of the shelving, she gingerly tiptoed toward the back of the closet. Reaching out her other hand, palm forward, she flinched as a tingling warmth enveloped it. Reflexively, she tried to pull back. That served only to accelerate the feeling of heat up her arm. Taking her other hand down from the shelf, she grasped her entrapped forearm. Leaning backward, she tugged at the invisible force that ensnared her. Her eyes widened as a circle of energy formed on the wall, its edge expanding inwardly toward its center. As the grey of the surface was replaced by a shimmering, silver fluid, Tempora slid unrelentingly toward it.

Enn had overcome her initial shock and hastened toward the door opening. An eery glow emanated from it, casting a shadowy figure against the opposite wall. Pressing her back against the bulkhead, she cautiously peeked around the door's edge. Drawing in a short gasp, she fought the urge to enter and aid her time traveling companion. Enn's *time* had not yet come.

With a loud snap and flash, the corporeal form of Tempora dissolved into countless particles of light, disappearing into the silvery vortex.

Enn stood before the entrance, hands on hips, and murmured, "Like my travels, perhaps yours were prematurely ended. We may see each other again."

CHAPTER 15

A youthful P'Teel began her presentation with a tour of the control center's various stations.

"You are as much a man of science as you are a leader of your people, Del. So, marvel at this feat of engineering. At this panel you can monitor the inner workings of our environmental controls. Geothermal energy rising from probes deep in the planet's crust channel power to a series of generators. By heating waters from the underground river D'Kor that nourishes much of our planet, mighty turbines create electricity tc operate lumen panels, among other devices, throughout the complex. Conduits of the same heated water pass through exchangers to stabilize the temperature of our a r. Left on it's own, the subterranean climate would be a chilly 50 therms and quite dry. Ducting enables the warmed and humidified air to remain balanced at 70 therms and 45% hydropoints."

"An understandable alternative to our fusion powered infrastructure and hydroelectric facilities, given the absence of combustible fuel and flowing streams. Ingenious!"

"Of particular note is that the crystalline matrix of our lumen panels duplicates the spectrum of Polluxan light. No matter how long we remain within the confines of the facility, it is as if we never left the surface."

"Which raises an interesting question ..." the chieftain interjected, "... why go to the trouble?"

"As I alluded while we enjoyed each others company by our hearth, meteoric collisions are looming. Chances for your people's survival on the surface, though greater than those who challenged the savagery of space, are slim. The plan for our salvation is to seek refuge within this underground city!"

Mitron shook his head slowly from side to side in an attempt to disperse the cloud of disbelief. Finally, he protested, somberly, "Certainly what you have accomplished here is most wondrous. But if what you say is true, the impact of a multitude of meteorites on Gemini will throw enormous amounts of dust into the atmosphere. It will blot out our sun, creating an unnatural winter of devastation. Crops would be all but destroyed. Our food stores would quickly be exhausted. Even if you could house our population, how would you feed them?"

P'Teel answered, almost gleefully. "We are capable of drawing vast volumes of air through energized metal mesh - electrostatic precipitators - if you will. The particles are drawn to the charged surface and held until the polarity is reversed. Continuous cycling of the screens allows them to release the airborne dust into collection vessels. The captured soil is then conveyed to our growth chambers to nourish our subterranean fields."

"Truly remarkable, I must admit," mumbled Del. "Your people have been quite innovative … and busy."

"My liege, you must understand. What you see here has been the work of *generations*. We do not come by the moniker of *Stargazer* lightly. Our studies have long portended the impending calamity. It is only right that we take steps to save our people."

"Which is to my point!" he exclaimed. "There are tens of millions of souls scattered across our planet. Even if your tunnels riddled the entire mountain chain encircling our globe, there would not be room for them all!"

P'Teel sighed. "Dear Del, your heart is as big as your hope is misplaced. Did Ravar intend to save *all* Geminians? Even if you had depleted the royal coffers, he could not have built enough ships to evacuate the entire planet.

Hard choices had to be made by him. Just as hard choices will be made by *you*. To that end, my followers have also taken measures to aid you."

She toggled a control, activating a display embedded in one of the consoles. The screen glowed with a warning.

RETINAL SCAN REQUIRED.
FOR EXCLUSIVE EYES ONLY.
GAZE AT THE SYMBOL TO
ACCESS.

Mitron stared at the icon.

<~^^~>

A list of names and positions appeared, slowly scrolling for him to read. Some he knew. Many, he did not.

The chieftain raised his eyes from the monitor, fixing them on a distant point somewhere beyond the rocky wall before him. His visage hardened, as if it were extracting the very minerals from the stone surface that separated him from his people. P'Teel could tell his mind was in turmoil, and sensed his choice would not be in her favor.

Her decision came more swiftly. She knew she must act.

Filling the silence, the mistress of mysteries whispered, "A select number of representatives from the various tribes will be invited to join us. There is little time, but it will be used wisely. Over the coming duo-decion, privileged personnel will be notified. They will secretly slip away to come here. As you have so astutely concluded, even with our massive effort, we cannot comfortably co-exist within these confines as we would on the surface. So, we have prepared other means to survive."

A wave of her hand over a crystal control node shifted the contents of the screen from names to an image of a hidden catacomb. Instead of a network of sequestered tombs, the recesses contained modern-era suspension capsules, reminiscent of the gelatin modules aboard Mitron's vessels.

"Many will enter these, to be awakened after the holocaust. And you, my love, will be the first to embrace the sublime peace of slumber."

P'Teel raised her hand, palming a neuron-suppression disc, and laid it gently on Mitron's forearm. As it discharged through his body, nearly twice the mass of hers, she skillfully guided his bulk to the floor using a Tei Lan martial arts technique.

*   *   *

Pollux rose and fell over the Geminian mountain range for over a hundred times as the surface of the planet endured a barrage of meteorites. The sequestered elite of Gemini gave little heed.

P'Teel's plan had worked remarkably well.

Dignitaries and chosen ones were safely secluded within the confines of either their private quarters or the personalized suspension tubes within the catacombs. The Stargazer clan served as impeccable hosts, keeping the food supply flowing and equipment functioning.

The infrastructure operated as designed, with fresh air, energy, and environmental control delivered to all.

Except for those remaining outside.

As the hell from the heavens raked across the terrain unmercifully, 13% of the populace perished. Most would have survived the minor impacts, as the erratic pattern of the majority of meteoric missiles missed the major cities. Certainly, the atmospheric damage from the dust heaved into the sky caused calamitous consequences, but the effect could be managed. The Geminians were nothing if not an adaptable race.

Unfortunately, one circumstance was beyond their control. It was the 3000 tred wide crystalline-granitium composite object that served as a near planet-killer when it struck in the middle of T'Bok Vri.

The impact crater was 45 kilotreds in diameter. Despite the bulk of the meteorite disintegrating from heat as it pierced the Geminian atmosphere, the effect of the strike was significant. The circular tsunami of debris roiled across the continent as the thermonuclear cloud rose into the sky. For two full seasons, the particulate persisted in the air. Attacking the elderly and immunocompromised first, it's insidious effects lingered to afflict a majority of the people for just under a full revolution of Gemini around its sun.

Those favored souls safely ensconced within the confines of the mountain tunnels stayed healthy and well. At least physically. The psychological scars of surviving while others perished, however, would plague many for much of their lives.

P'Teel hoped that would not be the case for Mitron.

His suspension vessel now rested in the infirmary within the heart of the subterranean complex. Medical technicians scurried about making preparations for his awakening. P'Teel unconsciously stroked her abdomen, feeling the kicks of their as yet unborn daughter. Lately, the baby's movement was directly proportional to the stress level of her mother.

At the moment, it felt as if she were performing a masters level gymnastics routine.

Beeping from a nearby monitor signaled an elevation in the patient's biometric readings. The figure's stirring within the capsule confirmed it.

Mitron was awake!

Before the attendants could reach him, the magistrate of Centar lifted himself from the gelatinous goo and hoisted himself to the ground. The only sign of a synthetically induced sleep was the need to steady himself with one hand resting on the capsule's edge. One aide offered him a hand towel to wipe his head, face and neck, while two others meticulously and almost reverently focused on the rest of him. A half robe was provided, allowing him to turn away, don it, remove his sodden medi-shorts and complete the process with a modicum of dignity.

P'Teel tentatively approached. Pivoting to face her, his understandable rage at being clinically incarcerated drained from him.

"I would demand to know how long I have been in suspension, but it seems the answer is at least forty-five decions, given your present state," Mitron deduced.

"Fifty-one of the sixty, actually." P'Teel corrected.

"I shouldn't be surprised - you carry it well. Come to me," he commanded, with open arms.

P'Teel's trepidation evaporated as quickly as had his rage. Holding him firmly, her head pressing against his broad chest, she whispered, "Please allow me to explain, my lord. My intentions have been honorable, if not overly headstrong. The scarcity of time fueled my swift action."

A flick of Mitron's wrist signaled the attendants to disperse, providing the two some privacy. Unused to obeying anyone but their mistress, they instinctively chose correctly and departed.

The chieftan's hands slipped from P'Teel's back to rest on the sides of her shoulders - their grip just a little firmer than usual. The enchantress responded obediently to his silent demand for an explanation.

"As I noted prior to your slumber, my plan of saving the best of our people within the confines of the mountain chambers has been executed. I was compelled to suspend you first, because I feared your heroic compulsion would disrupt what needed to be done. You were able to dissuade the bulk of our followers from adopting Ravar's solution for survival. I did not want the irresistible influence of your leadership to repeat itself and disable mine."

The rhythm of her praise mingled with her message exerted a hypnotic effect on Mitron. It had taken much time, but her skills at influencing him had become quite adept. She continued.

"Those within our protection have been well cared for. Had we not been successful, I alone would have shouldered the blame, providing you with a level of plausible deniability. But our efforts have been rewarded. The facility has performed as designed. Soon, we will raise the others from their sleep, and emerge once more onto the surface."

"That is admirable, dear wife. But what of the others? Those not favored by your selection process."

A somber veil descended upon the priestess. But she resisted looking away from him. Peering deeply into his eyes, she defended the consequences of her actions.

"Truly, there is devastation and destruction. Though the bulk of our planet was spared, along with the nomadic people inhabiting the outer regions, casualties were unavoidable."

P'Teel deflected the focus of his question, avoiding the reality of the deadly statistics. Answering instead with a defense, "Should we not be grateful for the salvation of the selected ones - the best of our race? Would the destruction of all we have achieved on

Gemini be preferred? Was the destiny of our people to reside in the hands of those few Ravarians cast out into the void of space? It was a gamble, to be sure. You, yourself refused to fully support construction of more space arks. Left to the vagaries of chance, those within these confines could all be dead. The meteorite could have been a planet killer! Thankfully, it was not. We will be able to recover. The opportunity to rebuild, mightier and more magnificent than before, awaits us."

Amidst the swirling vapor of her hypnotic spell, Mitron discerned a kernel of truth. Yet, he was compelled to protest.

"Your words ring true, but at what cost? If, as you say, those still alive amidst the turmoil of poisoned air and depleted resources go on to survive, will they not rebel against us? Their suffering is intolerable! Rightfully or wrongfully, they will seek to assign blame. We who have avoided the pain they have endured over these past several seasons will bear the brunt of their rage."

P'Teel countered, "The bombardments have ceased. The dust storms have subsided. Even now, Pollux shines its life-giving rays through the dissipating clouds. Certainly, some will never forgive, but many will soon forget. Especially if we are the ones to bring sustenance to the body, and to the mind."

"I understand how your clan's accumulated surplus of stores and crops would be welcome relief, but what is this you speak of as to healing their *mental state*?"

"My lord, history has shown in times of deep crisis, people hunger to rally behind a strong leader - a leader that delivers a philosophy of hope for a better future. In that way, the populace can find solace in dealing with the blight of their present. Some leaders rise, creating opportunity amidst adversity's threats. I believe you are such a leader. Your innate skill to appeal to the masses need only the foundation of a guiding philosophy to deliver true *change*."

"And what *is* this philosophy, enchantress? Is it one you employ to garner such loyalty amongst your followers?"

"The simple answer is, *yes*. But I truly believe it can grow into so much more. It is true, those that do not understand our ways are fearful of them. They shroud any attempt at clarity in rumors, superstition, and fear. By reducing our beliefs to a simplistic label - *Fire Arts* - it is easier to react with scorn and derision to that which they do not understand.

But our philosophy can be *so much more*, if the right leader were at its forefront!"

"Tell me more of this belief system," Mitron implored.

"True, as with many philosophies, we reserve the right of self-preservation, and so empower ourselves with what some call mystical abilities, or Fire Arts. But behind this misrepresentation propagated by the uninformed is a more cerebral set of doctrines.

Through meditation and control, one can suppress the aggressive impulses that so often erupt within us. In their place, a sense of peace can emerge. This first level of empowerment, if spread amongst the people, can overcome the infighting and self-destruction that lead to the demise of a civilization."

Mitron's resistance was wavering, but not fully overcome. "The would-be followers must first not just hear, but *listen* to such a profound message. Yet, it is difficult to speak to them while they carry torches and arms."

"Aah, mighty warrior, you certainly know a more successful means to overcome an enemy. Rather than face them head on, you convert them from within. That is the beauty of what we have already achieved. The people within these walls will be eternally grateful for what you have provided. They will become your disciples, going forth, infiltrating the bands of survivors. By sowing the seeds of our beliefs, the fruit of wisdom will grow strong around them."

Revelation began to dawn within Mitron. "It *just might be possible,*" he mused. "*Suppress the warrior, allow peace to emerge. It's as if two conscious beings reside within us. By separating the two a greater good can be achieved. If they follow me, a new era of prosperity could arise.*"

Looking deeply into the flames of P'Teel's eyes, he relented to her persuasive charm. "What you say, dear wife, can become a reality. Under my guidance, the people *could* rebuild their lives. By unifying the great tribes, a civilization of wonderment would emerge. But I have my own thoughts about this philosophy you describe. Perhaps there is room to build upon it. What do you call it, if not the Fire Arts?"

P'Teel smiled broadly. Taking his face in her hands, she whispered serenely, "It is called *Phoenos.*"

*   *   *

The priestess left her husband to contemplate the future of the Geminian race, encouraging him to put his thoughts to parchment. She wove her way through serpentine passages, opening secret barriers, squeezing through hidden niches, to finally arrive at her destination.

As a child, her mother would leave her to her own devices, allowing her to explore the mysteries of the perpetually growing complex. As the facility expanded, some sections were left to embrace obsolescence. Those were her favorites.

The one she now entered was naturally formed, versus the carved and reinforced ones used most commonly by the Stargazer guild. She liked this one in particular.

Its environment was somewhat primitive. Trickling water from fissures nourished a collection of mosses and fungi. Through her training, she knew them to be edible, and quite tasty. Veins of rubidium crystal traced a convoluted path from the surface to convey a radiant glow contributed by Pollux's grace.

During her earliest visits to the cavern, she would depart feeling refreshed and energized. As she matured, she found solace in its confines, often attaining a meditative state that opened her mind to new ideas and impulses.

Of late, her trances yielded dream-like images. Visions, compelling her to make choices. As she sat cross-legged, open hands resting on her knees, the wispy visual impression in her mind's eye did something never before achieved - it spoke!

"Open your eyes, P'Teel. It is time for your awakening."

The priestess obeyed.

Before her, a small silver pool had formed where none existed before. A trickle of mercurial liquid crept from a hidden stone fissure, snaking its way to nourish the growing disc.

The voice continued. "You have performed well. Since childhood, you have grown, and learned. You are now ready for what lies ahead.

The path can diverge, yet your efforts will ensure success. Mitron will benefit from your influence, as will your lineage.

Your soon-to-be-born child, Kronia, will also provide benefit. Adversity breeds strength. There will be struggle. It will take what you refer to as *time*. Yet, despair not. For I will guide you along the journey. We will find the one way, and the Other."

Awestruck, P'Teel watched as a glowing mist rose from the metallic surface. Pulsing light oscillated within the construct as it shifted and morphed. Shapes appeared, then folded in upon themselves, only to emerge more complex. It was as if the substance were trying to decide which form suited its purpose best.

Finally, a glistening humanoid figure coalesced. Not quite solid, but more than a mere transmission of holographic light.

Unable to contain herself, P'Teel stammered, "Wh-What … Wh-Who are you?"

Responding, the figure exuded a sense of serenity and comfort, saying, "You, my child, may call me, Chrislar."

CHAPTER 16

Plant Manager Morgan Descartes sat at his work console, eyeing his new technical superintendent. There was a curious appeal to her, despite being an insectoid.

Clesk was the product of cross-species genetic transfer studies still underway on Earth's moon. Efforts to combat viral infectious outbreaks on several populated planets led to the program. Generations of developing insect control chemicals had spawned breeds that were hyper-resistant. Those breeds were found capable of fighting off viral infections as well. An outgrowth of the science was to incorporate into humans the genetic sequences that gave the insects their superior immuno-response. Social outcries of "not in my backyard", though, led to the only solution acceptable to all.

Put the lab on the Moon.

As is the case with many scientific endeavors, all factors could not be controlled. One such study involved the use of embryonic stem cells as the host for modified insect gene sequences. Thousands of iterations were trialled. A majority of samples failed miserably. Some generated viable proteins with curative properties. One resulted in meiotic cellular reproduction. A result that could not be duplicated. But it was successfully sustained.

True to the phrase "miracle of life", Clesk was born.

Her early development had occurred under stringent laboratory conditions. Despite the cosmos being an enormous place with infinite possibilities, some things never changed. Like the reaction of the broad population to a being such as Clesk. Discrimination. Hence, a controlled environment made possible by the Lunar Science Complex seemed the perfect solution.

For a while.

During an un-announced tour by a Solar executive, Clesk had been discovered. Watching her perform her exercise routine in the partial-gravity gym of the Moon had been astounding. A review of her exemplary scholastic abilities had sealed the deal. After undergoing a corporate indoctrination program, she would be an ideal candidate for a life crystal plant assignment.

Descartes, for once, was grateful to Corporate for intruding into his personnel affairs. He watched as his new manager went about her duties. Mostly humanoid in shape, she did have some unique and advantageous attributes. Instead of skin, her body was covered by a smooth, black, chitinous membrane. Multi-faceted, metallic-hued gold-green eyes perceived wavelengths invisible to humans. Retractable mandibles were held close to her jawline, accentuating her cheekbones to provide an exotic allure. Vestigial antennae - at least believed to be - were pulled back from a sleek forehead and wound into a French braid.

Most notable were her appendages. Her legs and one pair of arms were articulated like humans, with knees and elbows bending the same as those of her mammalian progenitors. Her additional pair of arms, though, sported mantis-style scissors with vise-grip strength. As such, she kept those tucked to her body beneath her corporate issued uniform vest. The effect was to provide a shapely, hourglass profile that garnered Descartes' attention.

"Morgan, stop staring," Jefferson Brown admonished. The *Darwin*'s personnel manager hovered around the control room, looking for areas that just might need his involvement - or as Descartes would say - *meddling*. "I just got you more accepting of exobiological employees with our reptoid friend Helicon of Clio. Now you have a problem with Clesk?"

"No, you Martian headshrinker, I don't. Actually, she's kind of attractive. Being an insectoid, she doesn't like reptiles either … and she kind of reminds me of my lander."

"Wow! Time for another cultural sensitivity seminar for you! You just likened one of your staff to an old Earth Apollo program Lunar Excursion Module - knowing full well Clesk is *from the Moon!*" the personnel manager scolded. An African-American moved by his parents to Mars at an early age, Brown was used to his plant manager's weak attempts at insulting him personally. His patience, though, did not extend to crass remarks about his employees.

"Seriously, J.B., get a sense of humor! I'm just being a misoxenogist to get on your nerves! In fact, I prefer Clesk over Starn any old day. After all, Starn is just a *human!*"

"Holy Hellas Basin! You're impossible. Just a human that has empowered another life form with *only his mind*!"

"Well, yeah, I guess there's that. From what he tells me, though, he doesn't want that to be his thing anymore. The director of the IAD contacted me personally. He wanted to make sure he wasn't stepping on any political toes if he took Starn into his organization. I said, 'go for it'. It's just as well. The chemistry within the plant's team didn't feel right with Starn instead of Nimon. I know it sounds crazy, since they *are* the same person. But, the balance of our staff just seemed 'off'."

Jefferson Brown, often a thorn in his plant manager's side, for good reason, hesitated before responding. More thoughtfully than usual when it came to Descartes, he replied, "I must be rubbing off on you, Morgan. Listen to yourself talking about 'team dynamics'. To be truthful, I agree with you. Starn is still working through some issues. He really isn't the same person as Nimon, by the way. A common mistake made when it comes to interacting with identical twins, biodgen Duals - or clones, for that matter…"Brown added, looking over his shoulder at Saffron 2 or Esstu, as she was called. One of two Angellian clones employed along with their primary on the *Darwin*, she was busily performing her duties as communications technician.

Seeing an opening to change the subject without bruising Brown's ego by interrupting his mini-lecture, Descartes interjected, "Speaking of communications, any thoughts on our orders to head back out ... *again*?"

"Well, let me see if I've got this straight. After rescuing Dr. Edison from the renegade Castorians and witnessing Nimon and Starn *talking to each other in the same clinic room* ... still creepy as far as I'm concerned ... we got orders to go traipsing off to the other end of the galaxy to the Legotians' homeworld. But instead of picking up Novas to return her to Corporate for a debriefing on the status of the Gemini-Solar-Castor negotiations as planned, we're told to reverse thrusters and come back to Gemini. 'The Legotians aren't ready to release Novas we're told. *'Release Novas'* - sounds like she's being used for their own purposes, is what I think. But I digress. So we're told to head *back* to Gemini -without Novas- because your new buddy in the IAD says the situation with Nimon and Starn is *unresolved* - whatever that means. Yet now, as of a little while ago, after picking up Dr. Edison, IAD says the *real* issue is some Geminian insurgent named T'Poch. And she just happens to be half-way *back* out into space on her way to Castor aboard the very renegade ship whose butt we whipped. Is that about right?" Brown concluded, his arms folded and foot tapping, waiting on a reply.

"Ummm … pretty much. Of course if we were using only thrusters, none of this would be possible," Descartes quipped, theatrically sweeping his arm through the air to take in the control room as he keyed in on Brown's verbal artistic license. "As a matter of fact, all this bouncing around in space has been quite lucrative. We're finding this quadrant to be one of the richest concentrations of cosmic particles for our process. Our yield of converting them into life crystals as we space-fold has been exceptional. I've asked our Technical Superintendent Clesk to look into it as to why. And, thanks to that very same space-time folding technology, we should arrive in the sector just ahead of our Castorian friends before they reach their homeworld."

*　　*　　*

"And what was that all about?" pressed T'Poch. Having returned from Vice-Executive Talor's conference room, she looked quizzically at P'teel as the door to their quarters irised shut.

P'Teel held out her hand, signaling her ward to place the memory doubloon into it. "This is most intriguing, my child - if not disturbing. The events presented here are in conflict with those chronicled in another record. Our benefactor within the Council of Elders saw fit to share with me information from Nimon's trial. If I had it, I could show you. As it is, I need you to dissect *this* recollection for anomalies. I sense something beyond our mystical science is at work here."

"It will take some time. No doubt, discretion is of the utmost importance. I will need to construct security protocols within the ship's central computer to isolate my work from prying eyes. Once done, I will have the full power of its processor core to unveil the secrets residing in the memory doubloon."

"Very well. I will use the time to explore this vessel and its people. I suspect there is much to learn from them before we arrive at Castor." With that, she returned the data coin to her disciple and departed.

Several rotations passed as P'Teel came and went, often wordlessly so as not to disturb T'Poch in her efforts. She brought meals to her ward, as would a mother bird nurturing her fledgling. She found it to be a pleasurable diversion to wander the levels of the spacecraft, prodding its technicians for bits of information. Often, she would provide her own insights as barter, weaving a network of informants and confidants.

Upon returning once again to the r shared quarters, she marveled at the display that greeted her. The trappings of the room, spartan as it was, had been pushed aside to create a miniature arena. Hologram projectors had been strategically placed on the walls at critical points. In the center, stood, or rather performed, T'Poch.

It was as if a Tei Lan martial arts master were practicing a kata, but the movements were aimed at manipulating data instead of striking an opponent. Computer subroutines took on three dimensional shapes projected holographically around her. She spun and dodged, plucking one from behind her just as it spiraled away. Repositioning it with another polyhedron to her left, she formed a complex architecture of pulsing matrices. Vaulting over it, she swiped at a nexus of swirling discs. Scooping them together, she hurled them like shurikens at the structure floating before here. Striking it in a tetrahedral pattern, the form collapsed in upon itself into an image of a data doubloon. Palming it as it drifted toward a panel in the wall, T'Poch snapped her arm forward, plunging it into the display screen.

Images sprang forth from the holo-projectors, as T'Poch took a cross-legged seating position at the room's center. She narrated to P'Teel the events that were being displayed. P'Teel looked on, ravenous for the information T'Poch was about to reveal.

*   *   *

Tempora emerged from the quicksilver portal, solidifying at its edge, a comet trail of twinkling photons disappearing behind her. Looking down, her hands at her sides, palms out, her radiance slowly dimmed as her corporeal form took shape. Still wearing her tribal garments, the leather border of her linen skirt skimmed the floor as she lightly strode away from the pool. Air currents from her passing disturbed a pile of ash stretching outward from its edge. A gold rosette glinted, as if winking up at her.

"Well, the mystery of the disappearing assassin is solved," Tempora mused to herself. *"I must have hurled him into the next eon*

instead of against the back wall of the closet. It seems time travel can be disagreeable to some."

As she pondered Tark's demise, wondering why she survived and he did not, she became aware of a conversation. Surrounded by shadows, she edged toward the sound. Moving closer to the source, the words of Chrislar, the Legotian, could be overheard. Soothing, hypnotic, he was attempting to calm an enraged female standing before him. Looking more closely, Tempora recognized the woman.

It was Novas of Gemini!

Immediately, a wave of fury swept over the Castorian Executive. The last recollection she had was of the temptress being swept away into the omnivator by her father.

"But that was on board the Destiny, over a kiloseason ago. And her hair, now, silver streaked and cascading to her shoulders. It is as I first saw her in this very chamber. Not as it was a short time ago, cropped and platinum-tinged -at least my short time ago."

Tempora, disoriented, attempted to make sense of her situation. She listened more closely as the Geminian berated Chrislar about her *time* in Gemini's past - but with *Mitron*, not Ravar.

Chrislar implored Novas to understand. "You *have* been in the presence of Mitron. What you experienced was *real*, not imagined."

As the Geminian struggled to comprehend, the Castorian more quickly grasped the meaning of her exchange with the Legotian. "*While I have been on board the Destiny, after its launch from Gemini, this one has been stumbling in the time of Mitron, prior to the momentous departure. I have been seeking to save lives while she has been preoccupied with a crystal and its connection to Phoenos.*" Her attention again turned to the Geminian's vitriolic complaining.

"If I *were* to believe you, Legotian, that would mean much of what Geminians know to be their history has been distorted. Ravarians left under *peaceful* circumstances. Their belief in the Phoenos was a righteous one. And, one half of the crystal that holds the secret of Phoenos is somewhere among the followers of Ravar!"

Tempora could no longer simply stand by and listen. She had done that for too long! She had been in the shadow of her father her entire life, never recognized as the heir-apparent to lead Castor. Her primary goal for the negotiations with the woman and being before her was to alter that fate. She would be the force bringing Castor to equal footing in the cosmos with Gemini and the Solar Corporation. Successful talk would generate righteous action. But only if she were at the center of those discussions. It was time to step forward, into the light, to seize what was rightfully hers.

Novas' steely gaze turned to the newcomer. Its focus aimed at a silver pendant hanging at the end of a gold chain around Tempora's neck. It was identical to the one she had bestowed upon baby T'Poch when she had given her over to P'Teel so many seasons ago.

At least almost identical. Missing was the locket that would have held a precious life crystal.

"Aah… the heiress to the Chair of Castor… and a descendant of Ravar," Novas murmured.

Tempora fought to quiet the rage throbbing in her ears. She had come to the Legotian negotiations intent upon fulfilling her destiny - attaining the Castorian Chair, and satisfying an unrequited love. Yet, she had been used by the Legotians. Ripped from her present. Thrust into the past - the outcome of her efforts unconfirmed - only to be returned to suffer the menstruations of this Geminian bureaucrat. Her hand edged toward the half-sword hanging at her side. *"It would be so easy,"* she plotted. However, Chrislar's glance cast a nullifying sensation through her.

Novas continued, citing the legend passed down through her family, "The possessors of the two crystal halves could unite to form a formidable alliance in the galaxy. But I see from the adornment the Castorian wears, she has naught to offer this union."

Tempora resisted the intoxicating trance induced by the Legotian. Despite her effort, and to her dismay, the rage within receded. Her focus shifted. Chrislar's words directed toward Novas swirled in the eddies of her consciousness.

"You should now have the Ravarian mate to the crystal... as should your child, your blood kindred, possess the Mitronian half. Did you not return with it? The Castorian Executive standing before you has experienced her own temporal displacement. Her influence is pivotal, as is yours. You should have brought back what is rightfully hers."

Novas was visibly shaken. Fragments of her response filtered through Tempora's mental fog. "There is more … that concerns me. It is the dark truth about which I spoke upon my arrival. My kindred *does* possess the crystal, but that is not Nimon…"

No longer able to be suppressed, Tempora's seething fury blazed. The mists of Chrislar's calming influence evaporated. Unable to be restrained, she exploded, "Your blood kindred *must* be Nimon. Nimon and I can make that union a reality! We will use the power of the Phoenos as it was meant to be!"

Chrislar interceded once more. Raising his hand, palm forward and directed toward Tempora, he urged Novas to continue. Tempora momentarily regained her composure and listened, waiting.

The Legotian pulled at the threads of Novas' narrative about the plight of the crystalline halves. At the Legotian's prompting, Novas explained, "My first born Dual, my Singular Dualiity, T'Poch of the K'Tar has the crystal. It empowers her very soul. And my greatest fear is her lifelong mentor, P'Teel, has the ability, and most evil of desires, to use it … a desire for power that has spanned generations … and *I* foolishly provided her the seeds of knowledge from whence that desire was spawned!"

Chrislar paled upon hearing this new information.

The Castorian fumed!

"I do not accept this! *I* am the heiress to Castor's future! The Ravarian crystal should be in *my* possession! You speak of the Mitronian half being in the possession of a biodgen *construct*. You would have me believe that a Geminian *device* is destined to bond with a Castorian to lead my people to their rightful place in the cosmos? That cannot be! My father is dead. He has passed the chair to *me!* And what of the Ravarian shard? If this Geminian witch before me did not return it from the mists of the past, then where is it? What is my role to be for the future of my *people*?"

CHAPTER 17

Enn turned from the afterglow of the Castorian Executive's passage through the time portal. Critical to any successful leader was the ability to move from one crisis to another, especially if the one was beyond your control. She decided the situation in the Stellar Cartography Lab might better benefit from her influence rather than the plight of the Executive.

Upon entering the lab, she found Thresh replaying the computer simulation once more for Ravar. The trio of explosions on the primary asteroid body generated an energy profile in a table on the screen's inset display. The blast force spiked exponentially. A series of subsequent explosions cascaded back through the swarm. She marveled at the fine powdery mist that dispersed through the cosmos.

"Ah, Adviser Enn," Ravar addressed her in a professional tone, but with a glint in his eye,

225

"were you able to attend to the security matter?"

"Time's eddies favor you, my liege. It has passed with no future to speak of," she replied, enigmatically.

The High Chieftain chuffed, the corner of his mouth upturned with the hint of a smile. He knew when to press for more information from his enchantress, and when not.

"Then let's turn to more urgent matters. You've seen the display. Thresh, please provide the supporting details to my second-in-command."

The sub-chieftain turned from the console to fully engage the newcomer, and was startled. *"Her eyes ... the line of her cheekbone ... perhaps a sister?"* he mused to himself. Regardless, he instantly trusted her. He relayed the details of the proposal.

"So... thoughts?" Ravar inquired, after Thresh was finished.

Enn reached out and deftly stroked several command jewels on the console. A split screen display appeared. On the left, the asteroid swarm engulfed Gemini, pulverizing it. On the right, remnants of the exploded cascade peppered Gemini's atmosphere with a shower of shooting stars.

Pointing to the images, Enn replied, "I believe our choice is clear. We save Gemini."

*   *   *

Chrislar patiently allowed Tempora to vent her rage. As she paused, he looked at her and considered, "She was more than the Castorian Executive that had first appeared in the Legotian chamber. And unbeknownst to her, she would become *much* more. True, as she had so ardently spoken, she *was* the heiress to Castor's future. Rightfully, she *should* possess the Ravarian crystal. And, in one brief temporal adventure, she had nudged events ever so slightly along a more correct path."

The thoughts of his collective murmured their agreement.

"Yes, what had been cloudy has become crystal clear," Chrislar telepathically conveyed to his council. "From this nexus in time, just as *Novas* must address her present, before *Enn* secures her past, Tempora shall address the future. Our belief that Novas would bring back the crystal from the time of Mitron was misplaced. Its properties are more powerful than we theorized. It passes through time at its own pace, not to be altered. Perhaps the influence of Novas on the past is a more subtle one. Yes … her contact with P'Teel, her affect on both Mitron and most of all, Ravar. This is not yet complete. Yet her impact on the fate of the crystal halves has come to an end. Her purpose is a far greater one. She is with child. From this point in the time strand, she must return - but *after* she counsels Nimon, with our assistance.

As for the Castorian, her evolution approaches. It is *time* for the crystal halves to finally unite."

A brief silence ensued as Chrislar directed his thoughts to her, and her alone.

"Tempora, calm your fury. You have done much, and you have much more to do. You have affected the past. The future can also be influenced. Make your choices carefully, and what you desire will be attained. Embrace your destiny and re-enter the pool."

Despite her initial instincts to demand an explanation, the Legotian was mysteriously compelling. The executive's expression slowly softened, and with a gentle nod, she departed.

*   *   *

Once more Tempora's essence coalesced into her corporeal form in yet another time and place, although oddly familiar. Taking in her surroundings, she sardonically observed, *"Perhaps the cosmic thread that unifies reality is that all storage closets are the same?"* She fully expected to emerge once more into the corridor of Ravar's vessel. Yet, she recalled Chrislar's reference to the future.

Still clothed in the trappings of a member of the Stargazer sect - a chamois bodice partially covered by a linen stole and a matching linen split-skirt draping to the floor - she knew the look was timeless, at least on Castor and Gemini. *"Well, no clues from clothes or closet, so the only thing left is to step out and see what awaits,"* she concluded.

Clearly not the tight, maximum-efficiency, utilization-of-space designed ark that had been Ravar's *Destiny,* this ship was spacious. Instead of smooth-walled corridors, the wide passageways were more industrial in design. Although spotlessly clean, conduits and pipes ran the length of the walls, intermittently disappearing into penetration points to other sections of the vessel. The slight curvature to the walls belied the fact that Tempora was indeed onboard a spacecraft, as opposed to the traditional rectangular design of most land-based buildings. That and the almost imperceptible hum from shielding that deflected the relentless bombardment of space particles while in flight.

As she strolled nonchalantly from one section to another, she noted cross-corridors leading radially to a central core. Most of the activity by personnel seemed to be occurring in that direction. As such, she managed to walk unnoticed for some time.

Finally, the passage necked down to a scissor-style doorway. Next to the opening, a control screen emitted a golden glow, begging to be utilized. Standing in front of it, a motion detector prompted the pad's voice interface to ask, "Identification, please." A graphic of a hand appeared beneath the header "SOLAR CORP LIFE CRYSTAL FACILITY *DARWIN* - Access Protocol"

"*Aah...*" mused Tempora, "*...the most profitable company in the ten star systems, its most prized asset, and the bane of my existence!*"

She still harbored ill-will toward this vessel and its plant manager. Not to mention the accursed Nimon. She recalled how he had seduced her into gaining access to stealth technology developed by the Castor

Conglomerate. And in the process, he had stolen her heart. Despite being spurned, she believed that she was fated to bond with him and unite their two planets. The legend of the crystal halves had foretold it. Yet, to learn from the Geminian harpy, Novas, that he did not possess the Mitronian shard had been crippling to her hopes.

"Perhaps this is my opportunity to still fulfill our destiny?" she pondered. *"Surely he is here. Chrislar said to choose carefully, and my desires can be attained."*

With steely conviction, she raised her hand to the panel. She understood the system had no record of her, and her chances for entry were nonexistent. But often, Conviction overrides Chance.

The monotone voice responded. "Working … working … working. Print record not found. Activating genetic protocol."

The index fingertip on the hand graphic phased to an icy blue. "Ow!" Tempora exclaimed, jerking her hand away. A thin veneer of skin remained on the screen, leaving a sapphire circle on her fingertip. As she watched, the cellular layer that had been cryogenically microtomed from her was absorbed into the display.

"You want my fingertip … how about my fist!" the Castorian exclaimed, balling up her hand and drawing it back.

Before she could strike, the synthetic voice announced, "Familial correlation confirmed. Temporary clearance granted. Please proceed to section Zeta chamber 619 within 0.1 rotation to ensure clearance is not revoked."

And with that cryptic message, the door scissored open.

Stepping through, the ambience changed dramatically. Gone was the neo-industrial environs of a life crystal manufacturing operation. In its stead was a corridor with tastefully selected art on the walls and firmly padded carpet runners leading to a variety of stylized doorways. Next to them, nameplates identified the occupants and specified the chamber number. As she passed several cross-connecting corridors like those that had occurred in the production area, section numbers were posted with arrows to aid in navigating.

Lack of understanding the control panel's response did not deter her from at least acting upon it to find the chamber. She occasionally crossed paths with other personnel. Some were dressed in distinctive clothing, most likely representative of their homeworld like herself, while others wore a soothing forest green jumpsuit. Embroidered on each uniform above the left breast pocket was a *Darwin* facility logo. Beneath the stylized silver sphere with a blue Marquise cut crystal in its center were department designations. Occasionally she would receive an appreciative nod as they passed, but generally, she was ignored.

Working her way closer to the center of the vessel, the passenger chambers yielded to work areas in support of the personnel. Break rooms, a commissary, and recreation area spoke to the fact that the people were well cared for during their tenure in space.

Entering the Zeta section, she noted a more erudite design. A glass walled conference room with holographic emitters ran along one side of the corridor. Sporadically, smaller isolation cubicles provided the opportunity for private research and study. One station sported a simulator allowing biometric interfacing for immersive gaming and role play. Residence quarters were fewer, as if reserved for the elite among the facilities' staff.

Standing at an intersection of passageways, her back to a branch leading to an omnivator access point, she failed to notice two men stepping out on to that level.

Dr. Edison and Starn abruptly stopped when they saw her. Looking at each other, dumbfounded, they could not believe their eyes. As if from the mists of Germini's past stood a Stargazer! Edison was the first to comment, more to himself than Starn. "Could it be … her!?" Instinctively, he reached with his hand to halt his son's approach.

Hearing the two, Tempora turned in their direction.

She walked toward them, one leg crossing in front of the other, the skirt enticingly revealing her toned thighs. Dr. Edison succumbed to memories of passion from times past. Starn felt the ghost of his other self whispering cautionary words of forbidden taboos.

He peered more intently, noting the short sword at her side, the cut of her dress. Studying her face, he corrected his father, "No, not Geminian. Castorian. And a notorious one. She is the Castorian Executive, emissary to the Conglomerate Chair."

"And how do you know that?" queried the doctor.

"Since my resuscitation by Nimon, I share his experiences. When it comes to her, they are not honorable ones."

Edison murmured, "She looks so much like …"

Then he briskly shook his head as if to dispel a trance. Addressing Starn, he remarked, "Thankfully, you are here, and not your Dual. Let us see why *she* is."

*　　　*　　　*

Several rotations had passed since the *Destiny* had parted company from her sister arks. Her precious payload of hibernating Geminian evacuees were safely entrusted to the *Vector*. By design, although a strain on resources, each umbilical command module could support two payload cylinders.

Ravar paced the control center while Enn looked over Stev's shoulder at the navigation station. Keenly aware of his restlessness, she knew her liege and lover was a man of action, despite his skills as an engineer. He needed a distraction while the vessel made its way closer to the asteroids.

Pulling him aside she whispered, "My Chieftain, leadership alters the fates of millions. While your followers continue on in the two arks, we are on the brink of Gemini's salvation."

"Hmmpf. My followers..." Ravar replied, his tone dripping with skepticism, "... they are led by my nemesis, Mace. Who is to say I have not doomed the fates of my people?"

"There are always choices. One can destroy their enemy, certainly. Or, instead, win them over. That is the meaning of *true* victory. If achieved, the strongest of allies can be the result."

Pausing briefly to let that message resonate with Ravar, Enn continued, "I studied Mace's reaction when you told him your plan to destroy the planet killers. I saw the veil of doubt lift. In its stead, a glimmer of respect appeared. I believe for the first time he recognized you as the strong leader that you are. Your words of sincerity entrusting him with the safety of the arks was no small gesture, either. Your engineering prowess proved the umbilicals could be extended to cradle not just one, but two payloads. Granted, their speed will be significantly impaired. But that enables us to overtake and rejoin them *after our successful mission*. I might also add, the irony of increasing the load of responsibility to the man that wished to displace you as leader is not lost on those who knew of his scheme." She smiled ruefully at her mate.

Ravar's grim countenance softened ever so slightly. He caught himself before taking her into his arms and embracing her. In the interest of ship's decorum, he instead placed his hands firmly on the side of each of her shoulders. "From Stargazer to Adviser - the title serves you well, my wise one." Looking down at her waist, he added, "Let us hope our child is gifted more with *your* qualities, than with mine."

Decorum be damned, Enn raised her hand and stroked her lover's cheek. From the navigation console, Stev theatrically cleared his throat to interrupt the moment and said, "We are approaching the launch point, my liege."

Ravar savored the touch of his mate for a moment longer and then turned. "Initiate launch protocol. Once the third transport vehicle is fired, set heading to intercept our sister arks, maximum velocity."

Stev looked out of the corner of his eye toward the tactical officer. She winked at him and responded, "Ready on your signal." Her hand hovered over a control orb.

"Activate launch sequence in 3, 2, 1... now!"

What transpired next was far from spectacular, but no less pivotal to the future of a planet. Three umbilicals had been deployed. Each held a passenger transport module at its end. No longer expected to protect a live cargo, the inertial dampeners had been deactivated. This allowed for maximum thrust through the journey. The ion rings at the base of each missile cycled through the rainbow of red to violet as they built energy. Once white, to an outside observer, the vehicles bearing their explosive payloads wavered and simply vanished. Untethered by gravitational forces, the ionic field from the respective drive swept over the module. This negated any visible light from reflecting off an object. Hence, they "vanished". But in virtual space, as was presented to the technicians watching their display on board the *Destiny*, a much different image occurred. The Control crew collectively gasped as a streak of silver shot off each of the tendrils toward the asteroid swarm.

Stev was the first to recover, closing his gaping jaw. With a blur of motion, control board jewels were pressed and twisted. "Evasive course set for ark rendezvous, High Chieftain."

Ravar raised an eyebrow and silently mouthed to Enn, "Evasive?"

In answer, she announced, "Excellent work, each of you! Our simulations did not extend to what happens in space *after* the objects explode to release their fury." Looking over at Stev as he twisted in his chair to listen, she acknowledged, "Let us pray to the gods that we *do evade* any deleterious effects."

CHAPTER 18

Sequestered in a small conference room, its glass walls tinted for privacy, the Castorian Executive stared at one, and then the other, of the two men before her.

Her piercing gaze settled upon Starn. "We have not met, but I definitely know *you*." Sweeping her eyes back to Dr. Edison, she continued, accusatorially, "I see the resemblance..."

"We are father and son," responded Dr. Edison, as if to apologize for the fact his was the only cream-colored skin in the room.

"...with *Nimon*!" She spat. "After his subterfuge to abscond with the Castorian stealth technology, I did my due diligence. Because of *your* science..." she continued, staring icily at Edison, then turning to address Starn, "... I find myself in the company of *this simulation of life.*"

Starn recoiled from the venomous bite of her words. Of course, she had no way of knowing the recent events that had precipitated his role reversal with his Dual, Nimon. He debated as to whether to continue with the ruse or attempt to establish a relationship based on trust. Eying his father as he reflected on his parents' subterfuge, he concluded honesty would be the best policy.

"Executive, the part my Dual played in that less than honorable affair is regrettable. While undoubtably pivotal to your interests at that time, I believe what I am about to reveal will instead become your highest concern."

Looking at Dr. Edison, she disregarded Starn and replied, "I understand Solar Corporation and the servile minions that control Gemini place a high regard on their *biods*, but *I* don't. Must I endure *this*?" A flick of her wrist dismissed Starn as if he were an Angellian gnat hovering over her favorite cocktail.

Rather than pull verbal punches, the doctor decided to be direct. "Starn is as organic as you or I. Nimon is the biodgen. Only recently has this fact come to light. There was no intended deceit. Only through an unusual set of circumstances has my son been restored to normalcy. So, you can fume about one more instance of your being duped, or behave more civilly as your executive position demands. Tell us what you have to say. After all, *you* are the one that seems most out of place and owing of an explanation."

This time it was Tempora who recoiled from the verbal onslaught. Edison's revelation was shocking - on several levels. She considered the impact of what she had just heard. *"So, my infatuation with Nimon is misplaced. I know the taboo preventing organic and biodgen relations. Clearly that can not be the path to unify the crystal halves, as I thought. Secondly, for the doctor to share this information so freely is meaningful. Why does he trust me? I must know more."* Gathering her composure, she conceded to his directive, and explained.

"Where to begin... it has been quite ... *unusual*. You know of the Castor-Solar-Gemini negotiations, I am sure. The Legotian techniques for facilitation are, to say the least, unorthodox. Yet, they do get results. Through them, I am able to be here. Because of them, I firmly believe it is my legacy to unite our worlds," she stated, looking intently at Starn. "For it to be achieved, though, requires fulfillment of a legend. It is said that when our peoples separated, so, too, was split a mystical stone. The Mitronians retained one half, while the Ravarians held the other. In order to unify our people, the crystal must be unified, as well."

Pausing, she looked to see if she was convincing, or deemed to be mad. Starn was the first to respond, wryly, "Let us say, we not only know of the legend, but are intimately involved." He continued, "The stone represents more than *legend* - much more. It is also the foundation of biodgen *science*. What is a mystery is how the two realms of legend and science intertwine to unite worlds."

"Aah… I have given this much thought. At the risk of being branded a megalomaniac, I believe *I* am the answer."

Both men straightened in their seats, each dubiously eyeing the other.

Holding her hands out, palms signaling them to wait, Tempora continued, "Before you wholesalely reject the concept, let us consider it *rationally*.

The Legotians selected two people to forge an agreement. Myself and Novas. I alone am descended from the Castorian Chair and heir to lead my people. Can the same be said of Novas for Gemini? I think not." Before Edison and Starn could mount an argument, she continued.

"I have learned the Mitronian shard has been in the possession of Novas, and the results have been less than spectacular. Instead of fulfilling a generations-long legend to unite our peoples, she squandered the opportunity. The last blood kindred of Mitron, an Executive of the Solar-Geminian joint venture, and emissary to the Geminian Council of Elders, what better position could there be, than hers? With those resources, surely the companion Ravarian crystal could be united with its Mitronian mate. Instead, she used the gem's power for her own desires. Bestowing it upon a mere facsimile of life, her Dual, she has unleashed a beast of anarchy! Yes, I am aware of T'Poch and the K'tar!"

Edison and Starn both fidgeted uncomfortably in their seats.

"The use of the mystical mineral in biodgen science has been innovative, true, but fraught with complications," Tempora added, noting her words were having an impact.

"Doctor, you know better than anyone how the technology of bioduogenetics has been regulated, contained, doled out only to the privileged. Has that *ever* served humanity for the greater good? Rather, the free exchange of ideas and advancement has proven to be the far superior way. Isn't it interesting that the science has been applied along a single direction - uni-dimensional in the approach?

Only *synthetic* constructs have been exposed to the power of the crystal. Have you even wondered what could be achieved if a new direction were explored?"

Starn sat impassively, listening, giving no indication as to his acceptance or dismissal. Edison, however, nodded slightly.

Seeing an opening, it was time for Tempora to declare her ultimatum. "What has yet to be explored is the effect of the crystal on an *organic*!"

Dr. Edison, normally the skeptic, found himself strangely compelled by her argument. Again, he marveled at the similarity ... the eyes, the curve of her jawline, even the cadence of her voice ... "*did she not know? I must explore this...*" he thought to himself, "*and she provides the perfect opportunity.*"

"Though a man of science, Executive, I have found it wise not to ignore Fate. Often it presents itself in the form of coincidence - things happening for no explicable reason. For you to be here before us, at this *time*, has to be more than coincidence.

Consider the events. Starn is adamant that his commitment to empower his Dual, Nimon, is at an end. I was forced for the sake of Nimon to cease the possibility of his independent sentience. And how was it done? I removed the very crystal that you seek. Until a moment ago, you believed that by joining with Nimon, you might unify two planets. And now, here you sit before me, making a compelling case that *you* should embrace the power that gave him life. Essentially, in a very unique way, bonding with him as you believed would happen. Certainly *more* than just coincidence. Fate. A fate we must explore."

Rising from the table, Edison turned to his son, who sat speechless as to this extraordinary turn of events. "Starn, as an officer of the IAD, you will witness, and assist." Reaching out his hand toward Tempora, beckoning her to take it, he implored, "And you, lovely lady, come with me."

*   *   *

Ravar stared in awe at the view screen in the *Destiny*'s control center. The explosions along the visible spectrum were inspiring. Radial sphere's pulsed outwardly phasing from violet to crimson as the faster waves outpaced the lower frequencies. But much like a tourist more enamored with the picture just taken instead of the event itself, the High

Chieftain could not take his eyes off the simulator image on a side panel.

Beyond the visible range, whether that of human or the much more extensive, Geminian, existed an energy realm only detectable by elaborate measuring devices. When converted via complex algorithms to a digital display, the result was breathtaking. Essentially, the software created a new spectrum of visual sensations. Intoxicating. Hypnotic.

Stev, always efficient, broke the spell that transfixed his superior, and reported, "The projectiles required 3.4 centi-rotations to traverse the space from launch point to contact. With our ion drives at maximum, we extended the safety margin to an additional relativistic equivalent of 2.7 centi-rotations. With sensors fully energized, we have witnessed the actual and virtual result of the explosions. Calculations show our models to be 94.6% accurate - well within the margin to consider the exercise a success. We are now in the experimental region outside the purview of our simulations. The frontal wave from the blast cascade is upon us. Shielding is at maximum. Your orders, sire?"

Ravar drew in a deep breath, exhausting a third of the time before impact. He replied simply, "We wait for Fate to grace our efforts." The answer exhausted the remaining time before the omni-wave engulfed them.

*   *   *

Christi Pomeroy, *Darwin* Planning Superintendent, intently studied her holographic display. One of her duties was to chart the dimensional pathways taken by the life crystal plant during time-space folding. The process was far from precise. Much like travel in the ancient sea-faring days when natural elements could dramatically affect your course, space folding could be fickle. Normally, the mode of transportation was reserved for jumping *between* star systems, not *within* star systems. Catastrophes with first generation technology had provided cause for that limitation - except on rare occasions.

This was one such occasion.

Plant Manager Descartes had impressed upon her the urgency of overtaking the renegade Castorian vessels. On his personal authority, she had been cleared to plot a course from Gemini to Castor, all within the Pollux star system.

"Plot a course," she grumbled to herself. *"As if I were using a compass and straight-edge on a paper map. Why not just stick my wet finger out a window to gauge which way the stellar winds are blowing?"*

The cause for the superintendent's grousing was understandable. Time-space folding was often described in simplistic terms as taking a sheet of paper and bending it such that two points far apart are placed in close proximity. In this way, an object can instantly travel a great distance. This static model, however, understates the complexity of the process. If a single fold could be created, many challenges would be removed. But, that was not the case. A more representative dynamic model would be one in which multiple folds, or waves, are present. Picture a paper boat floating on a pond with swirling wind blowing across its surface. Whitecaps are formed. Some move across the length of the water. Others collide, neutralizing each other's energy. Into this chaos, the objective is to drop a stone to form a directional wave large enough so that it overwhelms all the others, carrying the boat to the bank.

Despite the risk - and never one to shirk her duty - Christi took on the challenge. In a flash of astrophysics brilliance, she postulated that she could fold the *Darwin* to a point *outside* the star system and then fold it back *into* the system at a different point closer to Castor. While this made sense theoretically, it created its own set of problems. It was not unlike an architect envisioning a unique structure while overlooking the mechanical hurdles for the contractor to make it a reality.

Operations Superintendent Mack Weber was the contractor.

At his station, he rapidly made process adjustments to the life crystal formation loops. Sequential jumps were pushing the thermal dissipators to their limits. Instead of two jumps, Christi had begged him to figure out how to accomplish three. They were phasing into the third and last one as the chronal regulator bank began to misfire.

"Pomeroy! Check your holovid! Our chronal bursts are reflecting back on us. What is going on out there!"

"Can't ... help ... you ... need ... to ... focus ..." the planner responded, feverishly adjusting for the rapidly shifting time currents washing over the *Darwin*.

"Clesk!" Weber barked. "Can you give us a hand?"

Plant Manager Descartes had to stifle a smile at the faux pas his Operations Superintendent just made regarding his Technical Manager's anatomy. *"More like give us a feeler..."* the plant manager punned to himself. He had been quietly observing his team in action. Wisely, he knew when to exert control, and when to let the experts do their thing. Looking over at the science console, he was interested to see how Nimon's replacement would respond to a crisis.

The lunar insectoid straightened stiffly as she turned from her own monitor. Facial mandibles were no longer tucked tightly to her head. Instead, they emitted a rapid chittering noise as they clicked together at hyper speed.

"Clesk, please repeat. This time in standard Solarian, so we can understand," Descartes instructed.

Chitinous pincers retracted smoothly to her upper jaws as Clesk responded, haltingly. "Apologies, sir. I have witnessed ... what perhaps humans might call ... a *religious experience*."

"Say again?" the plant manager replied, this time with less patience.

By this time, both Weber and Pomeroy had regained their composure after achieving a modicum of stability with the plant's operation. They both turned toward the science station, curious as to Clesk's meaning.

"I will explain. My Hexapoda biological matrix carries with it certain genetic memory. One such memory speaks of a concept my phylum describes as *"Forever Time"*. Over the millennia, we have demonstrated an ability to survive holocausts that eradicate other species. We believe it is because we have a responsibility. In a way, we are the eternal historians. Despite the crisis, our essence continues while other creatures disappear from existence. And with us, certain universal concepts survive.

One such concept is the *Fulcrum Event* in Forever Time. A single phenomenon occurs at a point along the time stream, and *always* occurs. Its existence extends into the past and the future. Truly, it manifests itself differently as it emanates along the timeline, but it is in its essence the same. I believe we have just witnessed the *Fulcrum Event!*"

"Ooookay ... I get the *religious experience* part. A lot of mystical mumbo jumbo that doesn't make sense unless you are a believer, right?" Descartes interjected, his insensitivity bursting forth a little more than normal given Jefferson Brown was not around to reign it in.

Either Clesk didn't hear or chose not to directly respond, her excitement building, as she continued her explanation.

"Let me co-co-compare Forever Time to Light. Both are all around us, but we only experience a fraction of it. Both are made of up of different parts. For Light, it ca-ca-can be either a particle or energy packet. For Forever Time, one co-co-component of it is Life. Just as Light has different wavelengths, so does Life. Similar to how science ca-ca-can measure distance with the speed of Light, some cu-cu-cultures measure existence with the speed of *Life*. Creation is diverse, with different organisms experiencing widely differing lifespans. One planetary rotation for you ca-ca-can be many generations for another life form. But there has to be some co-co-constant point along which existence is balanced. That is the Fulcrum Event. Going backward in time from the Fulcrum Event, the wavelength, if you will, of the life essence changes. The matrix of life spores become altered. For example, mammals on Earth ca-ca-came into existence much closer along the time line to the Fulcrum Event than did my genetic ancestors. As such, the life spores were different. And so, *we* are different. Yet, in many ways, we ca-ca-can be the same, *if* certain universal concepts survive. As I said, the Fulcrum Event is one such universal concept."

"Right … right …" Descartes broke in, trying to both calm the the new science specialist and anchor her into his frame of reality. "Uuumm, you still haven't told us what the event was that you saw, Clesk."

"Aah, of co-co-course," she half spoke and half clicked. "Please observe the main holovid projection pad."

All chairs in the control center pivoted toward its middle. A two tred diameter disc in the floor glowed to life. Instantly, a three dimensional image formed depicting the phenomenon that captivated Clesk.

"I have adjusted the sequence of events to progress in a lineal timeframe we can understand. What we are seeing has not only *already* happened, but *is* happening, and *will also happen* in the future."

Descartes placed a hand on his face and slowly drug it downward, as if to wipe away the brain fog that was forming from Clesk's explanation. He still managed to peer between his spread fingers at the images on display.

"What we are witnessing are three Geminian transport vessels - but in this case, *missiles* - hurtling from a first generation ark class spaceship. Their targets, an asteroid swarm on collision course with their homeworld. As the events progress, watch the cascade of explosions."

Clesk paused as the images formed a fireworks display of veritable stellar proportions. For effect, she simulcast an audio simulation and thermal projection to enhance the experience of the audience. Reflexively, the observers held up their hands to shield themselves from the light and heat. Descartes simply closed his fingers together, his hand already conveniently covering his face.

The technical superintendent continued. "You'll see the Geminian craft veer away from the event in an effort to avoid the blast wave - unsuccessfully. Watch as it is swept up in the current and carried much like our own plant traverses enormous distances in a relativistic short amount of time. Eventually, those waves engulfed us as we phased into our third jump."

Descartes, though fascinated by the images, still struggled with comprehending what he was hearing. Mustering the last bit of patience at his disposal, he stood from his chair and stepped forward to a point between Clesk and the images. He spread his arms, palms turned up, in a posture used by orators to implore their audience to listen.

"Dear Clesk, you are clearly brilliant, whereas I am not. I am but a practical man, seeking to understand. Let me see if I can repeat your explanation, in my own words. What you are saying is that we are witnessing that ship ..." Descartes pointed back toward the holovid without turning ... "even though generations old, saving Gemini from annihilation. And, more perplexing, we are experiencing the same spatial phenomenon from an untold time past as that vessel. Because ..." Descartes held up vertically an index finger to emphasize his point "... we are engulfed in Forever Time, which has allowed us to witness the Fulcrum Event explosion of an asteroid swarm. Is that about right?"

The insectoid science expert nodded vigorously, clicking her mandibles with glee. "But there is more!" She waved a pincher over her jeweled keyboard. A depiction of a crystalline structure and chemical formula replaced the three dimensional projection.

"My analysis of the particulate from the explosions reveals a complex structure of both crystalline and organic material. I suspect whatever was in the passenger transports left a genetic signature. The composite is identical to the ionic profile of the spatial elements we harvest with the *Darwin*. The only difference is the tachyon profile which changes over time. Just as is predicted when describing differences in Life waves emanating from the Fulcrum Event!"

A grin of understanding spread across Descartes face, as it would if a prehistoric hominid had just seen fire."You're saying the same essence that forms life crystals transforms through time to become the spore of life for many species?" he inquired.

Clesk buzzed deeply, a gravelly sound that passed for an insectoid whisper, and replied, "Not *many* - ALL!"

CHAPTER 19

Chaos ruled the command center onboard the *Destiny*.

Ravar was determined to take back control. Enn stood at his side.

"Deploy stabilizer umbilicals. Maximum extension!" The High Chieftain barked.

Stev's fingers danced across the bejeweled panel. All but three segmented coils disengaged from the lower drive module. While the three contracted within themselves, pulling the engine closer to the ark's primary section, the remaining umbilicals flared outward into space. To an outside observer, the ship had transformed into a mechanized shuttlecock. A spectral display of energy radiating from the arms interacted to create a photon veneer. The canopy formed by the appendages created a stabilizing effect. The vessel no longer tumbled nose over end through space. Instead, its rotational momentum around its central axis resumed.

Enn murmured her praise. "Nicely done, my lord. Among other things, you know your craft well."

Ravar cast a sidelong glance at her, marveling at her composure, and the sultry look aimed at him. "Your praise is comforting, *Advisor* ..." emphasizing her title to convey that now was not the time or place, "... but might you also venture a theory as to what is happening?"

Anticipating the need for information, Stev commented from his terminal, "Our data collectors are mute. It is as if all input has either ceased or is being deflected away from us."

Enn stepped over to his controls. After some deftly placed flicks and a few knob rotations, the view screen sprang to life. Using the opportunity to capitalize on the mystique ascribed to the Stargazer clan, she counseled, "Can you not feel it? Time is in flux. I deactivated the chronal sensor array. It was preventing the other detectors from functioning properly."

What she did not explain is that it would be some time before future technology developed measuring devices better equipped to operate during a space-time fold, which is what was enveloping the *Destiny*.

Stev sat staring glassy-eyed at the enchantress. Ravar broke the spell by saying, "Admirable. Can you also explain *that*?" He pointed at an image arcing across the corner of the display.

Normally stoic, even Enn could not suppress a look of surprise. "Astonishing," she whispered. "Stev. Please magnify."

The fuzzy image filled the screen. The object's appearance resembled a cored orange whose skin had been coated with a silver glaze. The "segments" were "D" shaped loops, the curve forming the outer support for the metallic skin and the backbone running along the length of the core. Rotating around its axis, it created a funneled glow entering one end and expelled from the other as it careened through space.

"The *Darwin* ... " the enchantress murmured, this time so softly no-one could hear, "... but how can this be?"

Her mind rapidly raced through the possibilities. *"Could the Legotians wield such power that they transported the life crystal facility back to this era? Could they have hurled the Destiny into the future? Are we under some mind spell created for a purpose only they understand?"* She shook her head, realizing the limits of her hypotheses. *"Everything in the universe does not revolve around the Legotians. Despite our future ability to utilize the marvel of time-space folding, we understand but a fraction of the science. Perhaps this phenomenon is* real. *I wonder if even Descartes knows what is happening?"*

Enn had not yet revealed to even Ravar the nature of her origin. As brilliant as he was, she could not be sure how he would react to her being an entity from the *future*, in many respects, a *meddler* in his life. This was not the time to change that. Certainly she could not explain that the *Darwin* was from the future without raising questions about her own existence. Instead, she played a hunch, hoping the *Darwin* would prove useful.

"Our Stargazer clan believed we were not alone in the galaxy. But had no proof. This appears to be it," she misdirected. "Stev, can you plot the trajectory of that object? Perhaps that knowledge will provide insight as to its nature."

Building upon her ruse, she pulled Ravar aside, leaving Stev to fulfill his task. "My liege, we are but infants in a galaxy of unknown wonders. On our maiden voyage, we have already seen and accomplished much. What began as an adventurous exploration for a new world has dramatically changed. My own presence was an unexpected event - hopefully a welcomed one," she paused, her silence an attempt to coax from him at least a nod of approval.

Casting decorum aside, he pulled her toward him. "I am at fault for leaving any doubt in your mind, my love. Those yet to know of our desires will eventually discover the truth. Let that time be now." He bent close, his musky breath, intoxicating, drawing her to him. His passionate lips, firm but gentle, melted her inhibitions. She raised her hands to his face, slipping one into his cascading mane, and pulled him even deeper into her embrace.

After what seemed an eternity of bliss, they parted. He looked down at her waist, lovingly, and professed, "You speak of adventure. Our greatest one will soon be upon us. In less than four seasons, our child will be here. What a joyous time that will be!"

Enn shivered, whether from the caresses of Ravar's hands along her back, or from the uncertain future that came with the responsibilities of a child, was unclear. Once again, Stev's timing was impeccable.

"My analysis is complete. The object appears to have originated from the same orbital plane as our own planet. Since our time reference is unreliable, it is unknown if it coincided with Gemini's presence along that path."

Enn nodded, appreciatively, commenting, "Of course. I suspected it did. My sisters theorized that we were not alone. Even proposing that beings had secretly visited us over hundreds of revolutions. Stev, more importantly, where does its trajectory lead?"

"Curiously, it coincides with a destination shared by our arks. When we embarked, our objective was to reach a planetary body never seen, but hypothesized by our High Chieftain." Stev lowered his head briefly, bowing to his superior. "Gravitational effects on bodies that *are* visible to us from Gemini can best be explained by the presence of another planet. It is theorized to be revolving around Pollux in a position diametrically opposite from our home world. Yet, for us to actually reach it posed a tremendous challenge. Despite our calculations, space is a big place." The sub-chieftain smiled at his understatement's attempt at humor. Ravar and Enn glanced at each other, stifling their smiles so as not to reinforce future attempts at comedy.

Enn, still unsure how they were viewing the flight path of a vessel from the future, was grateful for their fortune. Capitalizing upon it, she instructed, "With Ravar's permission, we should chart our course along the same route. Eventually, with detectors at their maximum sensitivity, we may chance upon our sister arks."

Stev, hesitant to be the bearer of bad news, cleared his throat and simply pointed to a small readout. Ravar noted it and astutely concluded, "Whatever act of the gods that enabled our flight into fantasy is dwindling in its effect. Our velocity has deteriorated from the `hyper range', for lack of a better term. I suspect we again must rely on the ion drives to continue our journey."

Enn, careful not to display an over-developed knowledge of time-space folding as only someone from the future might, speculated, "As we return to normal, it is unlikely we will see this mysterious object again. I'd like to think of it as a seadolph from ocean-faring days of old, sent to guide us through hazardous straits."

Always wanting to please, Stev commented, "The anomaly has truly benefited us, though, despite the momentary instability. Presuming the other arks continued as instructed, computations show we will intersect with them midway to our destination." Pausing to stare at Enn's midsection, his exuberance got the better of him. "By then the little one will be well into her sixth season and walking!"

This time Enn and Ravar could not help but beam with pleasure.

*　　*　　*

T'Poch, pointing to the almost life-like projection of Stev, the young azure-toned man dressed in a light, airy cloth shirt, said, "This spokesman is the focal point of several versions of the recording. In the one shown us by Talor, he describes a somewhat optimistic perspective of events. *Chairman* Ravar has appointed him chieftain. They have had some success with averting a catastrophic effect from an asteroid swarm. More importantly, as you will see, he praises someone called *Advisor Enn of the house of Mitron* and has a hopeful expectation regarding their efforts to avert a cataclysm on Gemini."

"All these being points of difference from the version shared before Kronia during the trial of Nimon, the other record I mentioned," added P'Teel, with a nod of approval.

"Precisely. Yet, after some delicate techniques reconstructing shielded data, the following exchange was revealed."

Passing her hand through a control beam from one of the emitters, a new set of characters appeared, performing a play of events from generations ago.

"Stev, you honor Enn most nobly. Her wise counsel with the meteoroid swarm, especially," praised Ravar.

"You are too kind, noble Chairman," replied the newly appointed chieftan, Stev.

"Yet, as leaders of our people, our role is not just to chronicle our adventure. We must use the opportunity to guide and motivate them. Now is a pivotal moment in our journey. It is time for a transformation. I, as the newly created Chairman, understand that the future is decided *now*. What we do will determine its success or failure. Success depends on the will of our people. That will must be driven by a common goal. But what goal? There are many of worth, and even more of trivial value. It is our task to chose wisely. It must be both challenging and inspirational. If easily achieved, it will fail to instill the fervor necessary for our people to succeed. That is why I have given it much thought and deliberation."

Stev held his breath in anticipation, not daring to interrupt his leader anc mentor. Eagerly, he waited, allowing Ravar to continue after a dramatic pause.

"That goal is for us to seek *retribution*! Retribution agains the one that exiled us. Retribution against *Mitron*!"

Stev shuddered at the forcefu passion radiating from the man before him. *"No, not just a man,"* he corrected himself. *"A demi-god! He was leading a whole people to salvation. They may be the last of their race, despite their best efforts to protect their home-world! And I, chosen by this man, am at a moment in history where I, too, can leave an indelible mark on posterity!"*

Clapping both hands on the shoulders of the new chieftain, Ravar continued. "Your message must be crafted to fuel the fire of retribution. Just as my loss of my beautiful Enn transformed me, the people must know of *their* loss. I have been changed. The scientist, Ravar, is no more. Through you and the other sub-chieftains, I, as the Chairman, will lead. Our followers must know a greater story of the impact of the storm. They must understand the events that transpired. Why we were forced from Gemini. Who caused the demise of many of our brethren and the progeny they can never have. *Mitron* is the villain! Weave the story into folklore that will infuriate the clans. From their fury, we will become united. Focused. Determined on becoming a power in the coming times. A power that will extend from our new world outward. Eventually returning to Gemini to claim our true birthright!"

Stev nodded briskly, stating, "I understand fully, my lord. I know what I must say." Turning to face the holo-cam, he pulled back his shoulders, slightly leaning forward, and reached out to posterity with his words.

"In honor of *chieftain* Ravar's -hiss- *dying* request, I, Stev, am continuing his chronicles of our journey. *The ion storm which engulfed our arks during the final orbital approach has taken its toll. All three vessels were heavily damaged, with radiation poisoning affecting all of us to varying degrees. Ravar, himself, was one of the many fatalities.*

-glitch- Our healers have -static- *nothing but grim* news. They expect that *many of those who survived will be sterile, with those who aren't doomed destined to live in fear of the radiation effects on their offspring.* As new chieftan, I *now know the grief that tore at the very soul of Ravar as he was forced to watch his people suffer... and all due to the spineless, peace loving Mitron. If the hatred for the Mitronians was a smoldering ember before, it is now a white hot coal never to be extinguished!*

-squawk- *The gods have decided to delay our vengeance on Mitron.* Our starwatchers tell me that the *devastating* storm during our arrival is of a cyclical nature. Their best calculations give us four seasons to prepare for the next one. After much deliberation, we have decided that for our people to remain bound to this forsaken world through repeated sieges by the cosmos would be an injustice.

Rather than shield ourselves, or seek protection underground as would vermin, we will -glitch- *rebuild two of the damaged arks from the remains of the third.* The *sixth* and last drone-probe sent out before *engaging the storm* has been faithful in its transmissions. The most recent data has identified a planet twenty seasons journey from here. We believe this oasis, orbiting our own star, but in a cycle always hidden from our homeworld, gives us our best hope for survival. It will be a difficult journey, but our *warrior* spirit will strengthen us. So that one day, we may return home to -hiss- our *rightful heritage, and deliver retribution upon the Mitronians*."

T'Poch deftly plucked a holographic icon from the projection to end it. "As my image enhancement emphasized the differences in this last soliloquy, it highlighted the damning lies put forth at the direction of Mitron."

P'Teel, all but cackling with pleasure, interjected, "Damning to be sure, my disciple! I did not think Ravar capable of such deception. True to his statement, his loss *must* have transformed him. From that faithful event, he built an entire civilization upon a *lie*! And it is that lie that will be the downfall of the Ravarians. When we reveal this testimony to the Castorian people, they will understand how they have been manipulated by the House of Ravar. They will reject that archaic establishment in favor of our leadership. We will reach out the hand of a new Gemini to clasp the open palm of an enlightened Castor. Rather than slap it away in rejection as taught by Ravar, we will form an ironclad grip of unity!"

CHAPTER 20

Dr. Nicholas Edison stood next to the operating table dressed in a violet sterile gown. Protective gloves, a face shield, and skull cap isolated the remaining exposed parts of his body from the patient. Across from the prone female stood Starn, dressed similarly. He was monitoring the vital signs on the sensor array suspended above.

Tempora was in a twilight sleep, bathed in a suspensor beam that prevented the slightest movement. The procedure required the added precaution of both general and local anesthetics, since it centered on a critical area of her anatomy - her spine. To complicate matters, it would be accessed through her abdomen.

In a hermetically sealed pouch on a side table lay the Ravarian shard - only a dozen rotations ago having been extracted from Starn's Dual, Nimon. Strategically placed electrodes penetrated the pouch, their microfilaments floating lazily in the suspension gel within the packet.

"Making incision now," Edison murmured, his voice muffled by the face shield. A laser scalpel snapped to life as it cut a horizontal path across Tempora's abdomen. "You should not feel a thing," he added attempting to comfort her during a most uncomfortable experience. Despite being unconscious, it had long ago been proven speaking positively to patients while under sedation had beneficial effects.

Once the primary incision was made, the doctor inserted several surgical retractors to form a clear path for the crystal implant. The combination of the cauterizing effect of the scalpel and the influence of the suspensor beam stabilized the sterile field such that bleeding was non-existent. A glance at the sensors showed all to be within an acceptable range.

"Bring up the implant's organo-crystalline profile, Starn, holo-display mode. The genome compatibilizer serum may need to be realigned." Starn adroitly manipulated the equipment in response.

The translucent image of the shard appeared. A cross -hair target slid over a section and then zoomed in on the stone's surface. The visual effect was captivating. It was as if a drone were flying deeper and deeper into the substrate. A glassy smooth surface quickly evaporated into a craggy valley interspersed with coiled protein chains. Plunging further into the sub-molecular level, crystal lattices appeared, cradling nucleic acid networks. Finally, atomic orbital clouds formed a tempestuous storm of pulsing flashes and energy discharges. The imagery eventually faded, leaving a graphical representation of the data obtained.

"Let's have a look at the receptor site, as well," Dr. Edison requested. Starn obeyed. The emitter smoothly slid the cross-hairs off of the crystal and positioned it over the opening in the patient's abdominal cavity. It focused onto a segment of spinal cord. In the absence of an inorganic component, the biochemical readout sprang forward very quickly. As the three-dimensional depiction of the DNA spiral took shape, a red icon appeared below it. But Dr. Edison was more interested in the genetic correlation figures between the shard and Tempora.

"How is this possible?" he gasped. Starn pulled his attention away from the glaring icon and studied his father.

"I know. The alarm is unusual. It indicates a chronal shift…"

"Not that. Look! 50.37% match between the organic component dispersed throughout the crystalline matrix and the Executive's DNA. Siblings share at most 50% DNA. A child actually carries a slight amount more DNA from the mother due to the mitochondrial component originating only from that parent. Particularly in cells requiring high amounts of energy such as nerve cells."

"I'm sorry, Father. You've lost me. I am more concerned with this alert on the display. What are you saying?"

"My Son, just as you carry slightly more of your mother's DNA, somehow, our patient here has a *maternal match with this crystal*!"

"That's preposterous! This crystal's origin dates back generations. Plus, how can a living being descend from an inorganic structure?"

"Listen to what you are saying, Starn. You of all people know the science of bioduogenetics is in its infancy. You, yourself, have gone beyond the boundaries that separate organic and inorganic life essence. You have empowered a Singular Dualiity!"

Starn raised his hand and vigorously massaged the back of his neck, as if to squeeze more blood flow to his brain in an effort to understand. Again catching his eye, the icon on the holovid continued to flash a bright red.

He punched a few keys on the control pad to extinguish it. Per the programming, the flashing stopped and an explanatory text appeared on the work table display.

Before he could read it, a computerized voice intoned, "Artificial Intelligence protocol enabled. Life crystal plant core processing has detected information from disparate sources of synergistic value. Shall I continue?"

Dr. Edison, observing the puzzled look on Starn's face, slipped into lecture mode, interjecting, "A life crystal plant is more than a manufacturing facility. It's a research facility, as well. Hurtling through space, it is exposed to phenomena that, if left only to the mind of a sentient being, would go unnoticed. So, the central computer core has programmed within it AI to constantly monitor data and run simulations. As with many innovations, they are the result of unique happenstance. *Serendipity*, if you will. In this way, the designers of the vessel have attempted to program *Luck*."

Starn half listened while he was reading the text on his console. Edison paused, resisting the urge to fold his arms from impatience, thereby compromising his sterile field. "Well, Son, what does it say? Or shall I hear it from the computer?"

Starn's jaw gaped open in shock as he continued to read rather than respond.

"Very well, then. Computer …continue," Edison urged.

"Data triangulation confirmed. Surgical center - Command center - Personnel records. Exploratory readings on patient show familial chromosomal match with chronal frequency shift. Recent data acquisition from Fulcrum Event as classified by Technical Superintendent Clesk show source of origin to be asteroid explosion cascade. Confirmed - singular genetic profile linking the following:

Fulcrum Event explosion: transport and asteroid

Crystal substrate: categorized as Ravarian shard

Patient: Tempora

IAD Officer: Starn Edison

Solar Executive: Novas"

The meaning of the words had not registered with Starn until he again heard them aloud. Knowing the answer, he was compelled to ask his father anyway.

"Who is Tempora?"

They both looked down at the immobile patient as Dr. Edison responded, "Apparently it is the Castorian Executive ... and your *half sister*!"

*   *   *

Always the pragmatist, Operations Superintendent Mack Weber lamented to Christi Pomeroy, "Although this metaphysical discussion on the origins of life might otherwise be fascinating, I've got polymerization loops that are on the verge of imploding."

"I hear you, Mack. This little excursion into Forever Time is unprecedented ... just like our triple jump. I've run several simulations on how to get where we want to go. It's not the *where* that's the challenge. It's the *when*. It's called space-time folding for a reason. Usually, we leverage the space factor, keeping time a constant. Essentially, we jump great distances in space over a relativistic constant time.

When we entered the Forever Time continuum, that changed dramatically. Both time and space are in flux. Theoretically, holding space as a constant, we could travel to any point along the time stream using the continuum as a conduit. But trying to hit both objectives of space *and* time is like patting your head and rubbing your stomach … while upside down on a centrifuge!"

Descartes, listening to the exchange, looked over at his Technical Superintendent. Apparently Clesk was susceptible to the power of suggestion, as she was attempting to perform the physical feat, sans the centrifuge, that Pomeroy had just described.

Clearing his throat loudly to snap her attention back to the matter at hand, he queried, "Clesk - any ideas to offer?"

She jerked to attention, smoothing her tunic with her pincers, while readjusting the two appendages hidden beneath. Suppressing a nervous chittering she replied, "Clk … clk … classic temporal dynamics suggest we need a constant upon which to base our navigational calculations. Life crystal formation occurs at a constant rate. As chance would have it, we performed two campaigns of equal duration of crystal production prior to entering the Forever Time continuum. I hypothesize that by triangulating an equivalent campaign duration for our third jump as the first two it will restore us to the time period we seek. The issue with Mr. Weber's polymerization tubes is they have been generating zero output since entering the continuum. Their calibration settings are designed for collecting more mature spore from our era. A refinement of their crystallization frequencies to account for newly formed life essence should restore production capability."

Descartes knew when to quit. His head still hurt from the last discussion he had with Clesk. He simply said, "Christi ... Mack ... please tell me you got that!"

In chorus, they responded, "Working on it!"

*   *   *

The recovery ward adjacent to the surgery room transitioned from a blurry haze to a clearer image. Tempora took inventory of her body and, to her surprise, felt no pain. A small table top to the right of her bed had been pivoted to within reach. A glass of cool water sat atop it, enticing her to take a sip. She stretched out her hand.

Fingers closed but grasped emptiness. Trying again, she watched as if she were a bystander to a holovid projector demonstration. Her hand passed through the container. *"Was this some perverse joke?"* she wondered, more angry than curious. Swinging her legs off the bed, she defied any common sense that told her it was too soon.

Her violet medical gown at least provided a modicum of propriety as it draped both her front and back sufficiently. The sices were open but for a thin tie that held front to back. Bare-footed, she stalked through the open doorway connecting recovery to the surgery arena.

A glass observation window greeted her with an astonishing demonstration. Dr. Edison was intently hunched over a patient, closing an incision. His son, Starn, busily handed him instruments when ordered. A video lens from above captured the activity for later study, displaying the live action on a nearby screen. But the source of astonishment was not the activity. It was the patient.

Tempora herself lay unconscious on the operating table!

The conscious Tempora raised her hands to the back of her head, as if steadying it so it would not float away from disbelief. She hesitated, debating whether she should continue forward. Common sense finally prevailed.

"Perhaps I did get up prematurely," she mused.

Slowly turning, she reached out to stabilize herself on the frame of the doorway. Her hands cooperated by *not* ghosting through solid material. Aiming herself in the direction of the bed, she was struck by another preposterous sight.

There she lay. Peacefully asleep. The monitor beeping a steady cadence.

Wavering, she felt her knees weaken. Her mind raced with thoughts of what was happening to her. *"I must still be under the influence of the sedative. Surely I am dreaming. But it feels so real."* Pausing to consider other alternatives, she thought, *"Maybe it is real, yet some phenomenon created by the Legotians. But to what end?"*

Remembering the counsel she received from Chrislar upon their first meeting as she struggled with being non-corporeal, she performed the advised mental calisthenics. Releasing the door frame, she raised her hands, palms up, to shoulder height. Sliding her feet together, she arched her back, turning her face upward, and closed her eyes. Inhaling deeply, she held her breath for a dozen heartbeats. She then exhaled slowly as she brought her outstretched hands in to her chest. Straightening her back while lowering her chin, she pushed her hands forward. Once fully extended, she spread her arms and resumed the starting position, palms up and head back. She repeated the exercise twice more.

At the completion of the third sequence, she opened her eyes. Surprisingly, she was once again in the recovery bed. Dr. Nicholas Edison and Starn stood on each side, peering down at her. Starn actually had his hand covering hers as it lay by her side.

Edison was slightly more aloof.

He looked at his patient through a self-imposed clinical lens. It filtered a suppressed twinge of resentment stemming from her apparently being born of his wife, but not him. The doctor had long ago accepted that his wife had a life prior to meeting him. After all, her life span was well over twice that of his. Yet, he couldn't help casting a shadow of disdain from the fact that here was a daughter whose existence had been kept from him.

Tempora was the first to speak.

"Was the procedure a success?"

Starn replied, "It seems so. How do you feel?"

Accustomed to doling out information on *her* terms and not those of others, the Executive opted to keep her recent episode to herself. Co-existing simultaneously in the past, present, and future defied explanation - at least for the moment. Instead, she proffered, "I am in no discomfort." Looking at Starn's hand atop hers, she raised a quizzical eyebrow and asked, "Is there cause for concern?"

He pulled it away, a flush of violet crossing his cheeks, and stammered, "W-why no. It's just that we discovered some interesting information that we should discuss ... *my sister*."

CHAPTER 21

. . . .

The *Darwin* shimmered into normal space. The control center personnel released a collective sigh of relief, as an appreciative nod from Plant Manager Descartes conveyed a sincere commendation to each of them.

"Where are we, Christi?" he eagerly implored. "More importantly - *when* are we?"

Planning Superintendent Pomeroy activated the holovid at the center of the room in answer. The translucent image showed the mercurial sphere of the life crystal plant slowly spinning in a stationary point within the natural orbital plane of Castor. "If we rested here for a planetary season, she would pass comfortably by us within reach of our landers." Continuing, somewhat smugly, using a photon pointer to illustrate, she added, "And that little duet of lights is the pair of Castorian renegade ships we wish to intercept. I'd say we are just about exactly *when* we want to be." She concluded by putting her feet up on her console, leaning her chair back, and triumphantly interlocking her hands at the back of her head.

"Nicely done ... *nicely* done!" Descartes effused. "Saffron, are we within range to communicate without a delay?" Descartes knew the primary of the threesome preferred to be called by her name, as opposed to Esswon, which differentiated her from her clone sisters, EssTu and EssThree.

"Absolutely, sir."

"Very well. Let's have a dialog with the leader of the tug boat, then."

Saffron snorted as she stifled a laugh at Descartes' reference to a nautical vessel of old. She could almost picture rubber tires hanging from the Castorian spacecraft as it pulled its sister barge behind it.

*   *   *

"*Sister*? Perhaps I am confused by your Geminian slang. You would consider me family? I carry the stone that was once nestled in the chest of your biodgen, most certainly. At best, that makes us second cousins ... once removed," Tempora quipped, in an attempt to lighten the mood. The consternation on the faces of the two showed her effort to be futile.

Dr. Edison minced no words. "Executive … Tempora, although early into the process, it is good that you are adapting so positively to the implant. Yet, there is another, more perplexing, revelation stemming from the operation. An organic component of the crystal has a genetic profile that defies explanation. We know so little about the shard. Recovered on a planetoid in a retrograde, non-ecliptic orbit around Pollux, it dates back to the time of the Castorian exodus from Gemini. Extraordinarily, so does the genetic profile. Even more puzzling, the profile matches that of my wife, Novas. Naturally, then, it shares sequences found in our son, Starn. Further analysis reveals … "

Tempora interrupted, "Doctor, I believe I have some insight into your dilemma. It involves the Legotians and the negotiations. They employ what can best be defined as *unorthodox* methods. As fantastic as this sounds, they can displace people through space and *time*! I myself have experienced it. And, more importantly where your mystery is concerned, so has Novas!"

Tempora fully expected the two of them to burst out laughing. Listening to her own words, even she marveled at how preposterous it sounded. Yet, they simply looked at her with anticipation. Finally, Starn uttered a simple request.

"Tell us more."

The Executive complied. In a rapid fire monologue, she recounted her short, but eventful, tale. From revisiting the ship where she was born and foiling the assassination attempt on Ravar, to engineering, yet not executing, the destruction of the planet killer asteroid swarm, she relayed her adventure. In deference to Dr. Edison's feelings, she glossed over the details surrounding Novas' presence on the *Destiny*. She mentioned only that she glimpsed his wife there, but only briefly. Instead, she explained her understanding of Novas' conversation with Chrislar - that she was expected to bring back the Ravarian shard, but did not.

"So," Tempora concluded, "I can place Novas with the opportunity to be in the proximity of the Ravarian fragment, but nothing more. How her essence became imprinted on its matrix is unclear."

Edison, having patiently waited for a pause after being interrupted, continued, "Analysis of the crystal matrix shows a property that, given the opportunity, as you say, would allow for the essence of Novas to be incorporated within it. You used the word *imprint* most accurately. We have learned through the science of biouduogenetics that life crystals enable organic bioenergy to be encoded into the crystalline lattice. Once attuned, contact with the individual sharing the bioenergy pattern results in the person's genetic structure being replicated at a molecular level. At some point in time, Novas must have activated the matrix of both halves with her mind and then subsequently come into contact with them. Clearly, the reason for her success with Singular Dualiity utilizing the Mitronian shard can be explained if my supposition is true. Most assuredly, this revelation is of significance, but it is not the primary question that is before us."

"It's not?" Tempora inquired. "Then what is?"

"The question, my dear, is *how did Novas come to be your mother?*"

*   *   *

Executive Stol on board the *Eclipse II* did his best to suppress his fury at the sight of the *Darwin*, languishing in space on his monitor. He resisted the urge to call battle stations to avenge the loss of his prior ship, the *Eclipse*, as a result of the infernal Terran's ploy. The only solace was he had the fool, Talor, who had destroyed the *Eclipse*, and his ship, *Spectre*, dangling at the end of a towing field.

"I wonder if I could maneuver the imbeciles accidentally so both ships collided?" he schemed to himself. *"Accidents do happen. Surely the accursed Legotians would not prosecute me for a simple mishap."*

Shaking him from his sinister reverie, the communications specialist reported, "The Solarian facility is signaling us, sir. Their plant manager is requesting the opportunity to present a proposal."

"Interesting. After our past encounter, he still acts as if there's a possibility for a business arrangement. The sheer arrogance of the Solar Corporation minion is astounding. But my curiosity is piqued. Accept the request."

The curved screen occupying a section of the command center wall flared to life. Filling it was the view of the *Darwin*'s more sophisticated control room. Standing at its center, Descartes, smiling, awaited the link to be activated.

"Ah, Executive Stol. So good to see you again. And in fine health aboard a new ship, I might add. I trust we can put our prior little misunderstandings behind us and discuss a proposal I have for you."

In a single greeting, Descartes had delivered a multi-layered message. As opposed to the last time they spoke, the Plant Manager was recognizing Stol's title as Executive, rather than dismissing it. He then hinted at the previous defeats Stol experienced -a blocked information piracy assault and the failed kidnapping of Dr. Edison- to gently remind the young Castorian as to who was superior. Yet, he acknowledged Stol's resilience while requesting they move forward in a way that could prove beneficial.

When required, Descartes could actually be an astute negotiator.

Beneath the violet flush of his skin and the fire in his red eyes, the Castorian managed a civil reply. "Plant Manager, I am intrigued that you would deign us with such benevolence."

"Why of course. My request is a simple one. The benefits to you can be great. I respect your time, so will be brief."

"Respect? Already you strain your resources. That is a treasure rarely found and even less frequently offered by your corporation," Stol responded, sarcastically.

Descartes chose to overlook the Castorian's tone, continuing, "On board your sister vessel, there are two Geminian individuals whose presence would be better served on the *Darwin*. I imagine you have your subordinate where you want him. As such, despite his harboring two fugitives, he and his personnel may continue on their way. "

Descartes paused for maximum effect. He hoped it would elicit a reply from the Executive.

It did not.

"Ah. A man of few words. We are not so different. Then let me enhance my offer. I am sure we can both appreciate the waste that comes with reflecting a capital loss on our ledgers. Though sometimes necessary, our superiors rarely understand. I suggest that if negotiations fail, capital loss on both sides will ensue. What's the sense in that?"

Unfazed by the thinly veiled threat, Stol simply smirked, cocked his head, and raised his hands in a shrugging motion, as if to signal, "Fair point."

Descartes resumed. "Speaking of superiors, I suspect your recent foray into Gemini's political affairs just *might not* be sanctioned by the Board of the Castorian

Conglomerate. Affairs of state can be so unprofitable. Surely, a low profile is preferable over what could become an interplanetary debacle?"

"And what do *you* know of Conglomerate matters, *Terran*!"

"Why, it turns out, quite a bit. Pardon me for dwelling on your *subordinate's* passengers. Did I not tell you about *my* guest? Perhaps a picture *is* worth a thousand words."

Descartes inconspicuously signaled Saffron.

A soundless inset picture popped onto Stol's screen. There sat Dr. Edison, Starn, and the emissary of the Conglomerate Chairman, Tempora, conversing in the conference room. What Stol didn't know was it was a security video taken shortly after the Executive had mysteriously appeared. Hence the lack of sound to enhance the bluff's effect.

"They seem intense about the topic of their discussion," Descartes conjectured. "I wonder if Dr. Edison is praising you regarding the fine accommodations your underling, Talor, provided while a captive?"

Stol's aggressive demeanor wilted as he fidgeted nervously from the sight of the emissary. Though having never met her, the

High Executive's reputation was well known. Those that had witnessed her wrath whispered of her cruel, relentless vengeance. Anonymity provided the only shield between her and her enemies. Stol's secret role as a renegade assisting the overthrow of not just Gemini, but Castor as well, was in jeopardy.

As was his life.

"You've overplayed your hand, Descartes," Stol seethed, inwardly. *"Whereas we just might have come to some arrangement, revealing me as a conspirator leaves me no alternative."*

Duplicitously, Stol's features softened in an attempt to garner favor with his nemesis. "Masterfully done, Plant Manager. Your argument is compelling. You can understand, though, I will need to confer with my Vice-executive on the *Spectre* to make the arrangements you have requested. It should require but one of your standard time units. "

"Understandable. I am known for my patience," Descartes granted. Christi Pomeroy snorted, as Saffron deactivated the link.

"That was too easy," Descartes murmured, as he failed to catch Christi's eye with his glare. "Clesk, direct a full sensor sweep at those two vessels. If they so much as discharge out a waste portal, I want to know about it."

Simultaneously, the communication specialist on the *Eclipse II* inquired of Stol, "Shall I establish contact with the *Spectre*?"

What had first been a fanciful idea born of wickedness transformed into a scheme of reality - and cruelty most cold. Stol answered, "There is no time. Those remaining on the *Spectre* will be remembered with honor." Stol commanded his operations technician, "Reinforce the towing field to maximum strength. When ready, on my command, activate the ion drive. Set course directly at the Solarian plant. On my signal, divert course 45 degrees to port once drive is engaged."

The technician knew better than to publicly question the order of his superior. However, according to command protocol, Stol's second-in-command was *expected* to do so, as long as she did so with discretion. He anticipated this, so signaled her to approach him.

Having only recently been promoted to the position of commander, Dafni had been instrumental in saving much of the crew of the *Eclipse*. During their prior encounter, she had recognized the *Darwin*'s ruse and reinforced deflectors to fend off much of the *Spectre*'s misplaced onslaught. This had allowed sufficient time for evacuation. Stol had survived. Dafni had been rewarded.

The two stood to one side of the command center. Stol spoke first. "Concerned, Dafni?" He breathed in her scent. He had resisted taking their relationship from professional to personal. *"Perhaps, though, once this episode was concluded,"* Stol mused.

She eyed him, coolly. Almost reading his mind, she concluded, *"He would have to be put in his place. But now was not the time."* Instead, she proffered, "I am confident you know what I am about to say, but it serves you, and the records, best for you to hear it aloud."

Stol nodded, "Please continue."

"The towing field will overload once the ion drive is activated. But not immediately. Essentially, the *Eclipse II* will leap ahead, pulling the *Spectre* behind it. An elastic effect will result. Talor's ship will be slingshotted forward. If timed correctly, our vessel will veer out of the way. Talor's will be whipped forward - into the *Darwin*. The few on board will perish, honorably. Talor, his staff, and the *two Geminian subversives*. As will all on the *Darwin* - including the Emissary to the Chair!"

"You are correct. I *am* aware. Yet the outcome you describe is but the first phase. Rumors say the Chairman is dead. With his Emissary out of the way, chaos will ensue. The two Geminians would have *their* insurgents fill the leadership void. In their absence, it will be a select few *Castorians* that grasp the opportunity to lead.

And I will be one of them!"

Dafni stared into the eyes of her unscrupulous Executive. *"Perhaps I have underestimated him,"* she reconsidered. *"If this works, my counsel won't be the* only *thing I give him in private."*

Without relinquishing her gaze, Stol commanded, "Activate the ion drive!"

CHAPTER 22

Clarions blared as T'Poch and P'Teel burst into the *Spectre*'s control center. Talor frantically bounced from station to station, barking orders - to no avail. The limited staff was sufficient to maintain a craft in tow, but not one experiencing an emergency.

Clearly, being yanked into a collision course with the *Darwin* qualified as one.

"What is happening?" P'Teel shouted.

"The accursed facility, *Darwin*, is what's happening. They sit between us and Castor. From what we could intercept from their transmission to Stol on the *Eclipse II*, they want *you*! He responded as if he would comply, but his actions say otherwise."

"First the authorities try to apprehend us on Gemini, and now they send their Solarian minions after us!" spat P'Teel. "You and your followers swore you would provide us safe passage and asylum! What is Stol doing instead?"

"On the surface, it would seem he has strengthened the towing field and is accelerating to elude your would-be captors. Upon further study, his vector is *not* to escape. Instead, it is a collision course!"

"Then break free and take our own evasive action!" commanded T'Poch.

"If it were only that simple," Talor growled, through clenched teeth. He knew the value his guests provided to the K'Tar. It did *not* include telling him what to do aboard his own ship. "Our energy reserves were drained during the futile attempt to kidnap Dr. Nicholas Edison. If we could break free and escape, we would not be under tow in the first place."

"Then lead us to the escape modules. At least in captivity, we would be alive, instead of vaporized from the impact against the life crystal plant!" T'poch challenged.

"Launching under the effect of the towing field would shred the module to bits. You'd die instantly."

P'teel's hands began to glow a fiery crimson. Stalking toward Talor, she hissed, "Then I will have the satisfaction of seeing you die first!"

*　　*　　*

With less fanfare, but the same urgency, Clesk alerted his plant manager as to the criticality of the situation under way.

"It is confirmed. The *Eclipse II* has reinforced its towing field and is accelerating straight for us. With certainty, one or both vessels will collide with us. I have reviewed several es-ca-ca-cape options, with limited success," she clicked through her mandibles. "Our time fold triple jump has marred the surfaces of the wave capacitors. Mr. Crescent's maintenance staff requires a half rotation for repairs. That leaves only the ion drive as our mode of propulsion. Unfortunately, we are less maneuverable than our assailant due to our much greater mass."

"So we're like an apple bobbing in a tub waiting to be bitten, eh?" queried Personnel Manager Jefferson Brown, using one of his trademark archaic references that few understood. He had made his way to the Control Room as was his routine. He was a strong advocate of "MBWA - managing by walking around".

Descartes shot him a puzzled look. "Apple? What's that?"

"I forget, Morgan. You weren't raised on Mars. The last apples on Earth were over two hundred cycles ago - or should I say "years" - to coin another long forgotten term. They were successfully transplanted to save them from extinction from the blight of '02. Delicious fruit when prepared properly. Surely you've heard the *Darwin* described as a "cored apple"? A sphere with sloped ends feeding into a hollowed-out center ..."

"Spare me the history lesson, J.B. I've heard the description. Never bothered to understand the reference."

A loud chittering erupted from the direction of Clesk's station. Both Brown and Descartes snapped around to see what was the matter. "Look what you've done, J.B. You've got my Technical Superintendent all excited over the thought of fresh fruit. Not sure if she's considering eating it or pollinating it."

Before Brown could unleash a disciplinary tirade over Descartes' insensitive reference, Clesk proffered an idea to the staff. "Mr. Brown has struck upon a brilliant concept. The *Darwin as a cored apple*! I have compared the dimensions of the Castorian ship to our axial channel. If controlled precisely, it would pass through the core. However, only if aimed point

301

blank with no variation in horizontal yaw or longitudinal pitch. Ideally, entry through the stern after an ion engine burst to match speed would maximize success."

Morgan Descartes might be prone to the occasional boorish comment, but he was never hesitant to take action. "Mack, use thrusters to position us according to Clesk's calculations. Saffron, alert all personnel to secure themselves. Artificial gravity won't be able to handle Mack's maneuvers completely. Also, telepathically convey to one of your sisters that we need the Castorian Executive informed as to our situation. We need her to convince Talor to cooperate with us if we are going to pull this off! Christi, what does your navigational array tell you about the status of the renegade ships?"

"Stol's at least honoring his commitment to giving us a standard unit - whether he planned to or not. His ion boosters are taking a while to charge. He didn't factor in the drain caused by the towing field."

"Let's hope we put the delay to good use. Saffron, activate the communication link between the Castorian Executive and Talor when ready."

*　　*　　*

Before Tempora could compose a reply to Dr. Edison's query as to how his wife, Novas, came to be her *mother*, Saffron 2 burst into the recovery room. The more high strung of the three, EssTu wore her emotions on her sleeve, if her outfit had one. She had been sleeping in her room, since she was off duty. Upon receiving the telepathic download from her primary in the Control Room, she had leapt into action. Her quarters were around the corridor on the same level as the medical center. Grabbing a communication pad from her nightstand, she raced to her destination.

Unclothed.

Being a product of genetic engineering, no resource had been spared in endowing the Angellian clones with attractive humanoid attributes. Her blond hair cascaded in layers down to her shoulders, falling short of providing any cover for her full bosoms. Finely toned muscles presented a sculpted physique atop willowy legs. A complexion of iridescent ivory skin highlighted a form unmatched by anything nature could create on its own. Always the professional, Dr. Edison smoothly pulled a violet gown from a nearby shelf and deftly draped it over her.

Immune to frivolous trivialities such as modesty, Esstu ignored the doctor and delivered the information about the plant's situation. Her emotional entreaty as to the need for the Executive's assistance had the desired impact.

Tempora accepted the comm pad after Esstu established the connection to Morgan Descartes in the Control Room. "Executive, welcome to my facility, despite the circumstances. It turns out that your presence is most fortuitous. I took the liberty to use it to our advantage. Your employee, Talor, is aware that you are with us. I hope he will follow your instructions and save both our vessels from imminent destruction."

"I do not know him, but he certainly should know of me," Tempora retorted. "I would expect that to suffice. Let us proceed."

"Very well." Descartes signaled Saffron, who instantly alerted Esstu telepathically to activate the connection to the Castorian on the *Spectre*.

Talor's image coalesced on the viewer. Tempora, surprised, drew in a short breath, holding it as she studied him intently. He knew better than to speak first, so waited. Her mind flashed to another holovid likeness from a few rotations - or was it generations? - ago. "The navigator on Ravar's *Destiny* - this could not be him. Perhaps a descendent?" she queried to herself. Playing a hunch, she opted to use flattery instead of force.

"I sense you descend from a strong line of space farers, friend Talor. Might you be of the original lineage of the Arks - navigator clan?"

The hardened visage of Talor melted into one of awe. Even across space, it was as if she had peered into his very soul. It was a rare leader that could know you instantly, and in that moment, command undying loyalty.

"Some legends would say *navigator turned chieftain clan,* Emissary. My ancestor was graced by High Chieftain Ravar, himself. How may I continue to serve?"

"Your colleague does not share your loyalty. He betrays you. But you know that already. Your skill as a pilot is needed to foil his plan. Though they not be Castorian born, you *can* trust the staff of the *Darwin.* Will you do that?"

Talor looked past his view screen at the wizened enchantress whose hands still burned with an otherworldly flame. To whom should he swear fealty, one who threatened his life, or one who honored his heritage?

"Tell me what you require me to do, noble Emissary."

P'Teel hissed. Seeing her threat was an empty one, she lowered her hands as their fire dwindled.

*   *   *

"Commander Dafni!" bellowed Stol. "I ordered you to activate the ion boosters!"

"Would that I could, sir. The energy drain from the towing field has inhibited the ionic capacitors. Charges have just reached sufficient levels."

"Then activate the drive!"

"Ion stream increasing. Maximum velocity prior to towing field overload expected in five centiunits. Angular trajectory programmed. Once the field ruptures, the elastic effect will pull the *Spectre* immediately toward us with a multiplying effect. Our course change will allow it to slingshot past us and head directly at the *Darwin*. Recommendation - we should maximize the distance prior to impact. During their early development, life crystal plants were nicknamed `moon busters' due to their explosive capacity."

"Very well. Engage the quark core micro warp once clear. Put us at just outside orbital range of Castor."

*　　*　　*

"First you tell us the escape module would be shredded if launched while immersed in the towing field. Now you have us confined in the lander you used to aid our escape from Gemini. Does your bowing before the Solarians bestow some favor that enables this craft to better survive?" T'Poch snapped.

Stol chose to ignore her tone and instead ask for her cooperation. "Indulge me, please, for your own safety, and hopefully the survival of us all. My team and I need to focus. Secure yourself, as I am not sure this will succeed."

He then gave a staccato string of orders to his command crew. "Extend graviton plates. Energize at five per cent, but prepare for maximum output. Retract landing struts. Ensure hangar bay door is locked securely - I repeat - lock it down. Transfer *Spectre*'s controls to the *Wraith*. Prepare emergency separation sequence of ion drive module. Set umbilicals for defense posture. Give me a countdown on the projected time for the rupture of *Eclipse II*'s towing field starting at ten. Project the *Wraith*'s holographic image in relation to the *Spectre*. And finally, I commend you all!"

*　　*　　*

A different holovid display captured the full attention of the *Darwin*'s staff. Clesk gave the play by play. "Ion drive output has reached overload point for the *Eclipse II*'s towing field generators. Elastic recoil is underway. *Spectre* is accelerating toward the lead ship. *Eclipse II* is veering off. *Spectre* is on collision ca-ca-ca-course with the *Darwin*!"

Mack Weber cut in. "Tangential thrusters firing. Plant rotation underway. Aft crystal polymerization aperture coming into alignment. Firing Ion drive … NOW!"

Clesk chittered, in what his colleagues had come to understand was a sign of utter dismay, and announced, "Unfortunately, perfect alignment means little. The *Spectre* is pitching end over end. If it continues, it will saw through us unmercifully!"

CHAPTER 23

"… three … two … one … Towing field has ruptured!" reported the *Spectre*'s control technician. "*Eclipse II* has veered off. We are accelerating toward the *Darwin*. They have aligned their aft aperture with our trajectory. Against their desires, though, we are pitching end over end. Despite their engaging their ion propulsion it will be insufficient to outpace us. Our combined speed and rotation will cleave them in two."

The design of the Castorian vessel had not changed appreciably from that of the first space-faring vehicles. Its structure was comprised of an inverted teardrop with sinewy appendages extending to the conical ion drive at its base. Encircling the drive were concentric rings that rose up from just above the base to midway along the appendages. The exception for the *Spectre* compared to the original arks, though, was that there was no passenger module nestled within the mechanized tentacles. Instead, the spherical shaped hangar containing the lander was centrally located there at the point of the inverted tear drop. The bay door was actually a reinforced band that encircled the girth of the ship, opening by rotating such that a gap in it aligned with a gap in the fuselage of the vessel.

In locking down the bay door, Talor had essentially reinforced the hull surrounding the lander. By extending and energizing the graviton plates of the *Wraith*, tremendous force could be exerted against the fuselage. At 5% output, it caused the smaller craft to float within the hangar independently of the main ship. The holographic image displayed within the lander showed it maintaining its relative orientation in space stable inside the *Spectre* as the larger craft rotated tail over end hurtling toward the *Darwin*.

The Spectre's Vice-Executive was determined to thwart his superior's murderous scheme. Improvising, he commanded, "On my order, detonate the manacles holding the ion drive to the umbilicals!" He watched as the image of the lower module swung over the top of them. As it reached a twenty degree position from vertical, he barked, "NOW!" An instant later he directed, "Increase graviton output on all plates to 75%. Align lander gyroscope to keep us linear with the *Darwin*."

The result of Talor's cosmic choreography was nothing short of miraculous. The explosive force of jettisoning the ion drive reversed the cartwheeling of the *Spectre*. The mechanized tentacles retracted to their defense position, adding rotational speed as does a figure skater pulling in her arms during a spin. Passing through the vertical and back to a relative horizontal to the *Darwin*'s aperture, the effect of the graviton waves served as a braking mechanism. Once in proper position, the lander's gyroscopic program held it, and the outer husk that was the *Spectre*, oriented properly.

*   *   *

"I wouldn't believe it if I hadn't seen it with my own facets," marveled Clesk. "That is some fancy flying!"

"We're not in the clear yet," interjected Mack Weber. The Castorian ship loomed ominously as it continued a rapid approach toward his prized reactor loops. "I'm guessing your calculations didn't consider those umbilicals configured in that flared pattern, did they, Clesk?"

Her response was a rapid clicking, which Weber took as a "No". "I figured as much. As a precaution, I've filled the loops with inert foam. We'll know in a moment if it works."

Descartes' head snapped from Weber, to Clesk, and then the holovid in the center of the control room. "So you're telling me the Castorian is *not* going to pass through?"

No amount of hexa-celled foam could dampen the sound of screeching metal reverberating through the *Darwin* as the *Spectre* penetrated its nether regions. Life crystal loops splayed open as coiled tentacles raked across their surface. Sparkling fragments blew out the forward aperture like a party favor celebrating a new year. Alarms blared alerting personnel to the obvious - the plant was in distress. Automated safety protocols shut down power in the three radiating bands of work areas around the core. Fire crews were dispatched in case the plant's computerized crisis mitigating systems were insufficient. Department heads assessed damage to assets and employees and reported in.

On the *Wraith*, the situation was much less dire. Prior to impact, graviton plates were ramped to 105% of safe capacity, figuring the danger from them was far less than from being crushed against the bulkhead. Harnesses had performed effectively, keeping passengers' injuries to a minimum. Umbilicals had been sheared off of the *Spectre*, along with chunks of its hull. The resulting depressurization had not impacted personnel, as they were all safely ensconced within the intact lander. *Spectre*'s escaping moisture-laden atmosphere upon entering the vacuum of space formed frozen spikes in the *Darwin*'s tubular core. Serendipitously, the combination of mangled appendages and ice lances anchored the *Spectre* firmly within the life crystal plant's reactor conduit.

After a review of the damage reports showing no fatalities, Descartes had Saffron key the voice-only link to Talor. "What's your status, Vice Executive?"

"No serious injuries. We are secure within the lander in the hangar. Though other sections of the ship have been breached, pressure is holding in this chamber. It seems we are at your mercy. What are your terms?"

"We are not at war, Talor … at least not yet, despite the efforts of your passengers. My plant did not fare as well as your lander, unfortunately. Until we have fully assessed the situation, I suggest you make yourselves comfortable. Accessing you from the areas closest to our core may be problematic, as they experienced the most damage."

"I understand, Plant Manager. We will await your next communique." Talor terminated the connection at his end before T'Poch or P'Teel could voice their complaints. To his misfortune, as he, instead of Descartes, had to bear the brunt of their ire.

P'Teel was the first to lash out.

"Surely you don't expect us simply to sit here and await capture by the Solar Corporation savages, do you? We should be formulating a plan to infiltrate their vessel and commandeer it!"

Having been recognized by the Emissary to the Castorian Chair as well as successfully saving her along with the others, Talor was no longer inclined to act as lackey to a pair of less than effective subversives. But he *had* witnessed their formidable abilities, so elected to display some level of diplomacy. "To what end would taking over a crippled life crystal plant serve, enchantress?"

"Ransom, of course! Safe passage and amnesty, to start."

"And how are our small numbers expected to overwhelm a full complement of personnel on a life crystal plant? The first sign of weapons between Solarians and Castorians will surely bring the Legotians down upon our heads. Without weapons, I doubt we will convince the esteemed Plant Manager to meet our demands with words alone."

Before P'Teel could snap back at Talor, T'Poch intervened. She gently placed her hands on P'Teel's, absorbing the fire building within them. "My mentor, perhaps a frontal assault is not the optimum plan. We are like the Matryoshka nested dolls - trapped inside a lander, inside a Castorian assault vessel, inside a life crystal core, inside a Solar plant. Let us open them one by one.

I have an alternative plan I wish you to hear."

*   *   *

Tempora sat at the table in the med center break room sipping a cup of steaming Castorian mead. She had changed into a standard issue Solarian grey body suit after ending her entreaty with Talor. Figuring that if their efforts failed, she preferred her body not float through space for the rest of time scantily clad in a medical gown. Once the plant's safety protocol had been lifted, her jangled nerves called for a non-medicinal comfort drink.

It was having the desired effect.

Easing into a more contemplative mood, she wondered if her appearance on the *Darwin* had yet again been a well-orchestrated maneuver by the Legotians. *"Had I been absent, would Descartes have been able to sway the renegade Talor to aid in their survival?"* she pondered. *"And what of the Ravarian shard that lies nestled within me? To what end will it lead? Without its counterpart, I am but an unbalanced sword. Potentially useful, but not nearly as effective as would be when finely honed and shaped."*

Looking across the rim of her flagon as she lifted it once more, her interest shifted to a group at an adjacent table just within earshot. At first, it seemed Starn and Edison had expressed politeness by allowing her some privacy. They had not broached again the unanswered question as to how she came to be the child of Novas. To that end, she herself had not fully thought it through. But she had her suspicions. Thinking their curiosity would eventually overcome their civility and prompt them to join her, she soon saw why they resisted. Shortly after being seated at their separate tables, two more had joined the father and son.

One was dressed in violet medical scrubs, less revealing than the gown she had been given, but still indicative of his being a recipient of care. The other, in contrast, looked ready to assault a hostage stronghold. He was dressed in a black form-fitting thermal body suit, woven from polymer designed to disperse high impact energy. Sporting a sidearm as nonchalantly as would a mechanic carry a torque wrench, his utility bandolier stored more items than the same mechanic's tool box. Quite the contrast to the business attire worn by the Edisons. The doctor wore an off-white lab coat over a pale green jumpsuit. The son, a high-collared beige long-coat over matching black shirt and pants. The only notable evidence of accessories was Starn's belt. Wrapped and tied in a martial arts style, it held the coat closed at the waist. The weighted spheres at each end hung at his side, one slightly higher than the other.

Starn obviously wielded some level of authority over the two, as Dr. Edison simply observed their exchange.

"Director Starn, I understand your new role within IAD carries with it a sizable amount of authority. Any chance you could exert a little of it and get me released back to full duty?" Eric implored. He had been cooped up in the medical wing since returning from his harrowing experience with the rogue biodgen skier on Gemini.

Before Starn could reply, Dr. Edison broke his silence and proffered, "Supervisor, consider your situation as if it were someone *else* who had had physical contact with a biodgen exhibiting aberrant behavior. Isn't the policy to flame first and ask questions later? I confirmed she was infected. Due to the IAD policy I just mentioned, there are very few records of someone surviving a sexual assault as you have. The least you can do is allow us to monitor you for a while longer. It would be tragic if your comrade, Hal here, were forced to burn you to a crisp during a mission."

Hal fidgeted at the thought. In an effort to change the subject he interjected before Eric could reply, "Could we maybe address the main reason I asked for this meeting? I was monitoring frequencies known to emanate from rogue biodgens as standard protocol. I detected a signal maxing out the meter right after the Castorian probe ship slammed into the *Darwin*. What are we supposed to do about it? Our jurisdiction doesn't extend to foreign properties. And for that matter, since when did Castor develop a viable bioduogenetic program?"

Starn cast a wary sidelong glance at his father, as if to alert him it was time for full disclosure. "I suspect that the source of your readings is a *Geminian*, not a Castorian. As such, we have full authority to apprehend her. The primary reason we are attempting to apprehend the two passengers of the *Spectre* is *not* due to their political insurgency. We believe the lead agitator, T'Poch, to be carrying the infectious strain that we hope will not present itself in Eric, here."

What Starn did *not* disclose was he looked forward to confronting the vile creature for another reason. He hoped to wreak vengeance upon the witch that nearly took his life while acting as a sentinel at the Archive of Families on Gemini.

"Our challenge," Starn continued, "is devising a way to gain access to the *Spectre*. The Darwin is not designed to provide a means of entry through the vacuum of space from its shredded reactor tubes to a vessel lodged in its core. Plant Manager Descartes has made it clear the integrity of his facility comes first. Rescuing, or more accurately, *capturing*, the stranded occupants is the lowest of priorities."

"That's why I asked for your help," Hal pleaded. "Even if we attempted a spacewalk from one of the maintenance hatchways, we would be vulnerable. I wouldn't put it past those animals to take potshots at us using discharge from the waste ports! It sounds ridiculous, but frozen feces can do a number on an enviro-suit's integrity!"

Tempora, still listening to the discussion, couldn't contain herself any longer. "Let them come to you," she proffered across the room.

Starn looked over at her. "You've got something to add?"

Rising from her table, flagon in hand, she idled over to the group. "I said let them come to you. They want out of their involuntary cocoon as much as you want to get to them. If they are any kind of *respectable revolutionaries*," she said, sarcastically, "they're probably plotting a way to get over here and take over the facility. We need to be patient and observant and see what unfolds."

Tempora paused for effect, looking in the eyes of each of her audience, one by one. Settling upon Starn, she added, "And, *my brother*, I know who, and *what*, T'Poch is. While with the Legotian, and our *mother*, I learned. True, T'Poch is an insurgent. Highly likely, she is a vector for a plague of galactic proportions. But she is *more*. I suspect there is a f*amily affair* you wish to resolve, as do I. Any plan we devise must ensure that *I first* settle a score with her!"

CHAPTER 24

"The Solarians are tempting Legotian intervention simply by confronting the Castorians," T'Poch explained to P'Teel and Talor. "Despite having a Castorian Executive on board, they are limited in what they can do. They must demonstrate some level of cooperation. Talor, you will present your plan for freeing your ship. They must listen."

"My plan? What might that be? We are inextricable lodged within the *Darwin*'s core."

"But are we? Your ship is uniquely designed. Though some are damaged, it has umbilicals that can be manipulated. Some, in fact, can pluck transport pods from space and deposit them into this very hangar. Others were used to convey personnel from the command module to the ion drive, now floating somewhere in space. Surely the combined resources of your staff and that of the *Darwin* can work cooperatively to free us."

"And how does that benefit you? Once we have established a path to freedom, they will demand you be the first to use it - straight into their holding cells."

"Precisely as I hope. Are you aware of the ageless espionage technique, "catch and release"?

"Please, elaborate," Talor responded with a quizzical wrinkle to his brow.

T'Poch cocked her head toward P'Teel, deferring to her mentor.

The wizened enchantress smiled appreciatively. "It is a bold approach stemming from the knowledge that it is easier to overcome overwhelming odds if the attack comes from within. By allowing the opposing forces to capture you, a focused application of superior skill can be applied in order to escape. If done effectively, it leaves a wake of chaos and destruction behind."

Talor stroked his chin, thoughtfully. "No doubt. You have certainly displayed `superior skill' that is most impressive. I imagine you just might be successful in your escape. But the question remains. How are you to be captured … alive … stuck within this `Matryoshka doll'?"

T'Poch resumed the explanation. "Why, with the smallest one first. As I mentioned, you have a passenger pod designed for transporting a three person payload. I suggest using one of the remaining functioning umbilicals of the *Spectre* to extract it from the hangar and place it outside the *Darwin*'s core. You as the pilot will accompany P'Teel and myself. Using the kernel of trust you've cultivated with our nemeses, you can convince them to allow safe passage into their lander bay. Once onboard, P'Teel and I will take care of the rest."

*   *   *

The foursome marched through the corridor on their way to the *Darwin*'s lander bay. Starn and Tempora, in the lead, were side by side. Dr. Edison followed a few paces back. Hal, the straggler, drew up the rear. He whispered a play-by-play on his wrist comm to Eric, who had reluctantly followed Starn's orders and stayed behind.

"All I know," he voiced softly, "is Starn must hold some special sway over the plant manager. After all, he was previously charged with special projects for the plant. What could be more 'special' than apprehending two known insurgents? Descartes and his staff have their hands full with repairs. By letting these three take the lead, it's more a 'family affair' than any official Solar Corporation exercise. Should their be casualties, it's easier to keep it off of the books."

Hal tapped a few control keys to dial down the volume of the surge of invectives coming from his supervisor.

"I get that you're worked up. But I can handle this. I'll lay back and see what unfolds. According to Starn, I shouldn't even be talking to you. Give me some space. I'll update you shortly. Out." With that, Hal disconnected Eric, knowing he was going to pay for that later.

Father, son, and sister came to a halt in front of the transparent metal-polymer window looking out into the hangar. Hal continued to lag back. True to his superior piloting skills, Talor smoothly arced the transport pod through the bay opening and nestled it to the deck.

More advanced than the pod design of old, this transport allowed the passengers to *sit* in series as opposed to *laying* in inertial stabilizing ooze. Talor only had to use the positioning thrusters to steer from the claw of the *Spectre*'s fully extended umbilical to the awaiting hangar. As such, there was no need for life support suits and suspension gel to protect the passengers from excessive gravitational forces.

Once the chamber's atmospheric pressure triggered the safety lock protocol to "Clear", two events occurred. The canopy of the Castorian pod slid smoothly backward along the projectile-shaped profile. Simultaneously, the hatch barring the *Darwin*'s "welcome" party irised open.

T'Poch was the first to disembark down the stairs, as they unfolded to reach the deck. She wore a shoulder-to-floor burgundy cape of Slotar skin, its scaleless texture shimmering under the lander bay lights. P'Teel, the eternally shadowy wraith hovering over her ward, followed close behind. A high-collared waistcoat of Vambor pelt, trimmed with the beast's fur over an ankle-length pleated linen skirt was a timeless style befitting an Enchantress of the Fire Arts. True to the universal code of a captain, Talor was the last to leave the ship. He had opted for a more practical look - a black oxidized flight suit of Castorian copper.

Across the hangar, the foursome from the *Darwin* stood as a single rank. Dr. Edison whispered a request, and with nods from Starn and Tempora, stepped forward toward the new arrivals. Hal moved further down the wall, taking up a flanking position to where Edison and T'Poch stopped face-to-face, a tred's distance apart.

T'Poch was the first to speak. "Do you even recognize me, *Father*?" she hissed, her venomous question dripping with a resentment that had festered for a lifetime.

"Of course, my child. I have followed your progress since that fateful parting long ago."

"And you think that absolves you and Novas from the guilt of *abandoning* me?"

"Dear T'Poch, it was not abandonment, but preservation that forced our actions. *Your* preservation." Looking over her shoulder at P'Teel with a steely gaze, he continued. "Your guardian surely explained. For you to exist - independently - your mother had to stay away. The proximity syndrome from empowering you required it. True, we might have had you for a few years if we had not given you up. But you would have left us much too soon. The brain wave interference from your organic Dual, Novas, would have aged you prematurely. By separating you from us, although excruciatingly painful, she was able to empower you to your fullest. Eventually, you, and she, became the *Singular Dualiity*, but one small step away from Phoenos itself."

"Your explanation reeks of self-sacrifice and noble ideals. How unfortunate it was that my mere existence caused you such hardship," T'poch retorted, sarcastically. "Do you think I care to hear your twisted rationale for what you did? This is not some endearing story where the child seeks a long awaited reunion with her parents. The concept of an idyllic family finally unified against all odds is found only in theatre and myth. The *true* story is found in the Archive of Families you and Novas hoped to keep hidden. But you failed. The facility's security measures and the anemic efforts of that *organic* cretin were no match for me!" She paused, casting a contemptuous glare over the doctor's shoulder at Starn.

Her half-kindred caught the look. Sensing a mounting threat, Starn moved forward to stand behind his father.

T'Poch bristled. "While you doted over the futile attempts at Dualiity by this *mongrel male*, my right as succeeding matriarch to the Mitronian lineage was erased! Even the Angellians, before cloning was forbidden, recognized that the fruits of the process possessed the same rights as the source. Think! What better candidate to continue the family heritage along the matriarchal line than me? I am the essence of my mother.

Genetically pure. Uncontaminated by any male pollutant. Bred from her body and mind to carry on the legacy of our noble guild. Yet, in the infinite wisdom of the Geminian Council, my rights, freedom, and dignity were *nonexistent*. The family line was sealed!"

Starn could stay quiet no longer. "As it should be! T'Poch, you denigrate males as if they are beneath you. Do you not understand that without them, the matriarchal line cannot continue? It is the union of two genetic strains that brings diversity and strength. True, you are born of my mother's body and mind. But only a shadow of her essence. The crystalline matrix within you weakens you. By carrying the Mitronian shard, you present a viral threat to the technology of bioduogenetics. The wave of economic collapse from the loss of biodrones throughout the star systems would be catastrophic. Your dream of uniting Gemini and Castor is but a nightmare that would destroy them. *You* think! You are not a messiah. You are barely more than a *machine!*"

T'Poch seethed. Her crimson eyes inverted to reveal the smoldering flame within. Slowly, she placed her hands behind her. Only P'Teel could see the fiery glow building within them. She knew the extent of the power growing from T'Poch's rage. If unleashed, surely the target of her fury would suffer. Yet, glancing at the IAD agent and the armament he carried, the risk of loss from an open assault was significant. This time, it was P'Teel who reached out to stay the use of Fire Powers during a confrontation. As she rested her hand on T'Poch's, she proclaimed, "Groka!"

Starn and Dr. Edison, flinched at the ancient Geminian command to halt - to proceed would be at the risk of death. The two Castorians and IAD specialist in attendance instinctively took their cue from their reaction, and froze.

P'Teel continued, stepping forward to stand between T'Poch and the two males of her clan. "T'Varek Kar! I invoke the Survival of the Ancients to settle this dispute within the family."

Talor and Tempora exchanged puzzled glances. As Castorians, they were unfamiliar with the nuances of ancient Geminian methods for settling disagreements. Tempora edged up closer behind Dr. Edison and whispered, "What is she talking about?"

He turned his head slightly to reply. "Before the coming of Mitron, the clans of Gemini dealt with conflict through strength. The claimants to unreconcilable opposing positions sought resolution through *combat*. Often, to the death. The victor would then act according to their newly won right. The loser, if fortunate enough to survive, and their supporters, would bow to the whim of the winner."

Extending his mini-lecture to a synopsis of current events, he explained, "The two positions before us are of galactic importance. On the one hand, T'Poch contends the actions of the Geminian Council have stripped away the rights of a sentient being, *her*. This decision is supported by the ruling matriarch of the clan, your mother, Novas, as is evidenced by the seal on the ancestral ark contained within the Archive of Families. T'Poch wants that decision reversed. Once done, all the power and wealth of House Mitron will eventually become hers. On the other hand, should the Council's view be upheld, the precedence of biodgen rights as subordinate to organics will be set. A blessing for some. A curse for others. Particularly T'Poch. She will be tried for sedition. If found guilty, she will spend the rest of her life imprisoned.

For the beliefs surrounding bio-duogenetics are complex and varied. They prompt followers to behave in conflicting ways. Mitronians propose that the Mind is the source of Life. As such, the biodgen shares the same rights as organics. Ultimately, Phoenos will manifest itself through Dualiity, enabling two lives to coexist in harmony from one mind. Should T'Poch's stance falter, so will that of the followers of Mitron.

Were T'Poch to succeed, it would be a blow to the Life Rightists among the known star systems. Any manifestation of synthetic life is abhorrent to them. They would welcome her failure as a sign that any form of empowerment of inorganic life is a travesty, an affront against the natural order.

Then there are the Materialists. Less enamored by the spiritual beliefs of Phoenos, they see value through the commercial use of bioduogenetics - whether biodgens on Gemini or biodrones within the Solar Corporation. Starn is of that camp. His position was even championed by his Dual, Nimon, before the Council. Should T'Poch be victorious, there will need to follow a reassessment of how biodgens are used. Perhaps new rights for the sentience of duotrons will have to be factored into the cost-profit equation used by Solar," he added, sardonically.

"And let us not overlook the perspective of the K'Tar, which is perhaps the most relevant, but contradictory, in this circumstance. T'Poch, a disciple of the K'Tar, argues for equal rights and recognition of her independent sentience for *her* benefit. Yet, the ultimate goal of the movement is to create a legion of *followers* using bioduotronics. Power through their *d e p e n d e n c e , n o t f r e e d o m .* With overwhelming force from their biodgen followers, a totalitarian rule uniting Gemini and Castor could be achieved. Should T'Poch fail, it could be the domino that leads to the collapse of the movement."

P'Teel's grating voice resumed, interrupting the doctor's monologue. "I am the senior surviving matriarch of clan Mitron. I side with my ward, T'Poch. As is the way of the ancients, only a contending *matriarch* can respond to my challenge of T'Varek Kar. Since Novas is not here, and she has no eligible delegate, her opposing position is forfeit! As such, I judge that we are free to go and passage to a safe haven must be provided. Castor should do nicely."

She smiled wickedly, as she turned to guide her colleagues back to the lander.

CHAPTER 25

. . . .

"You pride yourself too highly and presume much, P'Teel. Only someone in great need would do so."

A chill ran down the spine of the ancient one. The voice, tone, and timber triggered buried memories from the distant past. A Star Child from long ago had nearly foiled her plans. The words were reminiscent of her exchanges at the start and end of her early encounter with Novas those generations ago. How could they be present now?

Slowly she turned.

Tempora moved forward, a partial step in front of her half-brother and his father. P'Teel approached slowly, cautiously, as would a Centaurian leopard to its injured prey, unsure if it were a prize or a trap.

Tempora spoke once more, with a firmness born of nobility. "I stand as delegate for Novas as her matriarchal successor!"

The elder enchantress halted. Her chin lifted slightly as she peered down her nose at this upstart. "Yesss … I believe I *do* see a hint of ancient aristocracy in your features. A heritage from an acquaintance long since forgotten. He fled to the stars. You have Ravar's blood coursing through your veins, do you not?"

"I do." Tempora admitted. But she knew that meant nothing in relation to the rites of the Ancients. For her to represent Novas, she must prove she carried her lineage. Tempora did not have to trust Dr. Edison's science. When he announced she was the daughter of Novas, the image of her father with the Geminian aboard the Castorian ark cemented the fact in her mind. *How* it came to be was yet to be understood. But she knew it to be true. Novas and Ravar had been together those many generations ago. And if P'Teel was a contemporary in those days, it could be used to Tempora's advantage.

And use it she would.

"Look more closely, venerable one. I sense your intuition is formidable. If you knew Sire Ravar, then you would also know of his acquaintance during those troublesome of times. You heard it in my voice. What do you see in my eyes?"

At this point, P'Teel's caution was overcome by her curiosity. She stood a breath's span away, peering intently into the soul of her challenger. Unspoken, unheard - yet undeniable. P'Teel knew the person before her was her own blood kindred. She considered the ramifications. *"So, Novas did survive that fateful day. How and to where she disappeared is still a mystery. It seems a fair trade. She left me the the seed of knowledge that would blossom into the guiding doctrine of the K'Tar. As well, stolen from her grasp was the miraculous crystal that would eventually be returned to her. And for her efforts, she would be graced with child. Finally, one eligible to carry on the family line. But only if I acknowledge it. If I do, how does it benefit me?"*

T'Poch, at her side, murmured, "I have known you my entire life, my governess. If I can see it, so can you. She *is* of clan Mitron. Yet, do you sense what is all the more critical?"

The biodgen slowly reached out her hand, suspending it, palm outward, before Tempora's chest. The Castorian did not flinch, despite the pulsing aura emanating from it. Lowering her eyes to watch, P'Teel drew in a short breath. Simultaneously, a reflection of the energy appeared not only on T'Poch's breastbone, but on Tempora's as well.

"So, you carry the Ravarlan shard," P'Teel whispered, awestruck.

"How is this possible?!" exclaimed T'Poch. I, myself, Implanted it within the biodgen, Nimon, during our union. "

This time it was Dr. Edison who interjected, "And left him to die in the caves. Nevertheless, he survived - infected with your venomous essence. I saved him. And, at Tempora's urging, bestowed the crystal upon her."

On cue, breaking the contemptuous energy coursing between the parties, Tempora repeated, solemnly, "I stand as delegate for Novas as her matriarchal successor. What say you, P'Teel?"

The presence of the Ravarian shard changed everything. The bearers of it and its mate would fight to the death. A urified life crystal would be the trophy bestowed upon the victor. The outcome would be pivotal for not just the Mitronian clan for generations to come, but for the entire K'Tar movement!

"I recognize thee as delegate for Novas," P'Teel decreed. "You may stand in her place. But recognize this. The outcome of the challenge is of such great importance, so should be the combat. As such, it will be a *fight to the death*! Do you still wish to engage?"

Tempora eyed her adversary up and down. Though an enchantress of great skill, her age would be to her detriment. Not fully schooled in the traditions of the Ancients, Tempora at least understood that since *she* was the one accepting the challenge, it was *she* that chose the method of combat. She could require that no mystical arts could be employed.

"Not only do I wish it, I *demand* it!" Tempora answered, fiercely.

A sinister smile spread across P'Teel's face, as if Evil's blade itself slashed her from ear to ear. She hissed, "Your demands will be met, defiant one. And as is your right, you may select the weapon." Pausing for dramatic effect, P'Teel then raised her hand to stop Tempora just as she began to respond. "Aah, one more small detail. Because you are more Castorian than Geminian, in all *fairness*, perhaps you need be reminded of the Ancient's ways. Since Novas by proxy has selected a delegate, *so may I.*

I chose my ward, T'Poch!"

Starn could not contain himself, spluttering, "That's preposterous! A biodgen against an

338

organic! Tempora is no match for T'Poch's strength and stamina."

"But you would have your sister contend against a doddering old crone, such as myself?" countered P'Teel, with mock humility.

Before Starn could argue, Tempora raised her hand, signaling him to cease, and proffered, "Of course. The ways of the Ancients must be honored. And so, I declare the form of combat to be hand-to-hand - no mystical powers allowed ..."

T'Poch snorted, derisively, smugly smirking while folding her arms across her chest. She knew the organic was no match for her.

"... in a zero grav arena." Tempora punctuated her proclamation by holding her hand out, palm up, and pivoting in a sweeping arc to present the anti-grav training area in the corner of the hangar.

The biodgen's smile melted as would a comet's tail passing too close to a star.

*　　　*　　　*

The matte-black lander emerged from the cover of darkness as it settled gently on the pad. Jutting prominently out from the escarpment, the perimeter lights had been deactivated, making the exercise that much more difficult. The wizened magistrate sitting in the seat of honor behind the driver expected nothing less than perfection. Lowering her head and exhaling a long, slow breath, she dispatched her agents, one from the seat adjacent, the other in front next to the pilot.

Clad in stealth-mesh militia fatigues, the duo faded to nothing once they emerged from the cloak field of the vehicle. Speedily, they traversed to the edge of the tarmac and looked over the side. The escarpment's only luxury was a narrow path with precarious handholds down to a minuscule stone platform in front of an aged door. That would not suffice for what the infiltrators planned.

The leader unholstered a pneumatic pistol, loaded a ringed piton into the end, and fired it into the stone face of the cliff. Unwinding a length of cable from a belt-mounted dispenser, a carabiner was quickly employed to connect the cable to the piton. After a few commands via hand signals to her comrade, the trespasser launched over the edge and rappelled down to the door. She was surprised to see a relatively new piton and cable assembly leading further down the rocky path. Even more to her liking, the unexpected disabled access to the inner sanctum had been recently used. Rather than utilizing the micro-charges tucked in her utility pouch, she simply reached for the ring, pulled it outward, twisted it sharply, then pushed. The craggy surface once more separated along hidden seams. This time, hinges protested less loudly, allowing the door to swing inward. The dark recesses beckoned only the brave to enter.

"Tight security," she mumbled sarcastically. The sensor bracelet on her forearm silently agreed, as it detected no active scans. Pressing one of its studs, a heads-up display in her goggles luminesced a graphic representation of the items she was there to purloin, and their location, as she panned the room. Slipping out of her empty backpack, she undid some strategically located straps. The pack unfolded neatly to extend into a lightweight duffel bag, sufficient to carry away her haul.

The macabre scene within the room had no effect on her. She efficiently darted in and out the serpentine aisles, collecting articles of humanoid anatomy and placing them in the bag. Her display guided her to the required items - left and right leg assembly, upper and lower torso, both arms and hands. But a particularly valuable object was missing.

The head.

Pressing a few keys on her device, the range of the scanner extended outward. The yellow outline of room contents faded as a narrow, conical beam replaced it. It strobed rhythmically, casting its intangible touch into every nook and cranny. As it crossed a doorframe at the head of a spiral staircase in the corner, the pulsing increased.

Simultaneously, an indicator on the gauntlet blinked a warning. "It figures," she groused. "The most critical prize is in another room that has an active security system."

Undiscouraged, she left the heavy satchel where it lay and deftly climbed the stairs. Her night-scope goggles failed to show her the footprints in the dust on the treds. This time her pleasure was replaced with caution at finding a deactivated lock. "Surely not a trap," she contemplated. "That would require the suspicion that I was coming. Nevertheless, best be wary."

Lifting the flap of one of her pouches, she withdrew a palm-sized drill. The tungstinium bit made swift work leaving a hole in the wall adjacent to the doorframe. Replacing the tool, another pocket provided a thin probe with an optic fiber that she connected to a port in her goggles. Slipping the rigid end through the hole, she was rewarded with a clear view of the adjacent chamber. Thumbing a dial on the temple of her headset, the intruder sampled the images provided by a spectrum of frequencies.

"Hmmm … not so bad. A hover-drone with stun-tipped defense wand sitting dormant in its cradle. And in the corner, a remote activated pulsar musket retracted into its case. But no active system found. Curious. And neither aware of my presence … yet."

Studying their locations a moment longer to lock the imprint in her mind, she then retracted the probe, disconnected it from her goggles, and replaced the components in their pouch. From another, she withdrew a different attachment for the end of her pneumatic pistol. Nimbly inserting it into the barrel, she loaded the over and under assembly with two palm sized payloads. Taking a deep breath, then releasing it slowly, she pushed through the door.

Courtesy lights in the ceiling self-activated, slowly increasing to a soft glow. The interloper cocked her head, looking at the locations of the security devices. Facetiously, she whispered to herself, *"Mood lighting for what comes next, perhaps?"* But nothing came. *"Interesting ..."* she analyzed, *"... so far, since I do not appear to be a threat, no counter-measure is required. Or, could it be the defenses are designed to protect the resident only. Typical of the Terran scientist. He sees value in Life only. Protecting against the risk of losing material things is not worth the effort. All the better."*

The trespasser clipped her weapon to her belt. Raising her armband, she again activated the sensor beam. Immediately it signaled the prize could be found in one of the cabinets along the far wall. She eagerly hastened across the lab and pulled open the door. The whisper of released pressure allowed the chilled air within to waft around the thief in a cloud of condensation. The flat drawer automatically slid outward with a translucent dewar in its center.

The intruder flinched reflexively. As much as she had mentally prepared herself, the sight of a detached head staring out at her was unnerving. *"At least the eyes could have been closed!"* she grumbled. Recovering, she grasped the handles that she unfolded from the container's sides and hefted it off the drawer. Thankful her assignment was going so smoothly, she could not suppress a small smile.

Unfortunately, her gratitude was premature. The whirring sound of servo-motors alerted her to danger, but not soon enough. Her fears confirmed, the hands of the automaton behind her extended to tightly grip each of her upper arms, lifting her off the ground.

CHAPTER 26

Tempora stood just inside the perimeter of the zero gravity arena. Despite the grey body suit she had worn since leaving the *Darwin*'s medical center, her skin tingled from the energy coursing through the mesh screen at her back. She rocked slightly, left leg to right, to flex the newly-donned energy boots so they would better conform to her feet.

The mesh curtain was suspended in a circle from a slotted track in the ceiling of the hangar. Held taut, its bottom was affixed to a similar track in the floor. It would contain the anti-gravity field generated from emitters dotting the cylinder formed by the netting. Once activated, the boots served as boosters to propel the wearer off of the curtain, if they were the first to contact the surface. If not, the wearer would absorb a painful jolt of current.

Across the arena, her opponent prepared to enter. T'Poch unclasped the fastener at the neck of her cloak, letting it slip to the floor. Beneath, her backless, one piece black maillot streaked with white thread mimicked her tresses. Smoothly, she wound them into a braided ponytail hanging between her shoulder blades. She had opted for pulse slippers, held in place with flexible silver cord laces reaching to just above her knees. More stylish, but just as effective as the energy boots.

The audience of Talor, P'Teel, Starn, and Dr. Edison stood in separate pairs behind T'Poch outside the arena. Hal, not only skilled in monitoring biologicals during biodrone empowerment, also knew his way around the controls of the zero grav equipment. He stood behind the instrument panel along the side wall. In response to T'Poch's nod, he parted the screen to allow her to enter the ring.

Serving as unofficial referee, Hal announced, "Just a reminder - combat is hand-to-hand - *only*. Fight until one yields … " pausing to look over at the grim faces of P'Teel and Starn, "… or dies. On my mark, the fight will begin. It can only be stopped prior to its conclusion at the command of either P'Teel or Starn. If stopped by one side, victory will be forfeited. Combatants, are you ready?"

Tempora snapped to attention, curtly bowed, then turned with her left side facing her opponent. Sliding her feet shoulder-width apart, legs slightly bent, she extended her hands, palms up, toward T'Poch, as if to say, "These will be your undoing."

The organo-synthetic figure snorted in contempt. Turning her own body to mirror the Castorian's, she extended her right hand, palm up, toward Tempora. However, with her left, she reached backward to grasp the energized netting. The current sparked through the biodgen's arm, coursing across her frame and crackled as an ionized blue sphere coalesced, hovering above her right palm. Cackling, she then released the curtain and spit her response toward the IAD specialist, saying, "I am more than ready!"

*   *   *

The pilferer in Dr. Edison's arctic science facility looked at the shiny, metallic hands that held her aloft. *"Not a biodgen,"* she observed. *"Thanks for small favors. No sentient being guiding this mechanoid. Only programming. Most likely a simple household assistant designed to deter and detain. Such a pity, but easily replaced."*

Though her shoulders were pinned to her sides, she could still bend her arms. In one fluid motion, she cocked her head to the left, drew her sidearm with her right hand, bent it back over her shoulder, and fired. With a "pffft" and "splat", the cartridge exploded across the face screen of the utility android. Mechanized fingers relaxed from their captive. Feeble efforts to wipe away the sticky fluid to restore its vision were futile. The freed prisoner pivoted and placed the end of her weapon against the midsection of her adversary. Without mercy, she pulled the trigger again. The ooze exploded across the narrow articulated conduit that was the robot's waist. By the time the dripping stopped at the hip joints, the contents of the first projectile were having its full effect.

Time-released corrosives formulated specifically for metallo-polymer dissolved the face screen of the synthetic servant. Reflexively, the intruder looked down at her own outfit, expecting to see it smoldering from the splatter. But the gel's chemistry was very selective. Despite the absence of activity, she swept away the dried remnants of the gel from her own garments as she backed away from the robot. It rocked violently to and fro at its midsection while scratching helplessly at its head until it broke in two. The upper section flailed on the floor like a magma lizard left too long in the relentless rays of Pollux. The lower half spun aimlessly on its transport casters.

"Regrettable," she muttered, shaking her head at the pitiful display. But the trespasser had no time to mourn further for the device's demise.

The security drone lifted from its cradle and aimed a targeting laser directly at her breast bone.

*   *   *

"Begin!" Hal commanded.

Immediately, Tempora sprang along the fabric wall, racing in a spiral up a third of its height. Surprised, T'Poch stood immobile, watching what seemed impossible until realizing the abilities zero gravity endowed. Before she, too, could mount an assault, Tempora sprang off of the tight mesh. In a full lay-out position, she rotated her body toward T'Poch. Completing one and a half flips, she planted both feet on target. Instead of across the biodgen's face, the heels of the Castorian landed at the nexus of the left shoulder and collar bone. Tempora seriously doubted that any blow she could deliver would render her opponent unconscious. Her strategy was to debilitate her offense in the hopes of then being able to subdue her.

The would-be heiress to house Mitron actually grimaced from the blow. In her favor, the pulse slippers allowed her to slide across the floor, as she recoiled from the impact. Years of training had exposed her to hardship, but it had been some time since she had experienced pain from another. She wondered if her sparring partners had held back for fear of retribution. Taking a brief moment to rotate her shoulder to dissipate the discomfort, her hesitation proved costly.

Tempora's momentum had allowed her to pass by her adversary to land at the juncture of the net and floor. She twisted enough such that her coiled leg braced against the web. Using the impulse energy against her boot, she rocketed across the arena in flight. As intended, her knee delivered a crushing blow to the left shoulder blade of the novice zero grav combatant.

She was rewarded with the sound of a "snap" and guttural bark from T'Foch. The force spun T'Poch like a top until she collided into the far side of the arena. Sparks embraced her as the charge danced across her bare skin. Crumpling to one knee, her head hung low as she tried to gather her strength. Her left arm dangled at her side, useless.

Unmercifully, Tempora launched what she expected to be the final assault. Hovering slightly above the floor, she extended her legs forcefully, catapulting her body to a point on the netting above the duotron's head. Adroitly, she adopted a jump side kick pose, allowing her to ricochet off the curtain higher to the ceiling. Another acrobatic maneuver sent her to the opposite wall, where she completed the tactic by spring-boarding back downward, both hands forming fists aimed at the base of T'Poch's skull.

Surprisingly, the blow did not land. The Geminian enchantress had disguised her true condition, to some extent. Though her left arm was damaged, she still managed to roll on her right to avoid Tempora's strike. As the executive flew past, T'Poch grabbed the leg of her assailant. Planting her pulse slippers on the floor, the momentum of the Castorian organic missile was redirected, as the Dual pivoted and hurled her foe into the energized fabric. Continuing the counter-attack, T'Poch pounced on the stunned woman. Lifting her easily with her good hand, she slammed her repeatedly into the floor.

Dr. Edison and Starn recoiled at the sight of the physical abuse. Starn was tempted to yield for Tempora's sake. But the stakes were too high and need for vengeance too great.

As the brutal biodgen lifted her prey yet again, Tempora reacted. Twisting her body to allow her legs to wrap around T'Poch's arm, she simultaneously grabbed the hand at her throat with both of hers. Arching her back as her foot slid under her opponent's chin, she pulled the immobile arm forcefully across her chest.

The "crack" was extremely satisfying. T'Poch's cry of anguish, even more so!

The semi-stunned Castorian gave a kick to the side of the head of her nemesis to propel away from any further harm and regain her wits. Floating to the vertical center of the three dimensional arena, the executive weighed her options.

They would be limited.

The inferno that raged within P'Teel's champion would not - could not - be contained. The white hot glow flared around her hands, quickly spreading up both arms that dangled loosely at T'Poch's side. As the effect spread, debilitated appendages gained renewed, supernatural strength. Eyes blazed as would two crimson funeral pyres, consuming their dead. A sinister smile crept across the enchantress' face. Arbitrary rules and ancient customs would bind her no more.

Abruptly she spread her arms apart, then brought her flattened hands together in front of her, fingers aimed at her foe. Instead of a loud clap, the impact created a fiery wave hurtling toward its target. Tempora, shocked that even one as evil as T'Poch would discard all remnants of rule and honor by using her powers, reflexively raised her hands, palms forward, as if to deflect the onslaught.

She failed.

*   *   *

The drone's first tranq dart hurtled toward the interloper. Without concern for its contents, she hoisted the dewar in front of her as a shield. She was rewarded with a "ping" as the cartridge deflected off the metallic container, leaving only a scratch. She did not expect to be so lucky twice.

Desperation bred ingenuity.

A broad lab bench stood between her and escape to the level below. In one smooth motion, she slid the vessel across its surface while vaulting after it. Her militia fatigues, designed to evade detection, thankfully had a low coefficient of friction. Gliding on her hip and thigh, she overtook her prize, grabbing it as she landed between the counter and door to the chamber below. The dancing red dot on its surface was the drone's confession that its aiming system was unused to such an agile target.

There was no time to load and fire her pistol, so the intruder did the next best thing. Slipping a throwing star off the friction clip holding it on her shoulder, she flicked it through the air at the hovering menace. As it hit its mark, imbedding in one of the two lift impellers, she yanked open the door. Cradling the cryo-vessel in one arm, she plunged through the doorway and over the spiral staircase railing. Instead of plummeting to the floor, her free hand shot out to grab the curved handrail. Her forward momentum was immediately converted to an angular force, allowing her to careen in a spiral arc to the level below as the rail slid through her gloved hand.

Looking up to the head of the stairs where she had just exited, the persistent hover drone wobbled on one functioning impeller. A second throwing star missed the rotating blades, instead, imbedding in the device's body. The impact forced it backward into the domain of the lab it was designed to protect.

The trained thief had had enough. Keying a control on her instrument bracelet, she hoped to put an end to the nuisance. She was rewarded by a double flash and muffled pop from the detonated shurikens wedged into the floating mechanism. Listening further, no sound of whirring blades could be detected.

Satisfied, she hefted the dewar and its contents into the duffel with the other body parts. She hoisted it onto her back, grunting, securing it by placing her arms through the optional shoulder straps. Trudging to the antiquated door, she opened it, expecting to be greeted according to her prior instructions to her accomplice.

Instead, she found herself hurtling into open space, propelled by the concussion from the laboratory exploding behind her.

*   *   *

Fire, when considered at its basic level, is the result of three things: fuel, oxygen, and heat. When the fuel is heated sufficiently, it emits a gas that can combine with the oxygen.

This combination, or chemical reaction, releases energy in the form of heat and light. Both heat and light can be transmitted to cause other material to burn. Heat is transmitted when higher energy particles collide and transfer energy to lower energy particles. Light can also act as if it were a particle, but will behave as an energy wave, as well. Burning from directed fire will occur if the target absorbs sufficient energy from the source, either from the particles or radiation.

The fire emitted from T'Poch's hands had all the components to incinerate Tempora.

Yet she did not burn!

Practitioners of the Fire Arts had the supernatural ability to combine fuel and oxygen from both their body and surroundings to create fire. Its energy could then be propelled at a target via conduction or radiation. But the intended victim had to be of a substance that could be impacted by the particles or radiation.

At the critical moment of impact, Tempora was *without substance*!

The fusillade of flames focused upon the Castorian passed through her as she time-phased from the *now* to the *then*. The same power that manifested itself upon awakening from the crystal implantation surgery had saved her. How, she did not know. Yet, an object *did* bear the brunt of T'Poch's rage.

The Ravarian shard, it being a crystal, reacted differently to the bombardment of wavelengths. Diffracting some, it *absorbed* the impact of others of the photonic particles. As Tempora's body oscillated between moments in time, the gem was flung back against the charged netting. Ricocheting, it bounced up against the ceiling, only to be repelled back down to the arena's center.

T'Poch, seizing the opportunity, sprang into action - literally.

Coiled leg muscles launched her vertically. Rising faster than expected, her novice zero grav abilities betrayed her. She reached out to grasp the glowing stone, and missed.

However, this would be to her advantage.

Unexpectedly, an invisible force, like that of a magnetized child's toy, drew the long separated shards together. The pulsing fragment plunged into the Geminian's chest, vanishing without a mark.

CHAPTER 27

As the saying goes, the best laid plans of mayhem and misappropriation go awry - or something like that.

A few well placed throwing stars with concussion nodules seemed an appropriate solution to the problem of a pesky security drone. With one set of impellers disabled, what could go wrong by exploding the remaining functioning parts?

Enough could.

The blades still rotating flew off the body of the craft when the second star ignited. Spinning across the laboratory, they nicked a cryo-hose entering the compartment containing the dormant bioduotror, Nimon. No spark occurred, which was unfortunate. If it had, then the escaping liquid hydrogen would have ignited immediately. The resulting blowtorch of flame would have triggered the automatic fire suppression system. The sealant foam would have extinguished the flame and plugged the leaking fuel.

Instead, the liquid converted to gas upon leaving the hose and rapidly filled the room. The fractured core of the drone, after bouncing along the work bench, sat quietly going through a self diagnostic routine to assess its damage. Until it got to the step where programming required reinitialization of the power module.

Whether it be the metabolism of an enraged biodgen or the subroutine of a much simpler-in-design hover drone, the formula for fire works the same. Fuel - hydrogen, plus oxygen - air, plus heat - in this case, spark, equals fire. And with hydrogen, it means *plenty* of fire.

And rapidly expanding concussive waves.

The result - the intruder found herself abruptly thrust into the cold embrace of Geminian arctic air from the fiery explosion.

On the landing platform above, the companion in crime had obediently followed her instructions. He had just completed setting up the winch and cable to be used to haul up their contraband. The mechanism consisted of a tripod holding a motorized spool of cable attached to an articulated grappling claw. The operator had the choice of simply lowering it into position or, if a harpoon were attached to the launch barrel, firing it to anchor it into the surface of choice.

The launching of the claw attachment would require some rare, extenuating circumstances. Seeing his accomplice soaring through the air qualified. Quickly, he pivoted the assembly downward and fired.

She heard the "crack" of the discharge. Hoping it wasn't the harpoon, she flared her arms and legs to make a bigger target. Despite hurtling at one G toward the craggy outcropping below, the impact on her back was severe. Adding to the pain, the spring-loaded hooks clamped around her like the claws of a Castorian condor. When the drag of the winch engaged, snapping the line taut, what little breath she had was abruptly expelled.

Above, the marksman rejoiced at his success. Until physics intervened. As the cable drew taut, the payload at the end could not avoid acting as a pendulum. Though securely captured in the claw, ensuring his partner and her priceless loot did not plummet further, the impact to the side of the cliff was unavoidable. Helpless and panic-stricken, he did the only thing he could do. He turned to the lander occupants and gave the universal signal to disengage by drawing his index finger across his throat.

*   *   *

Tempora phased back into the "now" as she settled to the floor of the arena. Above her in its center, T'Poch was experiencing a metamorphosis. The fusion of the crystal halves within her triggered a transformation. Flames no longer launched from her hands at Tempora. Instead, they engulfed T'Poch herself, forming a fiery cocoon. As the blaze ebbed and surged, it was as if a living inferno in the form of a phoenix flapped its wings, celebrating its rebirth.

Starn, infuriated by his former assailant's ability to avert almost certain defeat at the hands of Tempora, reacted. "Hal, deactivate the zero grav netting ..." he barked, "... and blast that flaming witch!"

Seeing Tempora kneeling safely on the hangar deck, still recovering from her episode, the IAD specialist slapped the emergency "Kill" button. He hoped it would send T'Poch plummeting to the floor. The de-energized netting dropped, but the pulsating entity remained suspended. Sensing danger, the burning figure of T'Poch turned to cast her demonic gaze in Hal's direction.

He needed no further prompting to carry out Starn's order. Smoothly quick-drawing his sidearm, he cocked its lever to load three incendiary gel cartridges. "Let's fight fire with fire!" he quipped.

The first slammed into T'Poch's forehead, immediately followed by two to her center of mass. The impact released a metallic ooze that coated its victim before combusting with a white hot flame. As the two sources of incredible heat sought dominance over one another, the figure within writhed and twisted. Black veins of ash crackled across her body, then disappeared as if absorbed to spawn new matter.

Dissatisfied with the ineffectiveness of Hal's attack, Starn looked around for an alternative weapon. Spying a portable generator for recharging lander batteries, he ran toward it. He hoped its power cell, if hurled into the blazing biodgen, would finish her.

Starn's action did not go unnoticed. Drawing her attention away from helplessly watching T'Poch's plight, P'Teel shouted, "Cursed human gene splice! You ordered my ward's death! Let her fate befall upon you!"

The aged enchantress' hands flared with lethal radiation. Cupping them in front of her, a blazing sphere took form. She lifted it above her head and hurled it at Starn.

The infirmity of age and recent injury melted from the body of Dr. Edison as he realized P'Teel's intent. Launching himself between his beloved son and the fireball, it struck him full force. His lab coat, though designed to reduce the effects of radiation, thereby deflecting the fiery blast, provided no protection from the impact itself.

His sternum split with a sickening "Snap"!

As his father fell, Starn reacted. His hand loosened the clasp holding his ceremonial - and lethal - Ruga'r belt. Reaching across his waist with his left hand to grasp the sash a half tred from one weight, his right hand clutched the other end above the companion weight. He began spinning each in a counter-rotating direction.

Adding to the delivery technique, he twisted his body, left to right, imparting additional centripetal force to the ornamental spheres. The increasing tension served to stretch the unusual fabric, causing it to grow in length. The center of the sash pressed firmly against the small of his back, serving as a fulcrum against which to leverage maximum power.

At the optimal point in this weapon kata, Starn dropped his right shoulder and spun himself in a clockwise direction. Simultaneously, he raised his left arm over his head, that side of the bolo still spinning. It was as if he were mimicking an airplane in a steep bank, his arms the wings with propellers at each end. Three quarters through his pivot, he released the right half with a backhand throw. Instantly he followed through by letting go of the left weight with an overhand motion.

The action of the spheres spinning in opposite directions while hurtling toward their target caused the fabric between them to coil rapidly to form an unbreakable elastic cord. The writhing, serpent-like weapon struck its mark at two points.

P'Teel's legs were ensnared as the belt's other end wound around her neck. The rope between sought to return to its original length, contracting violently. Her back arched against the force, with no effect. A garbled scream was her only solace as she slipped into unconsciousness. Her incapacitated body fell to the ground, twitching in the throes of death from a futile effort to survive.

Still intently focused on the deliverer of her agony, T'Poch's fiery form turned to fully face her foe. The pulsating fire engulfing her ebbed into a more controlled aura.

She had absorbed the full effect of the napalm cartridges!

Slowly she glided downward toward Hal from her position suspended in the arena. The IAD specialist stood paralyzed, mesmerized by her ability to survive the inferno he had delivered upon her. As she neared, her arms lifted from her sides, hands extended as if to embrace a helpless child. "Let me comfort you," she solicited, with an evil smirk.

Just as her hands were about to cradle Hal's head in a blazing grip, she convulsed savagely. The mistress of the Fire Arts, first and only sustainable Singular Dualiity, looked down at her chest in shock.

A shimmering arm protruded from her. The fist at its end slowly opened. In its palm rested the intact life crystal - the Mitronian and Ravarian shards fused into one.

Tempora slowly pulled her arm back through the flaming biodgen automaton. Still phasing among the *then*, *now*, and *to be*, she gently inserted it into the waiting cavity in her own chest.

T'Poch turned as the fire coursing across her synthetic flesh dwindled to a glowing ember, finally extinguishing to leave an ashy layer. Barely a shell of autonomic responses, reflexive movement, and dying tissue, her lifeless eyes sought to connect with Tempora's icy stare. The seeker of Phoenos managed to convey a final, coherent thought.

"I am not … the One … but I leave … the Other."

Her body then crumbled into a pile of black and grey particles.

*   *   *

As the mountain face rushed at her at breakneck speed - literally - all she could do was close her eyes. Just prior to impact, and the snap of her neck, another set of eyes opened.

The aged magistrate was displeased. Taking a moment to reorient herself from her self-induced trance, her steely eyes finally settled on the pilot's, darting nervously in his rearview mirror. Without the need for prompting, he stammered, "The payload, and your Dual, are secured. They are being loaded as we speak. No damage occurred to the stolen items. But ... er ... *she* may be unrecoverable."

Silently, the honored passenger exhaled slowly again, nodding her head. A wave of anguish flickered across her face. Then another, more severe pang swept through her. Looking up, she responded, "It is as you say, and sadly, *more*. But, no matter. Our work here will be rewarded. I have the *Other*."

Abruptly, the passenger door adjacent to the pilot slid open. Realizing he had interrupted, he proffered, "My apologies, Revered One. We must go. The facility is ablaze. The authorities will be here soon to respond. I fear it will be a total loss."

"Again, no matter. We have what we came for. Despite *my* loss." And with the wave of her hand, Kronia's lander lifted from the pad. Looking below as her craft spiraled upward, she watched the flames engulf the complex, and the sarcophagus containing Nimon within.

CHAPTER 28

Starn knelt and cradled the lifeless form of his father. "This is not how it should be," he lamented to ears that could not hear. "Stories through the ages allow final, parting words. Even I came back from the brink of death. Was it not so we could reconcile the issues between us?"

The son stared at the father, as if waiting for a response.

None came.

Starn sighed, and continued. "Our last private conversation was heated. I regret that. You prophetically said 'time is rarely on our side'. So true. My mental condition, the dedication of you and Novas … Mother … to Phoenos - not the best combination on which to build a loving relationship. But I know, we *did* love each other. Yet, my identity struggle confused me. I felt that showing emotions was a sign of weakness. It is actually a sign of humanity. Ironically, I have learned to control them all too well. Much like Mother. Even now,

I should feel sorrow. Perhaps shed tears. But I do not - can not. Would she? How is she to know of your fate? Traveling into the past, will the present be of any concern to her? Grief is a sly affliction. Laying in wait. Attacking without notice. Perhaps in time, she will experience it - I will feel it. Express it without hesitation. Now is not that time."

Starn sensed Hal's presence as he quietly edged up behind him. A hand hesitantly reached out to Starn's shoulder in comfort, but stopped and was withdrawn before making contact. Without turning, Starn whispered, solemnly, "Notify Jefferson Brown that we need a detail to address two fatalities, my father and P'Teel. As for T'Poch, we need to follow IAD protocol to deal with the biohazard her remains present. Eric should be eager to help."

"Yes, sir. And what of Tempora? She *did* take a life - albeit synthetic. Our jurisdiction over her is tenuous at best, given her Castorian diplomatic status. Hell, we don't even know how she got on board the *Darwin* to be involved in all this."

As if on cue, a shimmering figure coalesced in the center of the hangar. It stopped short of fully solidifying, indicating it was more astral projection than teleported entity. Gliding just above the floor, it approached Tempora, who had regained enough of her strength to stand in wait.

Hal, backed away slightly. He warily kept one eye on the new arrival. Whispering into his wrist communicator on two channels to both Jefferson Brown and Eric, he slid his other hand to rest on his sidearm. Starn gently lowered his father to the floor and rose to face the apparition.

The image, dressed in a robe reminiscent of Earth's Greek philosophers, spoke so that all could hear. "I am Chrislar of Legos, advocate for the four-dimensional realm that defines your celestial system. Some know me …" nodding to Tempora, "… while the rest do not. But you do know the influence the Legotians can have over conflict arising among your worlds." He paused to let the magnitude of his words register with the listeners.

"The impact of what has transpired here is significant. Though the actions were limited to members of a single family, the *reactions* will reverberate across space and time. The K'tar is crippled, if not crushed," gesturing toward the ashes of T'Poch and the lifeless form of P'Teel. "Dualiity, a noble endeavor, seems at an end," glancing at Starn. "And perhaps the cosmic status of Castor and its mode of leadership is on the brink of change." He gestured again, this time letting it encompass both Tempora and Talor, who until now, had gone unnoticed during the melee.

"Which brings me to the issue at hand. As I said, this is a *family* matter. The Legotians need not intervene with corrective action toward Solar Corporation or its venture with Gemini. But Castor is another affair yet to be resolved." Chrislar paused once more, this time staring intently at Tempora. Reflexively, she raised her hand to her temple as his thoughts cascaded into her mind, and her mind alone.

In a breath's span, he conveyed his wishes to her. "Tempora, your role here is complete. Your presence elsewhere is of utmost importance, to you, your family, and your planet. Glimpse at the possibilities." A rapid-fire burst of images appeared as if a kaleidoscope exploded within her mind. Had she not previously been exposed to Chrislar's mode of communication, she would surely have gone mad. Though what he showed her were only *possibilities*, myriad and complex, she was convinced her part in them was pivotal.

Chrislar prodded, "I sense you know what to do. Advise your associates and we may take our leave."

Tempora solemnly stepped toward Starn, uncharacteristically extending her hands, palms up, to comfort him. Hesitantly, his eyes darting nervously from side to side, he raised his and gently grasped them.

"My brother," she started, with the utmost sincerity, "though birthed from the same mother, we have two distinctly different paths. Where she could not, you are poised to do great things for both Gemini ... and Castor. You find yourself in a unique position. Though male and of two worlds, with determination, you by right can assert yourself as the sole heir to the Mitronian line. Your Terran influence and position within the Solar Corporation only serve to strengthen your value. Drawing on these facts, it would behoove Plant Manager Descartes to utilize you in the negotiations underway with Castor. Negotiations that you will learn soon enough need replacements on both sides of the proverbial table."

She looked over at Talor. "As I said, I must follow a different path. I believed my destiny meant for me to be placed on the throne of Castor ... by any means necessary. I was wrong. It is true, I am meant for a leadership role for our beloved planet. But, it will be by *proxy*."

Talor looked quizzically at her, while Starn merely listened. She went on. "Talor, your lineage runs strong and deep to the time of Ravar and the migration of the arks. Your brush with insurgency can be overlooked, *if you swear allegiance to me*. For I deign to appoint you as my Executive Minister. I have influential people in place that were prepared to apply force to enable my ascension. I believe my sovereignty would be better accepted with less bloodshed."

Talor's face flushed a dark azure in surprise. He then bowed deeply to show his acceptance of her offer. Before he could speak, Tempora continued, "Chrislar informs me a flotilla of Castorian ships are enroute to provide aid to this vessel. It will be a worthy gesture upon which to build a strong relationship during the talks. You may be surprised at who you find among the envoys. Be open to the possibilities, and you will do well."

Releasing her hold on Starn's hands, and placing one briefly on the cheek of Talor, she concluded, "Now, I must take my leave with

Chrislar. I trust you both will heed my counsel. In *time*, we will meet again."

As mysteriously as she arrived aboard the *Darwin*, her departure was all the more intriguing. Walking toward Chrislar, his translucent form became brighter, pulsing with an eerie luminescence. The intensity grew until, even with the inner eyelids innate to the Geminian and Castorian species, all had to turn away. And in a flash, she and her Legotian escort were gone.

Starn, Talor, and Hal exchanged looks of bewilderment as the hallway hatch to the hangar irised open. Technicians with two gurneys swiftly glided in, descending upon the bodies of P'Teel and Dr. Edison. Eric followed the procession, carrying a device that looked like a cross between an industrial vacuum cleaner and beauty salon hair dryer. He veered over toward the remains of T'Poch.

Lowering the polymeric shroud over the residue, he activated the equipment. Unceremoniously, the particulate was drawn into the machine and hermetically sealed in a flexible pouch. Deftly, Eric removed the pouch and placed it in yet another cryogenic Dewar for safe-keeping.

The lifeless forms of P'Teel and Dr. Edison were handled with a higher level of decorum as they were gently lifted onto their respective gurneys. A violet sheet for each was unfolded and used to cover them.

Both Hal and Eric warily eyed their superior. Starn simply nodded his head solemnly, as if to offer one last farewell to his estranged father. Eric was never one to engage in sentimentalities. He opted instead to break the ice with an update of events happening beyond the confines of the lander bay.

Looking at Talor, he proffered, "Although crashing your ship into the nether regions of the *Darwin* was a dicey proposition, you ended up better off than your former boss."

"Former?" Talor queried.

"Yeah. Long range sensors tell an interesting tale. Turns out when you jettisoned your ion drive to control your cartwheel, it got sucked into the quark core micro warp vortex created by the *Eclipse II*. When Stol exited just outside orbital range of Castor, your little going-away present followed. Kablooey! No more rogue ship or rebels to worry about. Sensors also show a flotilla on its way from Castor. Descartes is about to burst at the seams figuring they're coming to pin the destruction of the *Eclipse II* on him. He muttered something about 'where are the Legotians when we need them!'"

Hal raised a finger to get Eric's attention, as if he were going to impart the wisdom of recent events upon his supervisor.

Before he could, Talor, blanching at this little bit of news, his earlier azure complexion draining to leave a pale blue, spluttered, "I'm already on probation from my last blunder involving Stol's near death experience. Now I've actually killed not only him, but his crew! The flotilla Tempora claims to be bringing aid will most certainly also carry with it a tribunal. What does my future hold? A position of power or imprisonment?"

Starn, still staring at the covered body of his father as the technicians wheeled it away, editorialized, "It was self-defense. Stol and company already established themselves as hostiles. Sending the *Spectre* into the *Darwin* was in effect using a weapon of mass destruction against a Solar Corporation asset … and personnel. You, Talor, are a *hero*. The Legotians have decreed the matter to be beneath them. And, if we are to believe my sister, the Castorians come bearing good will, not grief. You can start the process of ensconcing yourself in the good graces of the plant manager by informing him so."

An arched eyebrow from Starn punctuated his point as he turned to see if Talor would debate him. The Castorian simply nodded agreement, and responded, "Impeccable logic. I'll heed your input and go see him at once."

With that, he departed.

"Hal, Eric … we've got a lot of work ahead of us. I suspect there's quite a bit to be learned by analyzing the particulate in T'Poch's remains. It wouldn't surprise me if the nanotech within her held secrets to her extraordinary abilities. In that same vein, an autopsy of P'Teel might unveil some kernel of information on the Fire Arts she wielded, as well."

Hal and Eric also watchfully followed the departing gurneys. Hearing Starn's direction, they caught each other out of the corner of their eyes, both not quite believing the "business as usual" emotionally-detached approach from their boss. Exchanging almost imperceptible shrugs, they, too, headed for the lander pad exit.

Starn took a step to follow, then paused. Looking down, turning his head slowly back and forth, he rubbed the base of his skull. The unexplained chill that coursed down his spine was gradually massaged away. He then resumed his pace to fall behind his colleagues.

*　　*　　*

The heat of the blazing chalet raged against the backdrop of the frozen escarpment. Far below, the limited resources of the village's emergency response team scrambled. Unfortunately, the only two landers they had that were equipped with fire control capability would be hard pressed to make an impact.

Nature had other plans.

The glacial serac that had perpetually loomed over the remote lab had often been a topic of discussion amongst visitors to the area. "No wonder it was purchased for such a small amount! The owner must be a bold person to take such risks!" they would say.

And they would be right. Dr. Nicholas Edison and wife Novas de Mitron were not shy when it came to taking the path less followed. The facility, shirked by others, would serve them well as they explored the science of bioduogenetics and the quest for Phoenos. Ironically, its precarious location would provide solace to their son's Dual, Nimon.

The pyre hurled its flaming tendrils into the frozen fissures of the peak. Ice unmelted for millennia awoke from its timeless sleep with a groan. Stone flexed as steam snaked its relentless surge through unseen crevices. Pressure built until it could be contained no longer.

The mountain's icy monoliths cracked and swayed. A crystalline avalanche of snow rained down from the escarpment to blanket the inferno below. The patience of water drowned the impertinence of flame. Unsatisfied with the thick comforter of snow cast over the remnants of the facility, the goddess of ice, Khione, completed her mission. Dozens of frozen shards plummeted from above to lay an impenetrable barricade atop the site.

Far beneath the frigid pile, a seemingly indestructible sarcophagus, saved from the fiery onslaught, resumed its mission to sustain the contents within.

CHAPTER 29

Tempora expected to arrive in the Legotian's chamber. She hoped to get a better explanation for the surge of information Chrislar had revealed to her. What was fact? What was conjecture? What could be changed - if any of it?

"But of course not," she grumbled. *"As usual, I'm left to solve the enigma for myself."* She found herself in pitch darkness. *"Let me guess..."* fumbling around with her outstretched arms and grasping a rigid shaft, *"...either I'm back in the storage closet and this is a mop, or someone is very glad to see me."* Finding the lumen panel switch, she pressed it and confirmed it was the former.

Eying her reflection in a spare chromium rubbish container, she snorted, "Hmph, once again clothed in the trappings of a member of the Stargazer sect. I shouldn't complain. I'm actually growing quite fond of my chamois bodice, linen stole and matching linen split-skirt." Unconsciously adjusting the silver pendant on the gold chain nestled at her bosom, she couldn't help but twirl gracefully and cast a coquettish smile at herself.

Regaining a more solemn composure, she thumbed the dial to allow the door to slide partially open. Poking her head through the gap, she looked both directions up and down the hall. Seeing the way as clear, she emerged.

The timing could not have been more impeccable. Enn came around the curve of the inner bulkhead, like a morning sun rising above the horizon. Over three seasons had passed since she saw the Castorian Executive disappear. It clearly showed on her.

"Executive. I suspected the Legotian would have us meet again. My physicians demanded I get sufficient exercise. How better than to prowl the very halls where last I saw you vanish. What occasion prompts him to grace us with your presence?" Enn asked, glibly. " Surely our future negotiations found an alternative means to reach their conclusion. Although important, my *time* has been better spent here." The Geminian, with a gentle flourish, let float her open hands before the shimmering silver cassock that draped over her unborn child.

The Castorian slowly turned her head side to side, as if to free her mind from the conflicting emotions swelling within her. Tempora's last meeting in the _egotian chamber was not with *this* one. It was with an earlier manifestation, after her failec effort to return from Gemini's past with the Ravarian shard.

Tempora had been furious! But she, too, was now a different person. She had learned that the woman before her was *her mother*. *"How am I supposed to feel toward her?"* Tempora queried to herself. *"She did not raise me. She couldn't. Tragically, she did not survive my birth. To her, I am the Castorian Executive that railed against her until calmed by Chrislar's influence. She sees me as little more than a raving lunatic of an adversary, having no clue I am the grown daughter she now carries.*

And what of the truth? Am I to tell her? The fate of her Terran husband … her Dual … her very life!"

"Speechless?" Enn continued, seeing the would-be Stargazer struggling. She took a few steps closer. Looking more intently, she detected the concern behind the mask Tempora struggled to maintain. Cocking her head, the mother-to-be peered into the eyes of the troubled woman.

"I sense you are different from last we met in the chambers of the Legotians. Your fierce anger toward me is no more." Enn lifted her left hand and suspended it, palm outward, just in front of Tempora's chest. "Yes ... quite different ..."

Several heartbeats passed.

Then Enn gasped.

"You carry the Life Crystal! And it is One! How is this possible? The Ravarian shard is safely secreted away in a bejeweled locket of my design within my mate's chambers. And the Mitronian half empowers my Dual, T'Poch ... unless ..."

Finally, Tempora spoke.

"Executive Novas ..."

The former Geminian executive's palm closed to leave an index finger pointing upward, signaling for the Castorian to take pause. "*Here*, I am simply Enn. The life of mine you know exists *in the future*. Yet ironically, I have left it to exist in my own past. Until you arrived. Enabled by some form of Legotian contrivance, no doubt. Here to brandish my decision before me. Perhaps it is their perverse way to draw me back. Manipulate me once again to do their bidding. Distorting lives, societies, worlds ... *time* itself!"

Tempora could see her presence was disturbing, *Enn*. *"How strange to finally know my mother's name, yet not know her,"* she thought. *"While raised by my father and his servants, they referred to her with terms of endearment - my lady, princess mom, or your royal love. Sadly, all in the past tense. Gradually, they helped me forget. But father never did. In a way, that's why we grew apart. I served only as a reminder of the woman here before me, and of what he lost."*

The unrevealed daughter, shaken from her reverie, felt the intensity of her mother's fiery gaze. She knew it was less intended for her, and more for what she represented. The potential threat that the Legotians had sent her here for some unknown, nefarious purpose. Somehow, she had to gain her mother's trust.

"Exec ... *Enn*, know this. Whatever my reason for being here, it is for your *benefit*. True, it is made possible by the Legotians. And, unquestionably, I bear terrible news. But it is news that you need to hear." Pausing to see how the raw truth would impact her, she took a half step closer. Her arms were raised at her sides, palms up, as would a supplicant standing before her goddess. Noting a softening in Enn's countenance, she continued.

"T'Poch, your Dual, is no more. Though saddening for you, it was necessary. Despite her existence being a great achievement, she chose a dark path. I believe, deep down, you knew this. As bearer of the unified crystal, although momentary, the fires of her essence burned only to destroy. Yet, they *did* serve one noble purpose. Through them, the crystal was made whole again. Now, *time* will only tell if, as its bearer, I am able to bring its legend to life."

Enn's eyes warmed, not from the heat of anger, but from the dawning glow of understanding ... and recognition. "I hear your words, Executive ... or should I call you *Enchantress*, given your dress. But it is not those that convince me." She, too, took a half step forward. Her finger, still pointing, was joined again by its sisters, as Enn opened her hand once more. Reaching forward, she gently lifted the pendant off Tempora's chest, devoid of the locket that would contain a treasured stone. "I had this crafted on board this vessel. Its purpose, to cradle the Ravarian origin Life stone." Her voice wavered. "Ravar was true to his oath," she added, cryptically. She released it and raised her hand to lightly touch Tempora's cheek with the backs of her gently curled fingers.

"You have his eyes. And his determination. And the soul of a leader. How is this so?" Enn's other hand rested gently on her own waist. She looked from Tempura's face down to the growing life within her, then back to the woman before her. "No matter … I only know it to be true. Perhaps my failure in T'Poch will be balanced by my success through you. If only I had the *time* to know you."

A wave of pain washed over Enn as she quickly brought her raised hand together with the other to grasp her abdomen. She winced, drawing in a sharp breath, her knees buckling.

Tempora grasped her mother by the shoulders, easing her to the deck, preventing a harmful fall. A wrist band, to this point unnoticed, went from a sedate, verdant hue to a pulsing yellow.

"Mother, what is it!" the timefaring tempest exclaimed. "What must I do?"

Enn smiled through the pain. "Why … be you, my child. It is all a mother can ask." Another agonizing lance transformed the smile to a grimace. The bracelet morphed from yellow to red as its pulsing continued.

Tempora heard running feet from down the corridor. A team of three med techs came racing around the curve. A gurney wheeled in the lead with various devices swinging from it bore down upon her.

The female in front shouted, "What have you done to our lady?" Her clinician's coat flapped open, a surgical tunic underneath. A belt containing diagnostic implements accessorized her wardrobe nicely, except for the holster cradling several sizes of scalpels. Tempora fully expected to see one come flying her way if she did not respond correctly.

Enn grunted a reply instead. "She is a novitiate to my order. Other than I, only Ravar has rule over her. Keep her close as you attend me."

The lead medic knelt opposite Tempora and snapped commands to her two attendants. They gently lifted their chieftain's mate onto the gurney. Speedily they reversed course with their precious cargo, Tempora in tow.

*   *   *

Ducking through the doorway of the medical ward before it could close behind the attendants, Tempora nearly crashed headlong with someone she had not seen in many cycles. At least a younger, more vital someone than last she saw him in her era.

Ravar gently caught her by her shoulders, a rueful smile flickering across his face. "It seems I have a history of colliding with Stargazers." He tilted his head toward his mate as she disappeared into the next room, two more physicians descending upon her to assist. "Who might you be?"

Tempora looked into the eyes of her father, uncertain how to respond. She could not suppress the trembling that swept over her. Here was a man she barely knew, yet loved unconditionally. He had carried the weight of the Castorian people from the time even before they left Gemini. It had left litt e time to care for her. In his waning days before the future illness took him, she had tried her best to provide solace. But the same burden of the Castorian people had interfered once again.

One of Life's bitter ironies.

The sorrow in him she always sensed was already there. Yet, it was somehow fresh. The lines creasing the corners of his mouth had not had time to form. Her worry for him washed away her own trepidation. The maturity borne from cycles acting in his stead overcame the emotions of a little girl that needed her father's comfort.

He mistook her shaking as adrenalin-triggered instead of the trembling of anticipation. "Hopefully your sect is more polite than my dear Enn's. I often imagine her blow from our first meeting still has a lingering effect on cold days." Releasing Tempora, he chuckled as he stroked his jaw. "She has always been a fighter. But if I am to believe the doctors, this may be her last."

Crafting her response to be truthful but vague, the time traveler replied to Ravar's initial question before asking her own. "I am Tempora. I am here to serve and to learn. What do you mean, `her last'?"

A flash of pain crossed the chieftain's face. "I suppose it will become known all too soon. We have kept it a secret. Though united in our journey, there are still factions that won't hesitate to take advantage of any sign of weakness. My mate will not survive the birth of our child."

Tempora, though she knew the tragedy surrounding her birth, was shocked that it was not a surprise to her father - and most of all - that it could not be avoided. She exclaimed,

"How can you be certain? Surely, knowing in advance, something can be done!"

"Aah, one of the faithful of the Stargazer clan - the belief that all is possible. I wish only that that *were* true. Our best healers tell me Enn is a remarkable woman. She had suffered a physical trauma in the past, but miraculously healed. Yet, while the nature of her recovery restored her ability to bear a child, the outcome was fragile. Her neural network has become so intertwined with the child's, the procedure to deliver her will be fatal for my dear Enn."

"But the healers have known. Was there nothing they could do?" Tempora implored.

"In fact there was. But she would have no part in it," Ravar whispered, solemnly.

"What? Why not?!"

"Early in the pregnancy, they could have taken the child and Enn would have survived. But as she said, `That would be a life unworthy of living'."

Tempora staggered back against the waiting room wall, her hand to her forehead, as if that would keep it from exploding within from guilt. No child wants to be the cause of their own parent's misfortune, much less death. Despite knowing her only a brief *time*, there is something eternal about the bond between child and parent. Events can shape the relationship, the emotions, and the behaviors - sometimes leaving scars that are long to heal - but the bond still remains.

Ravar continued, seeing the impact of his words on the young woman. "My words wound you. Your grief is sincere. For that, I am both sorry and grateful, as, I am sure, is Enn."

Ravar paused and for the first time took in the full presence of the young woman before him. He noticed the pendant, now conspicuously dangling from her neck.

"The loyalty among your sisterhood is the inspiration for song. I cannot help but notice your adornment. My dear Enn had one crafted, very similar to that one. Most likely one of your clan's cryptic traditions. But hers incorporated a locket for a precious stone. A crystal shard, in fact. It represents a time we shared, a commitment we embraced. But it appears one we cannot fulfill. For, once she is gone, so, too, will be the stone. Like Enn and myself, the stone and pendant will be separated. As she has instructed, our daughter will receive the necklace. But as for the crystal, I will bury it, along with our mutual aspirations, so that it will never be found. Its mysteries, never revealed. I have so sworn, as Enn was my witness."

The once larger-than-life leader of a world sighed deeply. Lowering his head, the moisture forming in his eyes went unseen. A moment passed. No words exchanged. Then he drew in a sharp breath, drew back his shoulders, and raised his firm chin, as if readying himself for an enemy's blow.

Looking at the youthful enchantress, he remarked, "The legends around the Stargazers would have us believe they are otherworldly. Here to aid and guide us mere mortals. Despite powers that mystify, even they have limits. She and I both have known this day would come. Though I am gifted with great size, she is the stronger of the two. Perhaps some small bit of her abilities will pass to me so that I can bear to go on. For my people, my daughter, and for her."

Tempora felt for him, pondering, *"Even great men can be vulnerable. He carried the weight of loss, but it wore him down. Even now. She wondered what course Fate would have allowed had Enn survived? What would have transpired, in* time, *had another path opened?"*

Her arms tingled. Thousands of pin pricks coursed across them. She looked down at the backs of her hands. Then slowly turning them over, the palms. Nothing could be seen by the naked eye, but she saw. They wavered, as if phasing from this moment to another.

"No!" She exclaimed. "Not now! It is not *time*! I must stay! I must do something!"

Though a formidable warrior, even Ravar flinched in fear at the young woman's outburst. *"Had sorrow morphed to madness and overcome her?"* he wondered.

His concern was not unfounded. Tempora's face hardened with determination. She raised her arms as if to push the chieftain aside, saying, "Out of my way! I know what I must do!"

CHAPTER 30

As Tempora burst into the delivery room, the health care providers were conflicted as to what to do with the intruder. Training conditioned them to protect their patient. But as Ravar had said, Stargazers were shrouded in legends. Some quite fearsome. Succumbing to their reflexes, they backed away from Enn lying in the bed, as if a tred's worth of distance could protect them from the enchantress' onslaught.

Heartbeats later, reason replaced reflex. They turned first to Ravar, looking through the observation window, then Enn, who tossed fitfully from the pain overwhelming her. She seemed unable to acknowledge, much less address, the situation.

Tempora held her hands out to Ravar, open palms up, beseeching him. "I can save them both! It is my purpose! I know it is why I am here at this moment in *time!*"

The scientist turned prophet, as some would whisper, struggled. His rational self said this woman acted mad and should be forcefully removed from his dear Enn's presence. Yet, her commitment, her strength of will, was compelling. He recognized it in his friend and comrade, Mitron. And, looking upon his beloved as she fought through the pain, knew it to be one of her fundamental qualities, as well.

Inexplicably, this stranger seemed familiar. Without having a reason to justify it, he knew he could trust her. If *belief* alone could work miracles as the ancients taught, perhaps she could prevail.

Ravar signaled the medical attendants to leave the room. Tempora's gaze locked with Ravar's before tucking her chin to her chest, signaling her respect, obeisance, and appreciation with one simple gesture.

The executive, enchantress, and now, healer, turned to her mother. In a brief moment of lucidity as the pain ebbed momentarily, Enn looked at her angel of mercy.

"Though I know it to be true, I cannot see how it is possible. Even with the involvement of the Legotians. You are the daughter I never knew. How is it you are here, and also here?"

she queried, looking at her bulging midsection.

"There is much to tell. But no time to do it. Know this, though. Just as the life crystal shard enabled you to empower the creation known as the Singular Dualiity, the unified gem, too, is a source of even greater power. Through it, I believe I am destined to become the Duall Singularity - two timelines traveled by a single entity. Able to co-exist in *parallel*, and at times, *intertwining* streams of reality."

Enn's eyes widened. Tempora was unsure if it was a reaction to what seemed to be the fantasy of one insane, or in response to the new wave of agony building within her. Before it could consume her mother, Tempora rushed to her side.

Tempora adopted a pose as if she were a surgeon sustaining the sanctity of her sterile field. Relaxed arms with hands held just below her shoulders, elbows down, she might have been a messiah before a penitent flock.

An aura began to form around the Time Child. As she moved, a trio of images created made it seem as if she were in three places - the *now*, the *then*, and the *to be*. Her radiance expanded to encompass Enn. The mother-to-be relaxed, momentarily freed from the neural flames raging through her body.

Tempora placed her palms together, suspended over her mother's abdomen. As she then slowly moved them apart, strands of glowing tendrils formed, twisting and oscillating, barely contained within the luminescent sphere that surrounded them. Gradually, the chronal conjurer lowered the radiant orb until it engulfed the unborn child within her mother.

Tempora's brow furrowed in concentration, then smoothed. Her eyes closed, eyelids flickering as if in a dream. She found herself suspended on an endless golden net stretching in all directions. Between the filaments, the space contained an atmosphere of pulsing lights in a sea of darkness. More than two-dimensional, it twisted and curved back upon itself in places. In an effort to draw sense from the maddening images, she focused on a point in front of her.

One of the lights slowly floated up, as if to greet her.

It was more than a light, though. With effort, like trying to see an image backed by the sun, she could make out a shape. It was a child. Instead of the normal fetal position, it sat cross legged. An infant yogi, smiling gleefully at the prospects of a new friend. Tempora wondered if it could understand. So she asked.

"And who might you be?"

The diminutive figure, wondrous in its beauty, as are all innocents, cocked its head, to and fro. In reply, it gestured. A small closed hand went from its own chest out toward Tempora, opening as it stopped between the two of them.

The time traveller understood. "You offer to share your heart with me. We are one. You are me, and I am you."

The glowing babe brought its open palm back and closed it, except for its raised index finger. Bringing its other hand up to mirror it, index finger also extended, they were placed side by side. After a heartbeat, the hands gradually moved forward, the fingers slowly moving in parallel, but apart.

"I see," acknowledged Tempora. "I stand corrected. We are one, but only briefly. We will follow our own paths. Diverging, but in the same direction. Presumably along the way that is meant to be. Yes?"

The child smiled. Nodding slightly, Its palms came together in front in the universal sign of prayer. Or perhaps it was to say namaste - both good-bye and hello.

Tempora returned the smile and gesture. The figure before her responded by glowing more brightly. The intensity grew until its outline could be discerned no longer. The Time Child closed her astral eyes, not from discomfort, but because she knew it was *time*.

The experience for those observing through the delivery room window was quite different, but no less extraordinary. They saw the pulsating sphere phase into Enn as the throes of labor eased. After but a moment, the orb was lifted again by the enchantress. The Stargazer reached into it ever so gently. Pulling her arms back to her bosom, it prompted the audience to release a collective gasp.

Tempora cradled the newborn as it looked up at her, and smiled. Stepping to the head of the bed, she looked down at her own mother, reflecting the same smile.

For the first time she could remember, tears of joy streamed down Enn's face. She reached out to pull Tempora into an embrace. Mother, daughter, and baby shared a brief unity in body, mind, and spirit.

But the moment of tenderness was fleeting.

This time it was the medical team who burst through the clinic doors. The lead physician hovered over Enn, who now held the newborn. While showing Tempora the reverent deference she deserved, the other attendants still managed to usher the medical mystic toward the door.

The enigmatic enchantress complied.

Ravar, watching the commotion, knew better than to intervene. He yielded to the caregivers their moment to ensure the health of his beloved. Instead, he opened his arms and pulled Tempora into a grateful hug.

In a deep baritone overflowing with joy he proclaimed, "I know not how, but you have changed the course of my life! Misery beckoned me to become its eternal companion. Now I have Joy to embrace me, no matter Fate's plans!"

Tempora actually let slip a giggle as she basked in the good spirits of the father she had always hoped to have.

*　　*　　*

A dozen rotations had past and Starn found himself once again standing on the deck of the lander hangar. This time, the entourage waiting for the guests to disembark was more than twice as large as the one that had greeted P'Teel, T'Poch, and Talor during that fateful meeting.

At his back were his IAD companions, Specialist Hal Xkorp and Supervisor Eric Magnek. Mirroring their triangle to their left was Plant Manager Morgan Descartes in the lead, along with Personnel Manager Jefferson Brown and Plant engineer George Crescent in the rear. Recently appointed Executive Minister Talor posted himself in the background. He was still unsure how he would be received by the Castorian delegation. Unconsciously, he left himself an escape route to the hangar door

Descartes shifted from foot to foot. He was never a fan of waiting. Staring intently, he tried to will the lander stairway to lower from the craft's belly. Unsuccessful, he filled the time with banter. Murmuring over his shoulder to his Engineer, he prodded, "Guess we're going to see what the Castorians think of the work you've accomplished while their rescue flotilla made their way here."

George cleared his throat - or was it a growl? "They could have simply sent the parts and materials I requested. I don't need the likes of them poking around my plant. We've successfully cut away Talor's renegade dinghy and sealed the tears in the polymerization loops. Granted, we'll have to undergo repairs in an orbital shipyard to get them properly aligned. But I doubt this lot has the facility to do what we need. We could have been halfway back to Gemini while we waited for them to get here."

Descartes grinned sardonically, replying, "What would be the fun in that? Once again we get to be the guinea pig in Corporate's grand experiment to unify the cosmos. By kowtowing to the Castorians - gracefully - we set the stage for a merger of interplanetary proportions. Literally. Solar - Gemini - Castor: the big three becoming one.

After all, Castor has been completely isolated from the rest of the space-faring companies. Except for the recent couple of run-ins with Talor's deceased boss, Stol. Oh, and the not-to-be-discussed stealth device incident," he muttered, parenthetically, his smile growing wider.

Jefferson Brown couldn't help but pick up on the line of conversation. "Morgan, you're down right *sinister.* You love having the spotlight, even if it is shining up your plant's derriere!"

"That just happens to be where Talor left his probe ship!" Descartes retorted, stifling a chuckle at his own sense of humor, since no one else appreciated it.

Starn ever so slightly shook his head at the conversation. It didn't help. He had been diligently facilitating the pre-work negotiation sessions with Descartes and Talor. Data streams in support of the effort from Solar, Gemini, and Castor had been voluminous. But, between Descartes' cavalier attitude and Talor's paranoia over his future, progress had been slow. The arrival of dignitaries from Castor couldn't happen soon enough. Thankfully, the perimeter of the transport lander yawned open to spare him.

A security detail was the first to make their way down the steps. Although unassuming, the three females carried themselves with a subtle menace. Hal and Eric exchanged glances, as if to say, *"wish we'd been allowed to bring our weapons."* By mutual agreement, both parties felt armed guards were not the best tone to set for the talks. Of the trio, one took up position on each side at the base of the stairs, while the third floated around the hangar as if sightseeing.

The IAD team knew better - *defensive reconnaissance*.

After a pause - for the theatrical effect, maybe, but most likely to allow the guards to make their sweep - a cloaked and hooded figure emerged. Then two more followed, similarly clad. The leader wore a royal blue floor length garment trimmed in a red and gold filigree ribbon. Immediately behind, the first follower's robe was white with blue trim that matched the color of the first. Last in the entourage was a figure who, though shrouded in a simple grey hooded cloak, somehow conveyed movement in a way not unlike the security detail - subtly threatening.

The two guards had slipped away from their posts like mist in a breeze to materialize with their third comrade behind the *Darwin*'s welcome committee. The white and grey cloaked pair took their places on each side of the stairs behind the leader, who paused a few treds short of the waiting hosts.

In a gentle, fluid motion, the blue hood was eased back by the wearer's crimson gloved hands. The woman's nobility and stature radiated from her face. Framed with silver locks, a single ebony streak wound its way at one temple. The lines of many seasons of experience added, instead of detracted, from her beauty.

Starn was the first to react. *"Mother?"* he said with a whisper, unheard by those in his party, but somehow detected by her. Her head turned a fraction, crimson eyes transfixing Starn.

In his mind, a thought coalesced.

"Be open to the possibilities and you will do well."

The eyes of the former biodgen Dual held her gaze. He responded with silence.

Descartes, on the other hand, could not keep quiet. Under his breath, he sought counsel from his personnel manager. "J.B., does she look familiar to you?"

Stopping just short of presenting a full anthropological oral treatise, Brown replied, "Well, we know for certain from Helicon's work that the Castorians are directly descended from Gemini. Studies show that a small population developing in a confined environ will display dominant traits in a more pronounced way. Clearly an alpha of her group, she most likely comes from a dominant genome. Since you most often come into contact with Geminian alphas, it is only natural you attempt to see a pattern where one may or may not exist between her and others from that planet."

"So... you're also saying she reminds you of Starn, or more closely, Nimon?"

"At the risk of reinforcing your latent bigotry where all people of a particular race look the same ... yes."

Descartes scornfully glowered at Brown. But before he could continue their verbal jousting, their guest of honor introduced herself, speaking to the group, but keeping her focus on her son.

"I am Enn de Mitron. Wife to the Chairman. One of a select few original surviving sojourners that call Castor home. We welcome the opportunity to provide support to our distant blood kindred."

"Impressive," thought Descartes. *"In one brief greeting she first establishes her position of power, both historically as member of the Mitronian guild and currently as what could be called `senior executive' on the board of the Castorian Conglomerate - if not `Empress' in other circles. She then communicates her seniority and accomplishment as an original Geminian pilgrim that founded Castor. Lastly,*

she extends an invitation to accept her support as would a family welcoming a long lost relative. Well, I can be diplomatic, too."

With a flourish, the plant manager crossed his right arm over his abdomen, bent at the waist, and extended his left hand behind him and slightly to the side with palm up, all the while looking at the feet of his guest. "You grace us with your presence and assistance, noble Enn. I am the *Darwin*'s plant manager, Morgan Descartes. As appointed chief representative of Solar Corporation, we are honored to meet you, despite the unfortunate circumstances. I sincerely regret the loss of your ship, the *Eclipse II*, and its personnel."

Jefferson Brown's eyebrow raised at his plant manager's performance. *"Deftly done,"* he all but whispered out loud. *"Treat her like royalty, thank her in advance, but remind her ever so subtly in the guise of regret that it was her people that inflicted harm. A perfect balance between passive aggressive and obsequious. That's my Morgan."*

A twitch at the corner of her mouth was the only indication that Enn, too, discerned the nuances of Descartes' greeting. In an example of verbal aikido, she slipped to the side of the main thrust of the words, deflected them, and asserted her control over her sparring partner.

"Your magnanimity is appreciated. I, too, regret the actions of a small, unsanctioned collective. Hopefully my delegation will prove that we are actually a benevolent people. I will introduce them and you be the judge. But first, please do the honors."

In response, Descartes presented the names and responsibilities of Brown, Crescent, Magnek, Xkorp, and Edison, as well as Talor, in his new role as Executive Minister to his guest. A flicker of pain swept across Enn's face at the mention of Starr's family name. Unnoticed by almost all, it did not escape his keen eye. Instead of addressing him, though, the head of the Castorian contingent turned to Talor.

"Your reputation precedes you. Congratulations on your promotion from Vice-Executive to my daughter's Executive Minister. I was informed some *time* ago of her decision. However, you should know that she is on ... special assignment ... for the benefit, I should hope, of all of us. In her stead, you shall be in the service of the first of our group that I will introduce."

Enn pivoted gracefully, sweeping her arm with the twist of a wrist toward the white cloaked figure behind her. Stepping forward, as Enn had done, the person eased back her hood.

Talor and Starn exchanged puzzled glances. It was *Tempora*! Their same thoughts begged the question, *"But hadn't Enn just said she was on special assignment?"*

As if in answer, Enn proclaimed, "I present to you, heiress to the Castorian Chair, *Empirica*."

CHAPTER 31

Hal, select in the hangar among the only other two, Starn and Talor, who had actually witnessed Tempora's presence and then departure with the Legotian, blurted, "Hmph … twin sisters."

Empirica smiled and replied, cryptically, "No … not really. Something more. I will explain, in *time*. For now, suffice it to say I have looked forward to this meeting. We believe we have much to offer. Of course, aide with the current situation - but we bring change for the future, as well. As an example, please meet *my Dual*, E'Poch."

The grey cloaked figure repeated the unveiling motion for a third time. The staff of the Darwin released a collective gasp in awe. Standing before the entourage was a goddess brought to life! Her sapphire skin, glowing, darkened to a royal hue by rotations under the intense Polluxan sun, was flawless. Garnet eyes flashed intensely. Aquiline features, set beneath a flowing ebony mane highlighted with silvery white, dared any nemesis to approach.

Hal reacted again, yet much differently than his colleagues. Through clenched teeth, he swore, *"T'Poch*! I don't know how you survived! This time you won't!" His hand instinctively went for the holstered weapon that was not there. Trained to always be prepared, regardless of the restrictions for this meeting, he next reached for the flat blade strapped to the inside of his sleeved forearm.

Before the knife could be drawn, a steely hand gripped his wrist, pinning it to his chest. Another slipped around his back to clutch his shoulder, pulling him into a vise-like embrace. He heard a gruff whisper in his ear. "What do you think you're doing, rookie?!"

Eric, fully recovered from his injuries, welcomed the chance to exert himself. Especially if it meant inflicting a little friendly discomfort upon his subordinate. The senior IAD agent had never seen T'Poch, nor her fiery display prior to her disintegrating demise. He had only arrived in time to vacuum up her remains. So, he had no insight as to the reason for Hal's combative reaction to this new arrival.

"That's the rogue biod infected with nanotechnology! She and the stiff lying in the cryo-unit ended Dr. Edison and nearly took out Tempora!"

"Tempora? The one that looks just like Empirica, here? Maybe *you're* the one that needs to go into recovery this time. Having flashbacks, are we? A little post-traumatic disorder, hmm?"

Hal twisted his head around to look at his boss. "I'm not crazy," he spluttered.

Eric countered, "Look around you. Nobody else is alarmed. The *Darwin*'s three management musketeers seem fine. Talor and Starn were both with you when the witch was taken out. They aren't alarmed. So, stand down. Worst case, if you're right, is we see how this plays out, then take action. Got it?"

Hal grunted his agreement. More from the added pressure Eric applied than from a desire to acquiesce. *"Why hadn't either Talor or Starn flinched at the sight of this apparition?"* he thought to himself.

Talor, after having rescued P'Teel and T'Poch, had spent enough time on board his probe ship with the two to know them quite well. He also saw T'Poch's spectacular cremation. However, he was unaware that T'Poch was a biodgen Dual. Much less the

Singular Dualiity. *"No doubt a distant relative,"* he mused.

Starn, displaying the emotional control he mastered as the sentry outside the Fata-Akateer, Archive of Families, projected serenity.

Within, raged turmoil.

"Am I in some alternate reality? Buried in an avalanche of doppelgängers? My mother, grown older. My newfound sister - a twin, but not? And Life Mentor to a Dual coexisting in close proximity that is clearly designed after my mother's own Dual, T'Poch! Is this yet another way to lord over me the fact that she and her daughter could sustain a Singular Dualiity, where I could not? But for the fact an outburst would result in them institutionalizing me, I would thrash the three of them until I had answers!" he fumed, inwardly.

Enn, once again able to mysteriously divine the energy in the audience, suggested, "We have much to do and many questions to answer. I sense my dear Empirica is eager to meet with Talor and Plant Manager Descartes to immerse themselves in the possibilities that lay before us.

Mr. Brown, Xkorp, and Magnek ... as experts in personnel and the science of bioduogenetics, especially its failures and foibles, you might be interested to know that E'Poch is not the only biodgen among us. My security detail is currently being empowered by a single organic on one of the support vessels hovering several kilotreds away. No doubt you would find an in-depth interview with them fascinating."

Eric had since released his comrade. They both looked over to Personnel Manager Brown and shrugged. Jefferson, less averse to the company of synthetically enhanced beautiful women than the two IAD agents, smiled broadly and nodded.

Enn continued, as if she were a maestro conducting an orchestra through its symphonic movements, "As for Engineer Crescent, the supplies you requested are being ferried to your cargo bay as we speak. No need for any of us to look over your competent shoulder while you complete your repairs. No doubt you thought we would have an army of technicians descending upon you to give aid."

She laughed and added, "My dear husband likes to show off. Hence the flotilla, although it is mostly empty. Except for the minibots we brought along. You may be interested in playing with them. They are magnificent little devices that can be empowered with a headset - many at once - to perform the most mundane chores. I suspect you will be thoroughly entertained. Nevertheless, we stand at the ready should you need us."

Under Enn's gaze, George Crescent beamed his approval.

Once more she turned to Plant Manager Descartes, whose jaw had dropped little by little as she adroitly manipulated the assembly. Seeing her in action, a revelation flashed in his mind. *"Well I'll be damned … I recognize you now,"* he thought.

"Oh, *Morgan*, if I can be so bold. In the mean time, our ships will be performing training exercises. Would your command crew like to participate - virtually of course? It *is* our maiden voyage, after all. Until now, we don't get out much," she said, with a wry smile.

"Of course … Enn. Floating in space has been tedious. They can use the change of pace. But what of you?" inquired Descartes.

"It seems there is a family matter that needs my attention. My sources tell me that Starn and I "share ancestry". If you do not object, perhaps he can give me a private tour of your facility while we talk?"

"Why, of course ..." Descartes responded, the corners of his mouth upturned, as he suppressed the urge to finish it with "... *Executive Novas.*"

*   *   *

Two rotations had passed since Tempora had performed the miracle of parturition. The caregivers had allowed only Ravar brief visitations while they hovered over their liege and her new child. They had peppered the enchantress with questions surrounding the event. But, as a member in the Stargazer guild, she declined to answer. She stated somewhat firmly that the mysteries of her sect would go undisclosed and did not fall within the purview of the medical community. With a collective grumbling, the physicians relented.

Despite her victory over their attempts, Tempora entered the private ward, not knowing what to expect. The attendants simply nodded with quiet respect, then vanished as if shadows at dusk. She gazed upon the sight before her and could not help but smile.

Enn lay in her bed cradling the newborn. She had just finished feeding her. The baby slept, comforted by the fullness of her belly and scent of her mother. Enn greeted her visitor with high spirits.

"Please come closer ... *Executive* seems out of place ... *Enchantress* is much too clandestine ... *daughter* could be confusing ... " as she looked down at her baby, "...what *shall* I call you?"

"My governess, a Stargazer, named me *Tempora*. Perhaps she had some insight into my destiny?"

"Hmm ... perhaps. We are certainly going through a strange *time*. Your name, along with your feats, are but hints of what could be in store," Enn mused. "But know this, Ravar and I are eternally grateful."

"Most certainly. I feel every action I take has a profound impact on the future. Despite having lived aboard the *Destiny* as a child cared for by a Stargazer, I am not prepared for this. Events are not the same. Pardon me for being insensitive, but ... you ... were not here. Ravar - father - was very different. Withdrawn, dark, resentful. I'm not sure how much of this he should even know. Just saying it aloud seems bordering on insanity. Yet, being able to talk to someone about it is a huge relief!" Tempora gushed.

"You have much insight, despite your feelings of uncertainty. I, too, have struggled with the situation the Legotians thrust upon me … until recently." Again she looked down at the sleeping child. "But now, it all feels so *right*." She paused, as if drawing energy from the vast potential that lay in her arms. "As for sire Ravar, you and I are in agreement. Our origins enjoy the benefit of a shroud of secrecy. That should continue. I doubt that even in *our* era, the reality of time travel can be accepted by more than just a few."

Tempora also gazed upon the innocent bundle, so peacefully oblivious. She scavenged the deepest recesses of her mind for the earliest of her memories. "I don't actually remember it, but was taught that when I was just over a cycle old, our arks arrived at a planetoid midway in our journey. I have since learned the Ravarian shard was buried there, only to recently be discovered in our era. Most likely Ravar, still suffering from losing you, wanted to leave his life of science behind. It had failed you both. Regrettably, my existence provided little solace."

Enn winced at the thought of this dear woman - her *daughter* - suffering a similar fate as her son. She confessed, "Like Ravar, I too, allowed my misplaced sense of responsibility to others detract from what should have ben a responsibility to my *own child*. It shouldn't be, but the burden of a job, a mission, or even the future of a people seems easier to manage than doing what is right for your own family. Perhaps it's because the pain of being wrong when guiding your child is so unbearable, it's easier to provide no guidance at all. I don't mean to excuse my, or his, mistakes when it comes to nurturing our children. There are no excuses. Only sorrow. Sorrow for not expressing the deep love that we have for you."

Tempora thoughtfully considered the woman's words. *"Could the words meant for her son, instead shared with a daughter, substitute for the words of a father, never expressed to a daughter? Somehow, they do make me feel better."*

"Your sentiment touches me, truly it does. Maybe this little one will reap the benefits of your insight. But she is not me, nor I her. Somehow, I know that we are separate entities, with separate fates. As for my path, it was another four cycles after a time on the planetoid before we finally arrived at Castor. Without the shard and Ravar's insatiable desire to explore its potential, Castor was relegated to evolve into an impoverished, aggression-driven planet. Hence, our desire to enhance our position in the cosmos by negotiating with you, Solar Corporation, and Gemini. Unbeknownst to both of us, though, the Legotians had far grander plans."

Enn pondered over her newfound daughter's insight, glad to have connected in some small way with her. "Yes, it is hard not to feel like pawns on a four dimensional chess board. There is much I do not understand. Especially where your adventures with them are concerned. You bear the unified crystal. T'Poch is no more. Yet, there are events still unshared."

"I had hoped to spare you more pain. The loss of T'Poch was burden enough. But you have a right to know. After our last meeting in the Legotian chamber, you returned back to this period, while I was transported forward. I found myself onboard the *Darwin* as it pursued a pair of rebel Castorian probe ships. One carried T'Poch and P'Teel on their way to foment a revolt on my world."

"Wait ... *forward* ... the Legotians have the ability to move *bidirectionally* in Time?" Enn interrupted.

Tempora paused, struggling to collect words that could explain things she herself did not understand. She had glimpsed so much when Chrislar had touched her mind. "I am as much a newborn as she is when it comes to chronal displacement. I fear I cannot sufficiently explain. As best as I understand it, Time is *multi*-directional. Using a crude metaphor, it is a ribbon that can fold, bend, twist, and even fray into strands that loop back upon themselves. You and I met for the second time at a point between your two journeys. Relative to that moment, the *Darwin* was enroute to retrieve you from the Legotians, believing our negotiations were completed. I was sent forward to a point later where they were assigned to apprehend T'Poch and her subversives instead." Again, Tempora hesitated, allowing Enn to digest the fantastic story she was hearing.

With her extreme intellect, Enn grasped the labyrinthine concept while recognizing her focus should be not on the myriad of possibilities of temporal shifts, but on the actual events that transpired. She asked, "Please, tell me what happened when you arrived on the *Darwin*."

Tempora obeyed. She detailed her story from her first appearance to the fateful conflict in the hangar. Including the tragic loss of Dr. Edison. When she finished she stared intently at her mother, hoping her reaction would provide some insight into her nature.

It did.

No longer was she the executive, looked upon as an example of stony control and impeccably logical behavior. Instead, a new mother, but one seasoned by the remorse of missed opportunity with her firstborn. Compounded by the ill-spent potential of a misguided Dual. Yet, looking ahead at the opportunity for redemption with her daughter.

Novas yielded to Enn, and wept.

Tempora, moved by Enn's raw grief, offered comfort. Sitting on the edge of the bed, child still sleeping sweetly between them, the daughter wrapped an arm around the mother she never knew. Pressing her cheek against the head bent in sorrow, she whispered, "I never knew you, or my father as he is now. I would like to stay with you, at least for a time. Let me be the governess to your child. I can help you three navigate the turbulent times ahead. At least until you reach Castor."

Enn's gentle sobbing ceased. She raised her head to peer deeply into her newfound daughter's eyes. Tempora continued. "The crystal, unified, now resides within me. I believe my purpose, already unfolding, is to change the timeline that delivered me to this point. Through me, I can enable Castor, under your and Ravar's leadership, to evolve differently."

Enn paused to see if the mother, so often the counselor, could instead, heed her counsel.

Enn held her gaze, wordlessly imploring her to continue.

"With respect, I advise that you keep the precursor shard in your possession, instead of leaving it behind, as my time strand portrays. Use it to develop Castor as a technological cornerstone in the galaxy. Nurture the fledgling world so it can achieve its rightful place in the stars. For all our people. And especially, for the sake of her."

They both looked down at the child's flickering eyelids. So young, but already dreaming of greatness.

Tempora smiled and queried, "I am remiss in failing to ask … what have you decided to name her? Surely, she will follow her own path, so should benefit from her own, unique identity, no?"

Enn nodded firmly, having regained the composure of a leader, and answered, "I shall call her, *Empirica*."

CHAPTER 32

Starn had escorted his mother to his favorite place on the *Darwin*. Despite the facility hanging in space instead of hurtling along the crest of a time-fold, the view from the observation sphere was awe-inspiring. He most enjoyed the experience when the orb bobbed gently in the propulsion field that passed through the *Darwin*'s core during transit. The sphere's transparent walls and anti-grav floor, when activated, bestowed upon its inhabitant a sense of omnipotent power. *"Who other than a god could suspend themselves in infinite time and space just for their sheer pleasure?"* Even without the benefit of traveling beyond the Einstein barrier, the stellar panorama was breathtaking.

Enn ignored the scenery, and instead looked admiringly at the profile of her son. A simple pleasure, but one she had rarely enjoyed. He had overcome a great deal to arrive at this juncture in his life. Hopefully, her plan for his future would have at least a fraction of the appeal to him as it did for her. Steeling herself against the uncertainty of the outcome, she launched into the prologue of her appeal.

"I suspect you have countless questions, not the least of which is 'Who is Empirica and how is it that she has mastered empowering E'Poch, her Singular Dualiity, with no restrictions?' And perhaps 'Why does E'Poch look eerily like my own Dual, T'Poch?', who I learned is no more."

"True, that information is intriguing. But answer me a more basic one. How do you even *know* about T'Poch and the events surrounding her demise?"

Enn smiled ruefully and replied, "That answer is intertwined in those to the two questions I posed. The short response is - *the Legotians*."

"Truly, the being I witnessed appearing and disappearing on the hangar deck seems most remarkable. But please, elaborate."

"As far-fetched as it may sound, they have the ability to transport individuals through *time*. I have experienced it, and your sister, Tempora, has experienced it. More than once. After she departed with Chrislar from the tragic events that took my Dual and your father, she came to me. She told me of the confrontation. I, myself, was several generations into Gemini's - and Castor's - past. She ..."

Starn raised his hand to stop Enn's narration. "You speak of Tempora being my sister as a given. While in relation to your life, it has been countless seasons. For me, I learned of it only a dozen rotations ago. Even then, it was never explained."

"Forgive me. You are correct. I got ahead of myself. Which can be all the more confusing when explaining temporal conundrums. You know of my mission to negotiate a treaty with Castor under the guidance of the Legotians. What you do not know is that it was decidedly more eventful. Through their ministration, I traveled to Gemini's past. While much transpired, the most impactful outcome was my meeting Ravar, the eventual leader of the Castorian people. My heart overwhelmed my mind, and I fell in love."

Enn paused, knowing such a revelation from a mother to her son could be a shock.

Starn stared at her, stoically. After an uncomfortable moment of silence, he quietly commented, "Love. A foreign concept when applied to our family. The honorable response, I suppose, is to congratulate you on finding it."

If he had slapped her, it would have been easier to withstand. Instead, his words cut her deeply, wounding her to her core. Rather than submit, though, Enn was compelled to voice her position. "Your father and I were in love. And we loved you. Your best interests were always placed first in our minds. Yes, we were consumed with our work - to a fault, it appears, given your resentment. But there was still love in our family. Did it follow the idyllic outline prescribed by fairy tales and fiction writers? No. Because the stories of happily-ever-after characters are not real. Our love for you was! "

"Then why do I feel this way?" he replied, simply.

"Because the vagaries of Life with its uncertain outcomes and constant challenge always leave us wondering, `What if ...' . Would you feel differently if Nicholas and I had not explored the wonders of biodugenetics? If, instead, we had lived a simpler life, more mundane? *Definitely* you would. But on that path, you would have other questions. `Isn't there more? Shou dn't I be achieving greater things?' You are *our* son. You have always sought to be exceptional.

That is the legacy we provided. Unfortunately, at the expense of not satisfying the feeling of emptiness you describe."

Starn cocked his head slightly, digesting her words. A gentle softening of his features hinted that she was being heard.

Enn continued.

"I admit, before my experience reliving my life on Castor, my response to you would have been different. Less   sensitive. I was given a second chance at being a mother, with the birth of Empirica. That is the miracle that the Legotians made possible. You see, as hard as it is to comprehend, Empirica *is* Tempora … but not."

Starn cocked his head to the other side. This time, his features adopted a more quizzical appearance.

Enn, noting his puzzled look, attempted to explain. "Time forms loops and branches. One loop resulted in Tempora's birth and my death. She was raised by a father consumed with grief. In that regard, the two of you may share the same resentment toward a Fate where a family's love fell short of expectation. That woman became the one you know. Daughter to the Castorian Chairman. Relegated to leading a people from the shadows after his death.

But she, too, was gifted the chance to change *Time*'s course as we knew it. Aided by the Legotians, and the unified Life crystal, she arrived in the past. Her past. She successfully saved both me and *herself* during childbirth. *Empirica* was born. *Time*'s parallel loop formed a branch. One side led to the loop that created Tempora. The other side, we now follow. It enabled me and a more benevolent Ravar to lead Castor along a new destiny, raising Empirica along the way."

Pressing for a deeper understanding, Starn asked, "But what of Tempora? How can she exist as both entities?"

"Aah, in that regard, she is unique. The unified crystal within her transformed her into the *Duall Singularity*. A singular life able to coexist along dual timelines, simultaneously. Few are aware of the loops and branches within the fabric of *Time*. Along with the Legotians, it seems to be associated with those of us who have flirted with achieving Phoenos. Me, you, and because of the Life Crystal within her, Tempora. Ravar, and even Empirica, are unaware of my origin and Tempora's true identity. I ask that you allow our secret to be preserved."

"It appears my immersion in a life of the clandestine is to continue. A biodgen for cycles known only by a few to be organic, an officer within the Internal Audit Division, and now, one of a few acting as keeper of the secret of alternate realities. I will honor your request. However, Hal Xkorp and Talor saw Tempora with the Legotian. And then again, arriving with you as Empirica. What will they conclude?"

"The mind seeks to explain contradictions as best it can. They already believe them to be sisters. There is no reason to correct that."

"Elegant in its simplicity. Very good. Tell me, though, how did Empirica achieve what I could not? How can she sustain the Singular Duality, and at such close proximity?"

"My son, you *were* able to sustain a Singular Dualiity. If but only for a short time. And at great risk to your sanity, as you well know. That is truly a great accomplishment. Especially knowing what I know now, after so many seasons of work alongside Ravar."

"Again, I am intrigued. Please explain," Starn urged, impatiently.

"Your father and I were *so close* with your development. But we were too focused on the crystal part of the equation. We overlooked the organic component. Bear with me as I explain. As with most breakthroughs, Chance plays an important role. Among other pivotal changes stemming from my and Tempora's presence in the past, we orchestrated Gemini's very survival.

The meteoroid swarm that impacted upon our planet so long ago could have destroyed it completely, had we not intervened. We succeeded in destroying the largest of the projectiles. In so doing, the explosve wave front from the life crystal laden rock had an unpredictable effect. The released energy altered the chromosomal matrix of those exposed. The few on board the *Destiny*, Ravar's ark used to launch the missiles, developed enhanced biodgen empowering abilities. One being the power to manipulate more than one construct simultaneously.

In the case of Empirica, the effect was unique. You see, the energy field was not only composed of life crystal emanations, it had an organic element as well. *Mine*. One of the projectiles had previously transported me in a bio-gel. It contained my genetic matrix. The life crystal particles had the ability to imprint my genetic sequence. The result was the radiation was finely tuned to affect me differently.

Along with my unborn child.

Empirica is unique in that her prenatal exposure to the shock wave seems to have imbued her with the ability to overcome the distance requirement for empowering. By mimicking the work I had accomplished with T'Poch, this time with the Ravarian shard, and instead, using Empirica as the organic source, E'Poch was born. So to speak."

Starn shook his head, almost in disbelief from the fantastic story he was hearing. Finally, he interjected, somewhat cynically, "How ironic. While in my timeline, your Dual is destroyed and I abandon all hope of achieving Phoenos, a reincarnation of you is able to *succeed* with an alternate reality daughter. Do I have it right?"

Enn flinched. "You are bitter. How could you not be. I am sorry to hear of your decision regarding Nimon. Is it final? I believe with the advances in bioduogenetics that Ravar and I have achieved on Castor, you could be successful in your pursuit of Phoenos."

"Final? Such a powerful word. But yes, now that you ask, the decision is *final*. With father's death, Nimon's location and condition is a mystery. One that I have no desire to solve."

Enn glimpsed herself in the steadfast determination emanating from her son. She did not know the details leading up to his decision, but recognized it was unwavering. Her last contact with anyone of this era prior to her return to Ravar was a psychic link with Nimon, not Starn. She had implored the biodgen to save his Life Mentor, Starn. He had succeeded. But at what cost? It was clear Starn had no desire to pursue Phoenos. Yet, the legend had come true, as best she could determine. The crystal halves had been reunited. Not through her son and his biodgen, though. Instead, her daughter, Tempora, carried the crystal's power. And through it, she had returned to save *herself*. A self poised to reunite Castor and Gemini as the prophesies had foretold. If only Starn could be convinced to be the Geminian catalyst to fulfill his people's part of that destiny.

With Nimon lost, Starn was essentially free to pursue that fate. If too soon to plead for his compassion and forgiveness for what he felt was her neglect, could he be persuaded to listen to her for the sake of his *people*? She would try.

"Yes son, you have succinctly summarized how a Singular Dualiity has come to exist.

435

E'Poch is truly a marvel, but not the force that will unify our worlds. It is the *Duall Singularity,* Empirica, that is poised to unite Castor and Gemini by *peaceful* means, instead of divide them via insurgency as my Dual would have done. *If* … and only *if* … *you* agree to be part of the cause."

"Me? What role do I play in this grand plan? I have just discovered myself. How could I contribute to something so significant?"

"Son, your choice regarding suspending the search for Phoenos is rooted in wisdom - wisdom I wish I had at your age. My mission in life was misplaced. Rather than searching for Phoenos as taught by Mitron, I should have focused on being a mother. To *you*. I was unable to be one to Tempora, as I explained. But I have been blessed with a second chance. One I have treasured with Empirica. And one I would like to, in some small way, experience with you. Ravar and I recognize it is time for us to relinquish our positions leading Castor, but only if a succession plan worthy of our people is in place. You and Empirica are fundamental to that success. Working together, you for Gemini and her for Castor, a future of galactic importance can be forged. I can feel it with every fiber of my being!"

Starn could not help but be moved by the sheer force of will he sensed from his mother for her cause. Greater accomplishments in a world's history have been achieved with less. If only *he* shared her commitment. Pressing her further, he countered, "You act as if I hold a position within Geminian circles that could sway its leaders. I am but the firstborn male in our family line - and a hybrid as well. If anyone would have a chance at influencing the Council of Elders, it would be Tempora. She has no human half to contend with - and an argument could be made she bears the purity of the first families of Gemini - both Mitronian and Ravarian lineage."

Enn sighed. She knew she was to blame for Starn's lack of confidence. One of several things she hoped she could remedy if given the opportunity. Gently, she counseled him. "Tempora had hoped to take on the mantle of the Castorian Chair. It would have been a struggle among the various factions of Castor as it was. But *that* Castor is no more, since she saved me. With that change, Castor has evolved quite differently. No longer relegated to the scraps it pilfered through space piracy, in its isolation along this timeline it has grown strong. Our technological prowess, as you have glimpsed, can be a boon to the known star systems. We have been waiting for this moment to reconnect with our Geminian brethren. The time of isolation has finally ended. What better way to begin fruitful negotiations for an alliance than by providing assistance to the Solar Corporation's most valued asset, the *Darwin*. As for Tempora, according to her, the Legotians have other plans for her. A role she accepts and desires to fulfill."

"Hmm ... you mention this moment. Truly, it is pivotal. The K'Tar movement led by your Dual has suffered devastating loss. Both T'Poch and P'Teel - gone. I suspect, though, their organization had agents within the highest levels of Geminian power. The Council of Elders, from the memories left to me by Nimon, seemed divided on many fronts. I myself, met with Kronia shortly after my recovery. She would have me believe my success or failure with Nimon as a Singular Dualiity was of vital importance to the Council. I doubt she knows of my decision to forego the pursuit of Phoenos, much less the fate of Nimon, himself."

"You see ..." Enn pointed out, excitedly, "your insights into the machinations of Geminian power brokers are invaluable. Your importance is recognized, not only by the

Council, but I am sure by the Solar Corporation, as well. What better fac litator to our negotiations could there be?"

"I must say, your argument is compelling. Perhaps we take it one step at a time, and see. My role within Solar Corporation as an IAD director gives me access to Descartes' ear, which is good. My concerns do not lie there, though. It is more with Kronia and the potential difficulties she may cause that has me troubled. "

Enn smiled to herself, reveling in the small victory that was his consideration of her proposal. "Excellent! We have much to discuss. The least of which is how to manage Kronia, my *grandmother*."

CHAPTER 33

Kronia sat alone on the center throne of the Council of Elders. She found solace within the chambers, secluded deep within the mountain chain that marked the boundary of Gemini's immense desert, T'Bok Vri. Outworlders knew it as the Sleeping Giant. Visible from space, it had expanded mightily generations ago as a result of the the meteorite strike during the age of Mitron.

Rather than dwell on the influence of celestial phenomenon, Kronia contemplated how the generations of Mitron had impacted the planet. Only born daughter of Mitron and P'Teel, she indulged herself with a moment of satisfaction as she reflected on the demise of her mother. This luxury permitted only after the door of P'Teel's tomb had been hermetically sealed in the burial shrine that honored Mitron.

Some considered longevity a blessing, while Kronia thought it most definitely a curse. P'Teel had long outlived her husband. Perhaps it was the influence of the Fire Arts, of which P'Teel had been a most renowned practitioner. A pity. For often a daughter left to the rearing of a single mother finds herself the target of grief she had no role in causing. Such was the case with Kronia.

Even she recognized that what P'Teel felt toward Mitron was not *love*. It was more *opportunity*. Opportunity for *power*. Power that had been too fleeting from P'Teel's perspective. Kronia had heard the whisperings of the palace staff. She knew the marriage of Mitron and P'Teel had been orchestrated by the sinister manipulations of an enchantress. And not long after, Kronia had been born.

P'Teel welcomed motherhood. It provided an eventual legacy upon which she could bestow accumulated wealth and influence. But, she did not relish the responsibility that came with being a mother. The care and nurturing of her daughter were left to the servants. For P'Teel had higher aspirations. She felt that she should ultimately rule Gemini.

Yet, despite her elixirs, scheming, and devious power brokering, Mitron's force of will managed to dull P'Teel's influence on Gemini's development. Instead of a society built on domination and fear, the benevolent leader slowly transformed his aristocracy into a constitutional monarchy. Certainly, P'Teel retained a great deal of power, but not nearly that which would have been wielded had she had her way. Her resentment manifested itself with an even more intense focus on subversive control over the united tribes - to the detriment of her daughter's upbringing.

At least that's the way Kronia remembered it. She enjoyed a life of luxury, with no shortage of planned activities and training. The Fire Arts were part of that development, and another source of frustration between mother and daughter. Times had changed. The need for martial skills that could incinerate a foe had passed. As such, the capabilities within the Stargazer guild slowly atrophied. Kronia's skills were a prime example. Much to the chagrin and unbridled disgust of her mother. And so, Kronia's childhood memories carried with them a shadow of parental disappointment and youthful resentment.

As the heiress to the house of Mitron matured, she found other ways to demonstrate her individuality and prowess. Contrary to her mother, she saw the parliamentary system that governed Gemini as an opportunity, not an obstacle. Where P'Teel excelled at maneuvering the serpentine and shadowy corridors of quasi-criminal elements, Kronia basked in the light of the political elite.

She enjoyed the pomp and circumstance that had evolved around the elected officials of Gemini. Every planet seemed to have its Victorian era like old Earth. Gemini was no different. Balls, grand feasts, and summer cotillions were frequent forums n which Kronia reveled. Even the passing of Mitron failed to blunt her zest for life.

Although, the loss of her father did have an impact. Throngs of young, virile men courted her, but to no avail. Her eye tended toward the more mature. Perhaps an effort to replace the attentions of a father she never experienced. So, she found herself captivated by an elder statesman, and married.

Another source of disappointment for P'Teel.

Not because Kronia's husband, Moklei, was without influence. Nor was he lacking wealth. And though in the twilight of his life, he was still quite potent. Which, in part, was the problem. He blessed Kronia with two children, both males.

While sons Migil, and later, Morbet, were fully ordained to carry the house sigil of

Mitron through the halls of parliament when they matured, that was insufficient to P'Teel. The true heritage of a family, particularly one within the Stargazer guild, must be propagated through the *female* line.

So, another field joined politics to further distract her from the Fire Arts pursuit her mother would have preferred. Bioengineering. She was convinced the outcome of the procreation process did not have to be left to chance.

She required a daughter.

Her access to the rich and powerful within the governmental circles of the elite proved highly fruitful. She was not alone in her desire to influence Fate's hand when delivering a child. Instead of exhausting her own resources, she created and led foundations that drew funding from a variety of channels. And not just those with a penchant for the political, scientific, or educational institutions.

There was also religion.

Finally, some common ground with her mother. If only tangentially. Practitioners of the Fire Arts saw value in the beliefs of those who embraced the concept of Phoenos. They mutually espoused the ideal that the Mind is the source of Life. Ultimately, Phoenos would manifest itself through Dualiity, enabling two lives to coexist in harmony from one mind. In the earliest period of the doctrine, though, it was believed the goal would be achieved through purely organic means. As such, the ability to influence and eventually *design* a child became of paramount importance.

Kronia was at the forefront of the effort. Had it been a mission widely accepted within Geminian society, devoid of controversy, she might have enjoyed the sobriquet "Demigoddess of Dualiity".

But it was not meant to be. Fame had its downside, oft best avoided. No matter. She achieved her immediate goal. She bore a female child, Kolkar. And in what seemed to be an instant, Kolkar grew into a young woman and married Makon. They, too, had a daughter.

Novas.

So, as Kronia reflected on the generations within the house Mitron, with its trials and tribulations, she concluded they were for a greater purpose. She had held out hope that Novas and her pioneering of bioduogenetics would forge a path to Phoenos. The loss of T'Poch seemed to dash that hope. The probability of success from Starn and his Dual was slim. But they *had* provided an alternative. That alternative would be her ultimate achievement.

Stepping down from her cathedra, she traversed the chamber to a hidden control beneath a faux stone. Upon activating the biometric switch, a section of the rock wall slid noiselessly inward, providing an opening in which to enter. Treading resolutely down the passageway, an invisible beam broke, commanding the stone door to close behind her. Passing a small elevator, she elected to take an ancient spiral staircase, instead, to reach the level several floors below.

The craggy, rough hewn walls gave way to polished tile. The dusty environs of the chambers above were replaced by the smooth, antiseptic surfaces of a meticulously maintained medical facility. Kronia's journey ended at a revolving door to an airlock. Once the process of sterilization and pressure equalization was completed, she entered the laboratory within.

Enclosed within a hyperbaric chamber on an examination table, the immobile form of the assembled android lay peacefully. Optic cables exited the container at various points and terminated at a crystalline orb suspended in a transparent column a few treds away.

Kronia eased behind a curved control podium. After energizing a few select keys, a flow of pulsing light began to circulate between the two devices along the specialized conduits.

It was almost time. The essence of the union between T'Poch and Nimon had matured sufficiently. Eagerly it waited in its containment sphere. On the table before Kronia lay the culmination of decacycles of research into nanotechnology engineered automatons. The first attempt at uniting the two was at hand.

Once the guest arrived.

On cue, a shimmering image coalesced within the lab.

Kronia nodded with deep reverence. "Your timing is impeccable."

"Among the galactic elite, that is what we are known for. Is all ready?"

Yes, Chrislar. We may begin."

*　　　*　　　*

Tempora felt more fulfilled than she had ever felt in her life. Once again in the Legotian chamber, awaiting Chrislar's presence, she

447

reflected on the last five cycles she had spent aboard the Ravarian ark. She had proven to be invaluable to the success of the voyage. After the miraculous delivery of Empirica, her alternate self, by her own hands, Tempora had been elevated to Prime Counselor to the chieftain, Ravar, and new wife, Enn.

The first six seasons of the child's life had not been without event. Her mental prowess had developed at an accelerated rate. It constantly amazed Tempora, whose Counselor duties included being a nanny and governess. Her motor skills were also advanced for her age. So it came as no surprise when she petitioned, and won, the chance to accompany Tempora, along with her parents, on the first excursion to explore the planetoid when it was reached.

The timing of their arrival to the safe haven had been well calculated by Enn. The vessels narrowly missed a passing cosmic storm. Those same computations provided additional insight to Ravar. They revealed how long the wayfarers could enjoy refuge on the rogue wanderer before experiencing another life-threatening celestial anomaly. So, to avoid the devastation that the next storm would bring, they re-launched with less than a season left before the next onslaught.

Over the next four cycles, the arks traversed space to finally reach their new homeworld, Castor. Enn and Tempora had planned for that day. They knew the Legotians would eventually call for Tempora's return. To avoid the devastating effect it would have on Empirica, they concluded there was only one way to spare the child.

Tell her the truth.

Or at least as much truth as they believed a highly advanced 26 season old child could absorb. Was Tempora sent by a benevolent tribe to assist in her development? Yes. Would she at some point have to return to them? Yes. Could she travel great distances through a portal created by them? Also, yes. Was she a version of her own self from a future time period, as was her mother?

Too much truth could be a bad thing. That level of detail would have to wait for another *time*.

Tempora's departure from her little ward had been sad, but tolerable. She wondered if Empirica even remembered her once grown. Perhaps Chrislar might reveal what became of her in the alternate time stream that was created. *"Or is it actually my time stream now?*

There is much to learn about my new duties with the Legotians."

The intentional rustling of robes to gain her attention achieved its purpose. Chrislar spoke, "I sense you had a most fulfilling experience, Time Child. But it has filled you with questions. How may I help?"

"Yes. I have questions. As do all sentient beings," she whispered. "First and foremost, what is my purpose and does it matter?"

Chrislar, manifesting himself in the form of a Socratic scholar with a loose linen robe adorned with a royal blue sash, coyly responded, "That's two questions."

"A sense of humor?" Tempora replied. "I am surprised. I would have thought Legotians to have evolved beyond that."

"Humor is an important form of social communication. Laughing in the presence of others can indicate the situation is safe, if done with sincerity. It is one of the few luxuries left to a non-corporeal being such as myself."

"I see. And it can also serve to distract. You have conveniently used it in an attempt to avoid my *two* questions," Tempora added, with a whimsical smile.

Chrislar returned the expression, with sincerity.

"Your purpose is what you make of it. And it matters. Should you chose to continue as the Time Child, it will have galactic import. Your contribution has already made possible a reunification of Gemini and Castor. Surely that matters to many … and to you."

"It does, most assuredly. I only thought it would be with me in a different role. And what has become of little Empirica?"

"The possibilities remain endless … or limited, depending upon one's viewpoint. Many beings see time as linear. An action generates a response. Once done, they cannot return to that point in time. To undo it. As they move along the timeline, they can only perform other actions, which lead to alternatives.

In some sense, that perspective is correct, when considered by those on their short section of timeline. But Time is actually a *web*. An inter-connected collection of segments of timelines forming branches, loops, spirals, and even frayed ends.

You, Tempora, are no longer constrained to the time loop of your original existence. You have created a new branch that extends into the time web. But there are limits. There are permanent nexi that exist in the web -

unalterable. In what we call Forever Time, these permanent points provide stability. As an example, *you will always be born*. Yes, branches with different outcomes can, and do, occur. But your *existence* cannot be undone. You have created an alternate branch for yourself in the form of Empirica, while you, yourself continue. You are now a Duall Singularity. Existing along more than one strand of time, but still singularly you. As a result, an alternate branch is possible for the future of Castor and Gemini. And, most importantly, you can move from branch to branch and along each section of the time strand. Perhaps, one day, you can explore the space *between* strands."

Tempora resisted the reflex of her mouth gaping open in awe. Instead, she simply asked, "What is next for me?"

Chrislar hesitated, then confessed, "For those of us not restricted by the concept of linear time, it can be difficult to answer a simple question like `What's next?' Distinguishing between `what is done' and `what is left to do' can be paradoxical. What I do know is that a little girl has always needed your guidance."

Tempora wondered if Legotians experienced dementia. *"Have I not just returned from helping Empirica?"*

Chrislar smiled broadly. "Now that *is* amusing … the thought of a demented Legotian. No, Time Child, I have not lost my senses. You *have* already spun the segment of web creating Empirica. But think back to your childhood. Your mother was lost to you. A grief stricken father was mostly absent. Who raised you aboard the *Destiny*?"

"I have struggled with those memories. I recall she was a Stargazer, but cannot remember her name."

The Legotian gestured toward the silver Time Pool, his face brightening.

"That is a question I *can* answer," he responded, enigmatically.

"It was … and is …Tempora."

EPILOGUE

Chrislar watched as Tempora entered the mercurial pool, as she had done, and will do, for countless more *times*.

Turning, he left the Legotian chamber, and once again focused his attention upon Kronia on Gemini.

Straining to contain an awkward chuckle, he asked, "What's next?"

Kronia barely heard. She busily flitted from the control podium to various points where equipment connected the glowing orb and vessel containing the android.

The Legotian had become accustomed to the inability of corporeals to be in multiple places at once. Hence, their limited skill at focusing on two tasks at once. For an energy being such as himself, one able to traverse space and time, he found it satisfying to have the patience to be able to interact with them. Not all Legotians could. Those residing on the Collective Council certainly lacked the ability. That's why they relied upon him so heavily.

Despite his relative youth, he had accomplished much for them. He hoped Kronia's demonstration would further prove his worth to the Collective.

Kronia ceased her ministrations, turned toward her guest, and spoke, "Apologies, Councilor. I know how important this next phase is to you, as well as to me. I wanted to check the equipment's configuration one last time. To confirm, the android has been assembled. It is the culmination of decacycles of clandestine research by my kindred. Away from the prying eyes of zealots who would ban bioduogenetics altogether, the next developmental leap into synthetic life awaits."

"My compliments to you, Magistrate. You have been the linchpin holding our plans together. You are a focal point within Time's web. Your mother, P'Teel, certainly laid the foundation with her pursuits of the mystical power of the Mitronian shard. And your grand-daughter, Novas, pressed forward diligently to develop the technical possibilities. However, they created strain within Time's filaments. Through it all, you have invoked balance. Delicately traversing the strand that would lead us to this point."

The Geminian flushed a sapphire hue, pleased to be the recipient of such praise. The

Legotian continued, "Tell me, please, why you feel this is to be the culmination of our two endeavors, after so much effort?"

"As you alluded, the venture began with the mysticism of the Fire Arts made more powerful through P'Teel. She harnessed the ability to focus her mind through the rare element Fate delivered when the precursor meteor struck Gemini. What came to be known as the Mltronian shard, when wielded by an enchantress from our line, bestowed extraordinary abilities. Enhanced bioenergy blasts, telepathy, mind control, clairvoyance- to name but a few.

From her efforts, I then sought to apply a more scientific approach. By leveraging the resources of others, we learned how to synthesize the crystalline matrix. Granted, it was far inferior to the source crystal. Yet, the properties had an ability to enhance bio-organic processes. Natural selection yielded to scientific control for a chosen few. My daughter Kolkar being one such person to benefit.

Her reward - Novas was born.

With Novas, the seed grew and flourished to yield the fruit of our efforts today. She led the breakthrough that would become bioduogenetics. In so doing, it would be her essence that would manifest itse f within T'Poch. An essence purified by the synthetic construct that would become the Singular Dualiity."

Kronia paused to see if her narration was boring the Legotian. She knew from past encounters his focus could be divided. Invariably a side effect of evolving into a near omnipotent being comprised of pure energy.

Far from it. Chrislar's gaze was of an intensity bordering on manic. He had as much at stake as Kronia, apparently.

Possibly more.

He eagerly prompted her to continue by saying, "Truly a remarkable technical achievement. But, ironically, it took the influence of P'Teel's *mystical* influence to occur, did it not?"

"You are correct. Novas had mastered the ability of empowering her biodgen from a distance, as would others. However, it was P'Teel who conceived of implanting the Mitronian shard within T'Poch to free the entity that would become the Singular Dualiity. With a small contribution of medical facilitation on my part, I might add."

"No doubt, dear Kronia..." Chrislar interjected, smiling, "... as I said, you are the linchpin. But as I understand it, that essence needed to be enhanced, true?"

Kronia returned the smile, graciously accepting the compliment, and nodded. "Right, again. Through a serpentine sequence of events, the psychic essence of Novas would once again be purified, but via a different process.

Her son, Starn, would be the vector to deliver his mother's rare mental construct. He, too, would flirt with success in embracing Phoenos. With the assistance of the Institute of Meditative Phenomenon, under my leadership, of course. Over dozens of cycles, he would use the Geminian component of his genetic matrix to develop his own biodgen. That Geminian essence having originated from his mother, Novas. As a result, the biodgen known as Nimon was a *transmutation* of the essence of Novas."

Kronia could not suppress the gleeful smile blooming across her face. "I must say the elegance of how the two purified essences of Novas were recombined is nothing short of extraordinary. The bonding of two biodgens has been expressly forbidden and enforced most tragically. As such, facilitating their ... ah

... union ... took maneuvering. With Nimon enhanced by the implanting of the Ravarian shard, the distillation of Novas' essence was achieved. T'Poch captured it, her metabolism refined it, and I extracted it into that vessel so that it could gestate."

"Truly magnificent," Chrislar noted, glancing at the glowing orb. "Not unlike the device we Legotians use for propagation. What has taken us millennia of evolution to achieve, you are on the verge of creating in mere generations. To merge mental constructs to create a self-sustaining entity borders on godhood. When developed appropriately, the matrix of time and space become accessible. That is the culmination of our race's existence."

Kronia, normally entranced by the energy being's words, remained focused on the task at hand. At the pause in his narrative, she simply said, "Activating transfer now."

The cadence of Chrislar's speech increased, revealing his excitement. "I understand your goal, Magistrate Kronia. Create a super being that will swing the balance of power unwaveringly in your direction. Gemini will irreversibly become the dominant force in the galaxy. Perhaps with Castor as its companion. Some corporations will crumble, while others soar to preeminence. Power shifts among family houses will ebb and flow. The fate of specific individuals will forever change. Yet, the pivotal impact of your success may have escaped you."

Kronia's eyes flicked from the control podium over to her guest. Curiosity got the best of her. She monitored the power readings, to be sure, but at this point, there was nothing more for her to do. So, she yielded and donated a brief moment of her focus to the Legotian.

"And what might that be, Councilor?"

Chrislar sighed. Legotians had practiced behaviors to better relate to corporeal races. This was one. As would a mentor to a student, he explained, "Despite having the fabric of time at our disposal, shaping it to our will, we lack a basic means of satisfaction. Though we can appear in forms more acceptable to the races we encounter, it is a mere facade. What we lack is a simple pleasure. The sense of touch.

What corporeals take for granted, we have sought to restore - without sacrificing what we have achieved. We want it all! To be able to transfer our mental essence into a construct that gives us what we desire has been too long unattainable. You are on the precipice of changing that.

So, while the outcome of your efforts is of critical importance to you and your people, it is *even more* to mine. All that has transpired from the era of Mitron to now has been influenced by us to reach this point. And as I said at the onset, you have been the linchpin for this achievement!"

Kronia's emotions were in turmoil. Excitement, anticipation, anxiety - all prompted by the success or failure of the next few moments. Layered upon those were the unexpected feelings upon hearing Chrislar's words. Shock, dismay, resentment - reactions common to someone surreptitiously manipulated and used for the benefit of another.

"Could it be true? Had these … creatures … toyed with the fate of planets just for their own gain? The scale of their devious plotting was incomprehensible! My family, for generations, mere pawns in an interstellar match?" thought the venerated magistrate and matron of her line. *"Perhaps failure is the better outcome from the monumental efforts that have led to this point!"*

She failed to see the irony. Had her orchestrations within the Geminian government, the Institute, and her own family been similarly unscrupulous, only on a less grand scale?

Chrislar smiled. The Geminian may as well have spoken the thoughts aloud. Her mind was an open book to him. "Fear not, dear Kronia. You will see the fruit of your labors as sweet and delicious, much like the apple of legend."

Looking over her shoulder, Chrislar's smile grew broader.

The red eyes of the automaton flickered, then opened upon a new world. A whisper slipped from her lips.

"The mind *is* the source of life."

About the Author

Lawrence E. Maynard, or Larry to those who know him, enjoyed his formative years during the Silver Age of comics, Saturday morning superhero cartoons, and the interstellar exploits of Gene Roddenberry's *Star Trek*. His affinity toward science fiction translated into a pursuit of the applied sciences with degrees in Chemistry, Biology, and a Master's in Business Administration. Having completed a career of over three decades in the manufacturing, marketing, and management of building materials, polymers, and coatings, he is able to weave a sense of scientific realism into the fabric of science fiction writing. When not indulging in that creative art, he spends time traveling to visit his family and friends and supports people in pursuit of the American Dream, home ownership. He resides in Knoxville, TN with his wife of 46 years and looks forward to authoring many more science fiction adventures.